SEA OF WHISPERS

MELANIE MURPHY

To my boys—always dream big.

I have heard that the salt water within us—our tears, our sweat—have an innate desire to rejoin their native tributary: that vast blue expanse lapping on the shores of our ancient land. This magnetism, this invisible rope tethering us to the ocean, pulls harder at some than at others, but all of us feel it, whether we know it or not.

The deepest depths of the seas remain a mystery to human consciousness–their secrets, the unknown species scouring the ocean floor for scraps; yet the sea nourishes us. Its salt water heals all wounds. The tumbling waves–the ultimate reminder of how small we each are. Standing on the roiling shoreline, staring unabashedly at the beauty that extends beyond the horizon, forces even the most brazen to contemplate this beautiful world and her place within it.

The tiny fragmented seashells, the clumps of tangled seaweed, the beach glass worn smooth by endless tumbling in the waves, all manner of remnants washed up on the shore give us the briefest of glimpses into the true majesty that extends below the undulating surface. These items tell of long ago secrets, of a place that humans can never inhabit and can never fully know. These tawdry scraps that brush up against our ankles as we wade into the depths are tiny gifts, telling of a place where we may only visit, but never live.

From the craggy coastlines, to the sandy beaches, the ocean chisels away at our land, at our very beings, pushing itself into the crevices and cracks, filling up the voids of space and time–ever present, ever watchful. What skeletons reside beneath those whispering waves? Only the ocean knows.

Chapter One

CLAIRE

God she was tired. Who said being a working mom was easy? Claire guessed no one, as she watched her son and his best friend shooting hoops on her black-topped driveway. Jimmy had been bugging her relentlessly for a playdate, and she finally caved and called Kyle's mom, Trish, last night to invite him over.

"All the other kids have playdates all the time," Jimmy had said last week. "How come I don't?"

Maybe because all the other moms don't work 40 hours a week. Maybe because I don't get home until at least 6 o'clock at night … and that's on a good day. Maybe because all the other moms have time to sign up to be the Class Mom or the PTA President or a Field Day chaperone.

It made Claire a bit bitter to think about some of the other moms in the neighborhood, moms who could actually drop off their own children at school instead of enrolling them in the "Before Care" program. Moms who sipped coffee in their quiet homes and who took Yoga classes and got pedicures. Moms who picked up their children exactly at 3:25pm at Robert Moses

Elementary School in their LuLuLemon workout pants. Moms who weren't frazzled all the time. Moms who didn't have that overwhelming sense of guilt weighing upon their shoulders like a leaden scarf tied too tightly.

Claire and her husband, Joe, knew that this house and this neighborhood were above their budget, but they went for it anyway. The school district was top-of-the-line and their home, even though significantly more modest than most of the others–and in need of some updating–was situated on a quiet, tree-lined street. They splurged. Claire didn't regret it. Neither did her husband, even though he had to work nearly 60 hours a week at the office to afford the mortgage.

Despite her exhaustion and the fleeting feelings of resentment, she smiled a bit as she sat on the front stoop watching her son and his friend play. She was lucky, despite it all. A loving husband, a great little boy who would be turning 8 in two weeks. A nice life. The boys' laughter drifted to her on the gentle breeze and birds chirped. It was a mild day for winter and the sun shone warm and friendly on her upturned face. Her boss had given her begrudging permission to leave the office today at 2; it was the only way she could possibly accommodate this week-day playdate. Kyle was packed with social engagements every weekend, and Kyle was the friend that Jimmy wanted over. Just this once, Claire was determined to make it work.

She allowed herself to close her eyes for a second, to breathe. The briny scent of high tide reached her nose as she inhaled. She loved it here. It was home. She took off her black heels, laid them aside on the stoop and stretched out her legs. She hadn't taken off those shoes since she put them on 9 hours ago and her feet were aching and hot.

Shit! Her eyes snapped open as she remembered her laundry. She never switched the load over to the dryer. She groaned as she thought about the clothes, sitting, wet and crumpled, in the washing machine since last night. They were probably already beginning to smell mildewy and sour.

Getting to her feet she called, "Jimmy, Kyle. I'll be right back. I just have to switch over the laundry. You guys ok?"

"We're fine, Mom. Can you bring us out some snacks and some Capri Suns when you come back?"

"Sure. Be back in five."

Claire gave a fleeting look back as she opened the front door. She didn't like leaving Jimmy alone in the front of the house. Her husband always teased her and jokingly called her a "helicopter mom." But Claire had grown up in Queens, and as a child was never permitted to spend much time alone outside. Her own mother had been endlessly paranoid about the passing cars, "That car would run you down and the driver wouldn't even look back," she would always say. Claire's husband, who had grown up in a rural community on the North Fork of Long Island, didn't understand this mentality, as he himself was given all the freedom in the world in his childhood years. So, Claire found herself in a constant battle between her "city girl" upbringing and her husband's "country boy" frame of mind.

The sound of the bouncing basketball followed her. Bounce, bounce, bounce, bounce. Rhythmic and wholesome.

She walked barefoot down the narrow stairwell leading to her basement. Yes, there were other parts of the house that could use some modernizing, but Claire always considered the basement to be the "final frontier." When she and Joe first moved in, the space, with its brown paneled walls and built-in bar complete with red and green overhead lights had its appeal and they had hosted many parties down there where beers spilled carelessly on the shag carpeting. But once they had Jimmy and then moved the laundry down there, and the walking space dwindled due to the stacked bins holding old baby clothes and toys and books, the entire floor lost its luster and became simply a dumping ground. A dumping ground with spider crickets. Well except for Joe's office, if you could even call it that. It was more like a glorified closet filled with her husband's treasures–autographs, bobble-heads, posters, and other mementos of his beloved hobbies. Claire wasn't willing to allow the huge framed autograph of Mookie Wilson take up space on the living room wall, so Joe had carte blanche in this tiny space. And he loved it here.

Walking down the basement stairs, Claire shuddered as her eyes darted around searching for the brown, shrimp-like creatures with antennae as long as her pointer finger. She knew they were harmless, but they still gave her the heebie jeebies. She often joked with Joe that if he didn't call an exterminator, she would need to invest in a haz-mat suit to wear downstairs to do the laundry. She was only half-kidding.

She opened the washer door and got hit in the face by the unmistakable earthy smell of stale, damp clothing, so instead of switching the laundry over to the dryer, she added another cupful of Tide and turned the knob to 'Wash.' *What a waste,* Claire muttered to herself as she closed the door. She walked back up the stairs with snacks on her mind.

Claire opened the cabinets and pulled out a few snack-sized bags of Cool Ranch Doritos and fruit snacks–Jimmy's favorites–then opened the refrigerator for two cold Capri Suns. She thought ruefully for a second about how last week the box of Capri Suns had only cost three dollars, but when she went food shopping yesterday, the same box was almost five dollars. She hoped this inflation would level out soon. Her pocketbook was beginning to feel the pinch. And she simply didn't have time to do what her mom always suggested ... price hop from store to store to get the best deal on certain items. A good deal of her phone conversations with her mother these days focused on how she spent most of the day going to Key Food for grapes, which were on sale for 99 cents per pound, to Wegman's for chicken cutlets, which were on sale for 1.99 per pound, to Publix, which had Honey Nut Cheerios on sale for 2.99 per box. *It must be nice to be a retired Floridian,* Claire thought to herself. On second thought, even if Claire had nothing to do, she couldn't quite picture herself spending that much time clipping coupons and bargain-hunting ... she just didn't think she had it in her.

Still barefoot, and still dressed in her work clothes, she opened the front door to deliver the snacks to the boys. Squinting into the late-afternoon March sunshine, the first thing that struck Claire was that she couldn't remember the last time she had heard the sound of the bouncing basketball. And as her eyes adjusted to the sun, she saw the orange, dimpled sphere in question, rolling, rolling, rolling, down the paved driveway into the street. No one was there to stop it. The ball kept rolling and rolling and rolling, unobstructed, all the way to the other side of Maple Street. Claire's eyes followed the arc up the street, and then down again. The ball finally stopped at the lip of the Hansen driveway directly across the street with a soft thunk.

"Boys," Claire called. "Jimmy. What did I tell you about letting your ball roll into the street?"

Claire remembered last week, she had nearly brought Jimmy to tears when she yelled at him for allowing the ball to bounce into the street. A car had been passing at the time and the basketball had almost hit it. The car stopped with a screech to avoid the object and the driver rolled down her window to utter a nasty, "You need to be more careful!" warning. Claire had dragged Jimmy away from the curb by the sleeve of his sweatshirt and uttered the words her own mother had always used, "That car would run you down and the driver wouldn't even look back." She cringed as the sentence passed her lips and then drew her son in for a hug as the tears gathered in the corners of his hazel eyes.

Claire always felt guilty about the harsh reprimands issued from her mouth. Her worry often got the better of her–she knew that–and on more nights than she would like to admit, she went to bed feeling the hot pangs of regret as she stared at the ceiling above her. Self-admonishments like: *I shouldn't have yelled at Jimmy like that, I need to have more patience, I will be better tomorrow* swimming around in her jumbled mind. It was hard to be confident in her motherhood when she felt like she was being pulled in a million different directions. She constantly felt like she was short-shrifting something ... her job, her husband, her kid. She took on too much and as a result felt incompetent at each role she inhabited. Over a glass of wine and through hot tears, her husband would try to assure her ... especially after a particularly trying day. "Don't beat yourself up so much, Claire," Joe would say. "You're a good mom." Those phrases, no matter how well-intentioned, didn't help. Joe would often lament, "Nothing I say ever makes you feel any better." And maybe he was right. But in her heart, Claire felt that Jimmy didn't deserve merely a 'good' mom ... he deserved the best mom, a perfect mom. Sometimes, when Claire was being particularly hard on herself she would think that Jimmy certainly deserved better than her ... he should receive more than she could give. Sometimes Claire would wonder if this feeling of oppressive guilt was simply the natural byproduct of being a working mom? Too bad there weren't more working moms around ... she could use a female friend who actually understood her.

But now, despite the fact that she was trying to work on reigning in her temper, Claire was angry again. She was even angrier that Jimmy was ignoring her call, especially since Kyle was scheduled to get picked up in a half an hour. How would she look if Trish Yardsleigh pulled up and Claire couldn't find her kid? Probably not very good at all. Where were those two? Hiding?

"Jimmy, Kyle. Come out now. This isn't a game. And what did I tell you last week about letting your ball roll into the street?"

Claire searched behind the bushes, Jimmy's favorite hiding spot. She glanced behind the Adirondack chairs situated at the head of the driveway. Nothing.

She opened the gate of the white PVC fence leading to the backyard, calling, "Jimmy, Kyle. This isn't funny anymore. Kyle, your mom is going to be angry if she comes here and you're hiding."

She looked under the deck, between the arborvitaes that lined the perimeter of her yard, inside the work shed. She thought that Jimmy knew better than to go in there ... he had been warned countless times about the tools in there that could crush little boy toes, could chop off little boy fingers with ease. But the boys weren't there. Nothing was there. Only the chirping birds answered her.

Claire picked up her pace as she looked behind the wooden swing set, behind the garbage cans; her heart was starting to race. If Joe was here he would laugh at her. *Helicopter mom at it again.* But where were those boys?

Now she circled back to the front of her house.

"Jimmy! Kyle! Boys. Time to come out!" Now her voice was tinged not only with anger, but with a growing sense of dread ... fear.

In vain, she threw the front door open and plodded about the house, checking under the beds, in every closet, behind every door; she even pulled back the shower curtains of both bathrooms. Part of her knew the boys weren't in the house; she would have heard them if they had come in, but she looked anyway, with an increasingly frantic desperation. An eerie silence pervaded the space. No one was inside; she was alone.

Again, she stumbled outside, calling the names of both boys with an urgency bordering on hysterical. There was no response. Anxiously, her fingers crept up to her neck to stroke the smooth silver of the locket her husband had given her about a week after her son was born. She wore it every single day and only took it off to sleep or shower. It had become almost a nervous habit of hers to push her thumb against the cool metal on the back of the pendant. But as she raised her hand to the familiar spot, it wasn't there. Did she forget to put it on this morning? She dismissed the thought. She had more pressing concerns.

Again she called, "Jimmy! Kyle! This isn't a game. Time to come out now." Her voice was almost hoarse with overuse.

But the more she called, the more certain she became that this wasn't a joke.

Chapter Two

MIA

The ocean called to Mia. Growing up in an apartment complex in Sparta, New Jersey, surrounded by concrete and jughandles, she moved out the moment she could save up enough money. During her two years at the local community college, Mia worked a part-time waitress gig at the local Friday's and saved all her tip money in a manilla envelope stuffed under her mattress in her tiny bedroom. She didn't like banks, the lines to wait on, the forms to fill out, the questions ... all to gain access to *her* money. Yes, she understood the practicality of all the red tape, but she didn't have the patience for it.

After graduating with an Associates Degree from Sussex County Community College, some no-name institution that nobody had ever heard of, she knew in her heart that she needed to venture out in search of something else. Mia couldn't quite put her finger on what that something else was. She had a great family and friends where she was. Maybe it was the fact that she yearned to feel more like an adult ... and that was hard to do when she still lived in her childhood home. Yes, that was definitely part of her desire to move out, to start fresh, to find a corner of the world that was hers alone—a nook where she could properly take root.

But there were other forces at play as well. Forces that she couldn't properly name or identify–they were too elusive. She thought it possibly had to do with the ocean waves that crashed through her mind at night while she lay sleeping. The ebb and flow of the tide that washed over her psyche. But whatever the catalyst, the time had come to move on.

When researching a place to live, she typed into the Google search bar, *'best place for young people near the water tri-state area.'* The West End of Long Beach popped up first in the results. After reading the short blurb about the location in question on the website, she decided that she didn't even need to bother visiting in person. She was charmed by the location—a hidden gem tucked away on the south shore of a barrier island...a tiny, slender bit of green in a sea of blue. To her, Long Island itself looked like a kite tail attached to the larger landmass of New York. She could see herself there...on this minuscule speck of tan on the map that lit up her computer screen. So, she contacted a Long Beach realtor, told her that she wanted to be as close to the ocean as possible and was sent back five options of properties that were looking for tenants and that were somewhat within her modest budget.

The first listing, Mia dismissed immediately because it was a basement apartment, blocks away from the beach entrance. She didn't want the musty, dimly lit atmosphere that usually accompanies such accommodations, nor did she intend on living so far from the ocean. The second option was an East End, tiny studio apartment on the 5th floor of a huge apartment complex. Mia had come from the land of such monstrosities and had no interest in occupying what she viewed as a claustrophobic cell. The third property–a small second floor apartment on Minnesota Avenue, three houses away from the beach–boasted a partial view of the ocean and a much-coveted parking spot. But for these two perks, there were many drawbacks. The apartment was old, the wood floors were uneven and buckled at certain points, the bathroom sink looked moldy and there was a red, rust-colored stain underneath the faucet. Also, it was slightly pricier than the other two rentals. And these were just the flaws the pictures showed. Just as she x'd out the link to check out the next listing, her hand paused on her phone. A feeling crept in from the back of her scalp and lingered there, urging her to go back. Almost automatically, her thumb re-clicked the previous link and the slide show of that second-floor apartment once again graced her phone screen. Now Mia wasn't necessarily one likely to give into premonition, but she took the gooseflesh on her arms as a sign and said to herself, *Ok. This is it.* After all, this seemed to be the closest she would get to the ocean. So she made the call.

"Hello, Erica. I'm interested in the third rental. The Minnesota property."

And that was it. She agreed to send in her security deposit, along with first and last month's rent as soon as possible.

So it was that a few weeks later, on a windy March morning, with her little sister looking solemnly on, Mia packed her clothing, toiletries, futon, and other personal items into the smallest U-Haul trailer that she could have rented, and set out on the road to Long Beach.

<hr>

March in Long Beach is considered to be the end of the "down months." Only locals flock to the many bars and restaurants in The West End during the blustery winter months, where the wind seems to blow off the ocean with a ferocity bordering on anger. So when Mia turned her Honda CRV, pulling the U-haul containing all her personal possessions, left on Minnesota Avenue, it was not at all difficult to find a place to park in front of what would be, from here on out, her home: number 26. As she unloaded the cardboard boxes and clear storage bins from her backseat and trunk onto the sidewalk, the elderly couple who owned the home emerged from the sea-green front door to introduce themselves.

"Hi. I'm Dee," said the older woman, extending her hand to Mia. "And this is Bob," she continued, gesturing to the smiling man standing beside her. "I know we spoke on the phone, but it's good to meet you in person."

Mia looked at them both in turn. Dee's hair, although mostly white, had threads of strawberry blonde woven throughout, and her deep green eyes were piercing, perhaps even more so due to the delicate lines that crinkled up around the edges when she smiled. She was thin and petite, especially in comparison to her barrel-chested husband standing next to her. She was pretty and simple, the way that only older women can be when they shirk makeup and fashion trends.

Wearing only a thin, white t-shirt and faded jeans, Bob looked like an old salt–a head full of shaggy gray hair and a darker beard … more black than gray, obscuring most of his features, except for his deep brown eyes. Both of them radiated a healthy well-being, despite their age. And a hardiness.

Moving her gaze downward, Mia noticed that both Dee and Bob were standing barefoot on the cement sidewalk. Their feet must have been freezing.

Bob caught Mia's glance and said with a chuckle, "The cold doesn't bother us anymore. We've been living in this very home for over 30 years. This cement knows the shape of our feet."

With that tidbit of insight, Bob placed the silver key into Mia's palm.

"We have a few extras in our kitchen," Dee explained. "Let me know if you'd like a second set."

"I think one is fine. I'm pretty responsible," said Mia good-naturedly.

She was relieved that the landlords seemed so friendly and accommodating.

"Bob!" Dee scolded. "Help Mia bring up her things! Don't leave her standing out here to get frostbite!"

Bob sprang into action, "Of course, of course. Follow me."

The unloading didn't require very many trips up and down

the steep side staircase, and Mia was grateful for Bob's help along with his friendly conversation.

As they worked, Bob revealed that he and his wife were in their early 70s, that they had intended for the upstairs apartment to be for their kids. But according to Bob, "God never granted us any of those."

Mia felt uncomfortable that Bob was so forthcoming. She felt like she had to offer something personal about herself to keep up, so she blurted out, "Well ... sometimes kids aren't all that great. My little sister can be super annoying. I love her and everything, but ... "

She stopped talking when Bob gave her a wide stare revealing a deep sadness. Mia sensed that there was a story there, but she definitely was not going to ask. *Oh, crap. Wrong thing to say. Me and my big mouth.*

But Bob just gave a little shake of his head, as if to clear his gathering thoughts and moved on with his friendly banter. While setting the boxes on the kitchen counter, Bob explained to Mia that the West End of Long Beach consists mostly of 'state' streets, Minnesota, New York, Ohio, Louisiana, and so on ... and that most of those streets run north and south, butting right up to the ocean.

She also learned that every other street has a walkway to get onto the beach, "So you're lucky," Bob said. "Otherwise you'd have to walk over a block. And even though it doesn't sound like a far walk, when you're carrying a chair and a cooler and it's hot outside, it's much better to have an entrance right on your street." Bob continued, "Oh, and that restaurant on the corner, Minnesota's ... they have the best Taco Tuesday in town. I'm somewhat of a taco nut," Bob chuckled.

Good to know!

On their final trip down the stairs, as Mia went to step into the driver's seat of her CRV to return the U-Haul, Dee called out from the front door, "Would you like to come for dinner tonight? I can't imagine that you'll find the time to cook."

And even though Mia was looking forward to a quiet, solitary evening where she might enjoy a glass of red wine and maybe a pie from the local pizzeria she passed on her ride while settling into a new home, she already felt the rumbles of hunger in her stomach.

"Thank you," she responded. "I'd like that. Are you sure I'm not imposing?"

"Absolutely not," Bob responded. "We'd love to get to know you."

"Thank you. That's really nice of you."

"Okie dokie! See you at 6," Dee said.

Okie Dokie, Mia thought. Such a hokey phrase.

"Great! 6 o'clock. And now I better get going. I don't want to be charged extra for returning this thing late," Mia explained, gesturing towards the orange and white trailer that was hitched to the back of her SUV.

So, with the promise of dinner and more conversation later this evening, Mia turned the car around and wove her way onto Ocean Parkway headed towards the U-Haul Rental Center, eyes wavering between the road and the GPS directions on her phone.

Once she finished the business with U-Haul–she had not been charged any penalty even though she was a few minutes past the deadline for late fees–she felt as though she could finally breathe. Now she only had to unpack, find a job, make friends...easy, right?

The view of the setting sun over the Atlantic Ocean took her breath away as she drove south on Ocean Parkway. Such unfathomable radiance laid out before her. The highway seemed as though it were perfectly placed by divine intervention to allow the passersby a bit of beauty on their evening commutes. Nothing but sea and sky. Sea and sky. Wispy clouds reflected sapphire against the blazing gold hue cast by the butter sun as it sank into its shadowy bed behind the curve of the horizon.

This was what she craved. What she yearned for ever since she was 5 years old and could first recognize that powerful longing within her very being. The salt and the sun and the scattered, sparkling reflection of the rays as they skittered across the surface of the Atlantic–a handful of sterling glitter strewn carelessly across the cobalt waves.

Chapter Three

CLAIRE

Rich and Jeanne Gorman, the elderly couple who lived next door to Claire, allowed Jimmy to play freely in their backyard. A few years ago, they hired an architect to build a designer tree house for the sporadic visits of their own grandchildren. It was a stunning structure complete with blue twisty slide, tire swing, and Jimmy's favorite part, a secret hideaway. Claire couldn't even imagine what it cost. Definitely a lot. Perhaps they thought such extravagance would entice their son to visit more often. Well, it didn't. So they freely allowed Jimmy to come and go. Maybe they felt that it would replace the emptiness they felt ... Jimmy could be their surrogate grandchild in a way. And they certainly did spoil that boy. Cookies and lemonade, birthday gifts. Claire felt lucky that Jimmy had such a sweet relationship with the Gormans, especially since his own grandparents lived so far away. Jimmy was closer to Mr. Rich and Miss Jeannie (as he called them) than to Claire or Joe's parents, who had both moved down to Florida ... Claire's about 3 years ago, and Joe's about a decade ago. Could it really be that long already? Jimmy spent long afternoons next door on that impeccably designed tree house pretending that he was the captain of some giant flying pirate ship as he peered through the lush green leaves of his childhood paradise. Surely the boys were up there right now, two swash-buckling, sword clashing rapscallions of another time.

Claire held her pace back to a speedwalk: no reason to run. They were one-hundred-percent next door. They had to be. Where else could they be?

The PVC fence of her neighbor's yard banged shut behind her as she walked down the paved stone pathway into the Gormans' expansive backyard. She stepped clumsily on a small pebble, sending bolts of sharp pain into her heel. She had forgotten to put on her shoes. The backyard was eerily quiet; no screeching laughter of young boys, no rattling of small footsteps on wooden planks. Claire went to the structure and stood below it contemplating the treehouse situated above.

"Boys! Are you up there?"

No answer. They could be hiding ... trying to keep quiet to prolong their playdate.

Claire gingerly climbed up the rope ladder that was clearly not meant to hold the weight of a full-grown human. She pushed open the trapdoor underneath the floor and poked her head through. It was empty.

Now the panic overtook her, strong and urgent. She was not over-reacting; Claire knew that deep within her soul. She nearly choked on the bitter, acidic taste of the fear burning in her parched throat.

Not even paying attention anymore to her aching feet, Claire raced back through the gate, screaming, "Jimmy! Kyle! Boys!"

She stood in the middle of her blacktop driveway screaming their names, her mind blank, hoping against hope that the boys would come trotting down the sidewalk smiling sheepishly, but knowing deep down that they were gone.

Claire looked fleetingly at the orange sphere of the basketball still resting at the curb on the other side of the street. All she could think, in her jumbled, confused mind was *They were JUST here! They were JUST here! They were JUST here!*

Chapter Four

MIA

When Mia turned her CRV, now free of its burden, for the second time down Minnesota Avenue, the sun had sunk below her sightline, and a hazy dusk settled over the street. The house looked snug against the dimness and the street light blazed a friendly halo as she parked her truck beside the curb. Emerging from the car, Mia breathed in deeply, flooded with the feeling of excitement that oftentimes accompanies life's major milestones. *I did it*, she thought to herself. *I actually did it.* A feeling of pride swelled up within her as she looked at the darkened windows of her apartment. She envisioned Christmas lights hanging from the eaves next holiday season, maybe a wreath on the door. What color curtains would look best up there? Pale yellow? Or maybe a gauzy white? Or maybe just some sensible wooden blinds?

Glancing down at her phone, the time read five forty-eight. She had about ten minutes to run up to her apartment and freshen up before dinner with Dee and Bob. However, just as Mia turned towards the stairs leading up to her apartment, a cold sea breeze brought the rich, briny, slightly animalistic scent of the ocean to her nostrils. The wind seemed to wrap itself around her body, pulling her to the end of Minnesota Avenue and as Mia stood on the planked wooden walkway leading to the ocean, she thought that she could, that she *should*, that she *must* take a peek at the ocean. After all, that immense blue expanse that lay over those dunes was the reason she found herself here, the reason she uprooted her life with her loving family in Sparta. Well, one of the reasons anyway.

Pulling her winter coat more tightly around her slim shoulders, Mia walked the length of the pathway until the toes of her black Converse sneakers met the sand. The blustery day had made its way into a downright frigid evening and the wind whipping off the ocean caused tears to gather at the corners of Mia's eyes. She stood alone for a moment on the brink of the end of the world, contemplating the stark beauty surrounding her. Despite the cold, Mia unlaced her shoes and kicked them off, then rolled down her winter socks exposing her smooth bare feet.

She slowly made her way over frozen chunks of ice that had accumulated on the sandy expanse and crunched over the seaweed that had washed ashore. She walked all the way down to the place where the waves break, sending a fine mist of spray up to wet her cheeks. Mia ran her tongue over her lips relishing the taste of the salty moisture that had accumulated there as she watched the tide's relentless crashing. Bending down, Mia dipped her fingertips into the frigid water swirling in foamy circles at her feet. As she trailed her hands in slow arcs, she knew that she made the right choice. It seemed as though the water responded to her touch, allowing itself to be petted and caressed by a woman who had finally come home, come home at last.

Mia's quiet revelry was interrupted by a buzzing in her pocket. Snapping to attention, Mia retracted her fingers from the sea and reached into her pocket. Pulling out her phone, she saw her mother's smiling image displayed brightly on the screen. Her mother, who stood at the kitchen window and waved, trying to suppress tears as Mia, her oldest daughter, drove away from her childhood home. Mia had to answer.

"Hi, Mom."

"Sweetheart! Hi! Have you settled in yet?"

"Not yet. I returned the U-Haul and the landlord helped me unload the boxes. He and his wife actually invited me to dinner tonight–Oh, crap. What time is it?" Mia asked her mother.

"It's about 6:15. Are you sure you don't want me to come and help you move in and unpack. I'd be happy to–"

"Oh, no! I was supposed to be there fifteen minutes ago."

"It's ok, Mia, I'm sure they will understand. Call me tomorrow. Or tonight if you can't sleep. And again, if you want me to come and help, I'll hop in my car first thing tomorrow morning and–,"

"Ok, Mom. I got it. Thank you ... I love you, Mom."

"Love you more, my girl. I'll let you go now. Buh-Bye."

Mia took one last glance at the ocean before hurrying off to dinner. She felt guilty for being so short with her mom. Especially after her kind offers to help with the unpacking and moving-in process. Her mom was so well-intentioned. She would do anything for Mia, and Mia knew that. Mia made a silent vow to call her mom tomorrow and give her the full run-down. That made her feel a bit better and eased some of her guilt as she put her phone back in her coat pocket.

She bid the waves a silent farewell as she followed her own footsteps back the way she came.

Chapter Five

CLAIRE

anic. Breaths came in ragged gasps against her throat. Heart hammered against her ribs. Thoughts flew through her mind like a million birds in a single cage. A single tiny cage.

Think, Claire, think.

Her persistent calling had alerted two neighbors, causing them to emerge on their stoops with questioning looks in their eyes. Diane Dixon from next door rushed over, still in her bathrobe. Ever since her youngest son, Reid, went away to college, she stopped bothering to get dressed until right before her husband came home from work. After all, what was the point? And sometimes Claire smelled liquor on her breath, even on Saturday mornings when they sometimes chit-chatted on the sidewalk.

"Claire," Diane said, "what's going on? Is everything alright?"

Claire felt like a trapped animal. Her movements were jerky and her legs, desperate to serve some purpose, jittered and tottered her uneasily back and forth in the driveway. She wished her husband were here.

"The boys ... they were just here! They were just playing ball. They're gone!"

"Oh, dear! I'm sure there's an explanation," Diane responded, trying not to become infected by the terror rising in her neighbor. "Why don't you and I walk up the block a bit to see if they wandered off?"

Claire allowed Diane to lead her up the sidewalk to the stop sign. She hoped in vain she was overreacting. Her eyes darted crazily every which way, scouring for a place that she had not yet looked. Scouring every inch of her sightline for her boy.

It was eerily quiet on Maple Street. Claire felt like she was drowning. Diane's voice sounded far away and muted. All Claire could hear was her own heartbeat; she could actually feel her rapid pulse in her temples ... and all she could taste was the terror rising in her like a wave up through her intestines.

She thought of her sweet son, her baby boy, her kind and lovable Jimmy. Jimmy with his lopsided smile and deep dimples grooved into his perfect cheeks. She had a sudden and intense vision of having just given birth to this tiny soul. She had never felt love so keenly and deeply as she had when she gazed at the tightly swaddled bundle in her arms a little more than seven years ago, no, almost eight years ago. Where had the year gone? This recollection caused her physical pain, and she felt a violent longing, a desperate need to wrap her arms around her son, to hold him in her grasp.

This wave of emotion brought Claire down to her knees. She vomited into the flower bed next to the stoop, yellow bile emerging from the depths of her roiling stomach. Saliva hanging down from her mouth like cobwebs. Diane patted her back as she retched out the fear that consumed her. "Calm down, Claire," she distantly heard her neighbor whisper. "We'll find him."

"Them," Claire corrected. "Jimmy had his friend Kyle over, too. They're both gone."

"Oh, dear!" Diane exclaimed. "Claire, what are you going to do now? What should we do?"

Somehow, the vomiting brought Claire out of her shock and back to reality. She began to think more practically and rationally of what was to be done. Should she call the cops? Was that an overreaction? Would people think she was crazy? Did it matter? So many racing thoughts. Too many. With Diane next to her, Claire pulled out her cell phone and dialed Joe's number. He would probably be on the train home by now; he told Claire this morning that he was leaving the office early to come home and take a Zoom call with the sister company in Madrid. Joe was afraid that if he took the call at the office, he wouldn't end up home until ten o'clock this evening, and he had promised Jimmy that they would watch the Knicks game together tonight. Joe picked up on the third ring; the connection was staticky. Claire knew that happened sometimes on his evening commute.

"Hey, hon," Joe answered.

"Joe! Jimmy's gone. He and Kyle were—"

"Claire? Claire … the connection isn't great. What did you–"

"Joe? Can you hear me?"

"Uhh … yes … better now. Just got out of the tunnel. What did you—"

"Jimmy's gone … and Kyle … they were—"

"What do you mean, gone?"

"Joe, shut up and listen. Jimmy and Kyle were playing basketball out front. I went in to transfer the laundry over. When I came back, they were gone."

"Kyle? Kyle who?" Joe responded nonsensically.

"Kyle Yardsleigh. He was here, playing with Jimmy. I left the office early today. Remember I told you about the playdate?"

In all of her emotion, Claire almost forgot that she had left them to go transfer over the laundry. She had left the boys, alone, in the driveway … she had left two little boys in the driveway alone to go transfer the fucking laundry over!

Those thoughts were interrupted when her husband responded, "Claire, I'm sure they are around. Don't be a helicopter mom. Have you checked next door?"

"Yes! I checked next door! I walked up and down the block

screaming their names. They're gone, Joe. I only left them for a minute. I looked everywhere."

Silence.

Was her husband trying to hold it together to avoid making a scene on the train ride home from Manhattan? Did he really believe she was overreacting–that she was being a helicopter mom? She could almost hear the wheels in his brain turning as she waited for his response.

"Joe. Jesus Christ, Joe. Say something!"

"Claire–holy shit, Claire. My train should get into the station in 20 minutes. I'll be home as soon as I can get there. Call the cops, Claire. Now. Call them now."

Chapter Six

MIA

When Mia was seven years old, her parents loaded up the family sedan for a weekend trip to the Jersey Shore. Ocean Grove Beach is located on the south side of the Asbury Park Boardwalk and boasts a huge expanse of sand and sky. It was a popular destination for Sparta families because of its close proximity, and the large amusement park nearby was an added bonus. Supposedly, it had one of the largest ferris wheels in the eastern U.S., and Mia couldn't wait to ride all the way to the top. She imagined that she would be able to scrape her finger-tips against the sky.

Her mother, Lara, was a self-proclaimed beach bum growing up and was born and raised in the Hamptons, a prestigious upscale community at the end of Long Island's tail. She viewed the nearly two-hour drive to the Jersey Shore with a tinge of sadness and almost embarrassment. Very few people who grew up on the water ever actually move away. But Lara Rossi, formerly Lara Spalding had done just that. She never regretted her choice to attend SUNY Binghamton, nor did she regret falling in love with Anthony Rossi over black coffee and late-night study sessions. She sort of regretted the fact that her parents also moved upstate shortly after she graduated college, and therefore she never made the pilgrimage back home to her childhood beach. The Hamptons was just so far away, and without family there, Lara couldn't justify the trip, even though she longed for it. But looking at her girls' excited faces in the rearview mirror she couldn't believe that this would be their first time feeling the Atlantic Ocean lap against their tanned little girl skin and she couldn't quite shake the feeling she had failed them in some way for not having exposed them to the ocean earlier.

The drive wasn't memorable for Mia as she reflected on the weekend, nor was the room in the beach-front inn her family had rented, but when she walked up the wooden stairs and saw the ocean laid out in front of her in all its tranquil glory, something happened within her, a quickening of some sort. She ran down towards the water's edge and plunged herself deep into the cool depths. The water was so cold it almost took her breath away. This was nothing like the heated Saf-T-Swim pools in which Mia had taken lessons, nor was it like the raised oval enclosures adorning her neighbors' backyards. This felt like she had come home.

Her mother stood nervously on the shore, quickly shedding her beach cover-up to join her hasty and inexperienced daughter in the sea.

"Mia, be careful please. You're not used to swimming in the ocean!"

Mia did not respond to her mother's warning; she just continued to wade deeper relishing the squishy feel of the sand beneath her toes. Tiny brown fish nipped at her ankles. After taking the next eager step, Mia found that she could no longer touch the bottom of the ocean, and before her mother could reach her, a wall of foamy water crashed over her head, dragging her body down into the cool depths beneath.

Over and over again she tumbled under the water, scraping her knees on the ocean's floor. She felt the burn of saltwater as it rushed up her flared nostrils and into her open mouth, filling her throat with the salty brine. Just when she felt that she would be dragged farther out into the depths, just when she felt that she could no longer fight the powers surrounding her, she felt her mother's strong grip under her armpits dragging her back to the surface and onto the sand.

Her mother, crouching before her, rubbed her back as Mia spit and gagged on the water as it came back up. Her hair hung in wet clumps in front of her face; Mia could make out the sandy grains stuck throughout her course curls.

When she could finally breathe again, her mother said, "Mia, you have to respect the ocean. Mother Nature will always be more powerful than we are."

It was a lesson she never forgot. Not even today.

"I'm sorry, Mom," Mia choked. "I was so excited to go swimming. I didn't realize I was out so far."

"It's ok, Mia. You're lucky I was right there ... we both are."

Then the tears came, hot and heavy. They weren't tears of fear, more so they were tears of shame and embarrassment. The salt within Mia mixed with the ocean's residue on her wet, round cheeks.

"Don't cry, my little love. Let's go have a snack and then together, we can try again."

Mia's mother looked extra beautiful to her as she bent down and spoke softly. Her full lips, dark curly hair, high cheekbones and honey brown eyes. Mia hoped that one day she would look just like her.

Allowing her mother to lift her off the sand and swat the dried seaweed and pebbles off her bottom, Mia's mother led her back up shore to their bags, which, because of her recklessness, had not yet been unpacked.

Mia sat on her small pink beach chair with a bag of pretzels in her lap staring at the ocean. She felt a bit disappointed, but undeterred, as her little sister, Gabby, sat in the sand next to her, playing with a yellow bucket and shovel.

After lunch, Mia and her mother did try again ... with much more success. Mia waded into the ocean, more tentatively this time, holding her mother's hand. The two girls descended into the sea, floating over the crashing waves until they reached a calmer patch farther from the shore. Even when Mia's lips were blue and chattering, her mother had to almost drag her out of the water. She cried when it was time to pack up and head back to the hotel.

Mia trailed behind her family as they walked back up the sand and farther from the blue waves dancing in the sunlight. Casting one more furtive glance backwards, Mia said a silent goodbye. The sea answered her, crashing a tattoo of rhythm in her mind.

That's when it all began for Mia. The nightly crashing in her head ... sometimes serenely singing her to sleep, sometimes hard and insistent ... sometimes barely perceptible. Those waves played on rerun in her brain, daily, weekly, monthly, yearly.

And here she was, answering their persistent summons at last.

Chapter Seven

CLAIRE

Claire pushed the terror down far enough to pull out her cell phone to dial 911. Diane Dixon stood next to her, rubbing her back. At first she was grateful for Diane's reassuring presence, but now it was becoming annoying and Claire would have rathered she just left her alone and gone home, but there was no time, no space to utter those words.

"911, what's your emergency?"

"My son. My son and his friend. They are gone." Claire tried to keep the quaver out of her voice; she knew how important it was to communicate clearly.

"Ok, Ma'am. I am going to need your name and your address."

Kyle's mom, Trish Yardsleigh, took that moment to pull up to Claire's house in her brand new glittering black Chevy Tahoe. Shit! Claire hadn't even thought to call her to let her know what was going on. *911* was the only thought that blazed like a neon sign in her brain. Trish saw the panic on Claire's face as she emerged, cool and beautiful, from her SUV. The two women made silent eye contact as Claire spoke into the phone, "122 Maple Street, Oceanside ... "

Trish interrupted, "What's going on?"

Claire held her silent with a shaking outstretched hand while Mrs. Dixon, not knowing that Trish's son was the other boy who had vanished, said, "Shh. Claire's on the phone with the police. Her son and her son's friend are gone."

"Gone?" Claire watched Trish's eyes squint and then clear with a dawning understanding. Ignoring Diane, and ignoring the fact that Claire was on the phone, Trish grasped at Claire's shoulder, "And you didn't think to let me know? Where did they go, Claire? Where did Kyle go?" Her voice was rising to a shriek.

From the speaker, the three women heard the directive, "An officer will be there shortly. Please stay where you are." Claire turned to face Trish. Words failed her; she didn't know what to say, how to say it. Creeping up next to the terror for her missing son, standing beside the absolute desperation she felt, was a sudden twinge of shame, of shameful defensiveness.

"What happened, Claire? Tell me right now where my son is."

Claire's knees buckled as she crumbled to the pavement, her arms clutching herself in a sort of wild embrace, "I wish I knew, Trish. I wish I knew. One second they were here and the next ... they were gone."

"Did you check next door? Maybe they are playing hide-and-go-seek. I'm sure there's an explanation–"

Claire realized that Trish was going through the same list of rationalizations that she herself had gone through just a little while earlier. It hurt her to utter the reality of the situation. She was tired now, tired and drained. She thought that maybe she was in a state of shock. She couldn't even cry.

"Trish ... I looked everywhere. They're gone." Claire's eyes were drawn fleetingly to the basketball once more across the street still and bright in the 5 o'clock slanted sunlight.

When Trish didn't answer, Claire looked up at her. Her eyes traveled from her red-soled Louboutins to the Louis Vuitton bag that was slung across her chest, to the Ray-Bans tucked fashionably into the neckline of her silk blouse. When her gaze reached Trish's eyes, she saw the same fear that she herself felt, etched into her retinas, but she also saw something else. Something hard and bitter: accusation.

"Claire. What do you mean they were gone? Where were you when they just up and vanished? Why weren't you watching them?" Anger, blame, and bitter desperation radiated off Trish as her stare met Claire's.

When Claire didn't answer, Trish spoke again in a shrill, hysterical voice, "Well? Where were you, Claire?"

"I was downstairs, switching the laundry over. I was watching them! ... and then I realized I forgot to transfer the laundry to the dryer last night. I ran down so quickly. I was gone for just a few minutes—"

"Jesus Christ, Claire. You left them here? ... in the driveway *alone*? They're little boys for God's Sake!"

Claire thought fleetingly of a time a few months ago when the Yardsleighs invited her family over for a barbeque. The adults–she and Joe, Trish and her husband, Mason–sat in their elaborate backyard getting tipsy off pinot grigio while the kids rode their bicycles up and down the street in front of the Yardsleigh's restored Georgian colonial. No one thought twice about supervision then. Had Claire committed such an egregious sin by leaving the boys outside for the few moments it took to deal with the mildewy laundry? She had done it a million times before. All parents do. But does that make it right? Claire guessed that it's ok until something happens. Until something terrible happens.

With effort, Claire stood up and tried to put her hand out to offer Trish some comfort. After all, they were in this together, weren't they? When the other mother felt Claire's hand on her arm, she flinched as if she had been touched with a branding iron and pulled away.

"I have to call my husband," she spat out tersely and walked down the driveway.

Claire overheard snippets of the conversation, saw Trish gesturing towards her, wiping at tears. She thought about those crime shows she binge-watched on Netflix; didn't those make-believe detectives always say how crucial the first 24 hours was in the case of a missing person? Or was it 48 hours? She glanced at the clock on her phone. How long had it been for Jimmy and Kyle? 30 minutes? An hour? More? Time was ticking. Where could they be? Had someone indeed taken them? And if so, why? That last thought sent another wave of nausea through her. That urge to hold her son–to wrap her arms around his slender shoulders–returned so fiercely that she felt actual pain in her soul. *Oh, God ... if there is a God. Send him home.*

"My husband is on his way," Trish reported. Claire noticed that she used the word 'husband,' not Mason. So formal and cold. Were they strangers now? Claire didn't really care what Trish thought of her at this moment; all that mattered was getting those sweet boys back home. Getting her sweet little Jimmy back into her arms, where he belonged.

The two women stood in silence, next to each other, but miles apart. They didn't speak. What was there to say? The immutable fact of their missing boys hung above them like a storm cloud.

After about 15 minutes–or was it 15 hours? Time was doing a funny dance in Claire's mind–she glanced up Maple Street and was relieved to see the familiar Ford Explorer, with a logo on its side that read Long Beach Police Department, easing down the street. Most serious matters that involved the cops in Oceanside were handled by the Long Beach precinct, a neighboring city with its own full police department. Claire felt both relieved and terrified that this case was deemed important enough by the individual on the phone for the big guns. She hoped they could help.

Chapter Eight

MIA

Bob held out the chair while Mia sat herself at the oak dining room table.

"Thank you, Bob," said Mia.

All of a sudden Mia noticed that her stomach was rumbling; she hadn't eaten anything aside from the chocolate chip granola bar she snagged from her parents' snack cabinet before she made the trip to Long Island. Was that even today? Yes, it was. Leaving her childhood home, packing up the boxes in the U-Haul … it all felt like it happened ages ago.

Dee put a steaming platter of spaghetti on the table along with a bowl of meatballs, a fully dressed salad, and a loaf of garlic bread. Dee must have worked hard to prepare such a beautiful spread on such short notice, and Mia felt flattered that she would have put in such effort for her. She certainly didn't have to. Mia couldn't wait to dig in.

The meal tasted as delicious as it smelled, and even though Mia had many errands to run and boxes to unpack, she was glad that she accepted the offer of a home-cooked meal. It reminded her of comfort and home.

"So, what brings you to Long Island?" Dee inquired as she

sipped her glass of wine. The burgundy liquid glistened in the fading light.

"It might sound weird, but I wanted to be closer to the ocean," Mia replied honestly. "Ever since my parents took me to one of the Jersey beaches as a kid, I've always wanted to live in a shore town."

Mia felt momentarily foolish for sharing that bit of information with Dee and Bob until Dee replied, "Those Jersey beaches can't compare to this one. And that doesn't sound weird to us at all." Bob nodded his agreement as he wiped his mouth with a napkin.

"Heck, I couldn't imagine living anywhere else," added Bob. "I grew up in an apartment in Connecticut, nowhere near the beach. I ended up here when a friend convinced me to take an apartment and a bartending job with him at Fenley's. And I thought to myself, 'Hell why not?' I didn't have much else going on. A change of scenery would be good. That bar's not even here anymore. It's O'Malley's now, but the second I stepped foot in this town, I knew I'd never leave. I met some oddballs along the way, but overall, this place is home."

Even though Mia had just discovered this place, she could already see what Bob meant. There was something wholesome about this town, something that pulled at her soul, something magical and beautiful and right, and Mia wondered if that something had to do with those crashes that emanated through her brain even now while she sat here with this elderly couple.

Dee broke the silence, "As for me, I was born a beach bum. I grew up one block away. I never left," she giggled good-naturedly.

Mia took note of Dee's brown, deeply lined skin and imagined that once the weather warmed up just a touch, Dee would spend most of her time down the lane, feet in the sand, soaking in the golden sun.

Dee continued, "It's not only that I'm a sun addict either. There's science behind it. Did you know that centuries ago, doctors actually used to prescribe the ocean as a cure ... it helps depression and used to treat tuberculosis ... lots of other ailments too. All these beachside treatment resorts sprang up all over the world. Eventually they went out of fashion, but if you ask me, it's much healthier than all these pills people take these days. Why take medications when all you really need is a good ol' dose of Vitamin S-E-A? But I guess the pharmaceutical business wouldn't like that too much," Dee chuckled a bit.

"Vitamin Sea ... I like that. Well I think I could use some of that healing. I can't wait to spend my first summer here," Mia replied. "I can't wait to spend as much time as possible at that beach."

"I'm right there with you, my young friend," Bob added. "I'm not sure if you're a fisherman, but maybe you'd like to try your hand at the rod with me?"

Mia had never fished before, and was eager at the invitation. "I'd really love that," she responded to Bob's inquiring eyes.

"Great! I don't catch much, and what I do catch, I usually throw right back in ... unless it's something really good. Dee makes a mean pan-fried bluefish. But I am good for a beer and some chit chat."

"That sounds wonderful to me. Sign me up."

There was a comfortable silence that pervaded the room, and Mia glanced out the window noticing the fading sunlight over the houses across the street.

Dee must have seen Mia looking wistfully out the window, because she said, "Would be a nicer view if we could see the ocean, wouldn't it?"

"It's beautiful the way it is," Mia replied honestly. "Peaceful ... quiet."

"Well, you have a view from upstairs, not sure if you had much of a chance to look at it yet, but your kitchen window looks right out over the water."

Mia knew this only from the short description that the realtor had sent her about the apartment when she was still making her choice about where to live. But since she had arrived, she had only given the view the briefest of glances in between moving the boxes up and down the stairwell with Bob earlier.

Dee continued, "If you sleep with the windows open up there, Mia, you can hear the waves when the town is all quiet and sleeping. It's really quite lovely. As a kid I always slept with my window open ... all year round. My mother used to yell at me, 'Close that blasted window. You're gonna catch your death!' Ha! I kept it open even in the dead of the winter! I just couldn't get enough of that sound. Still can't."

"It's funny you say that," Mia said, feeling a bit emboldened from the warmth of the wine. "Ever since my parents took me to the beach as a kid, I haven't been able to get the sound of the waves out of my mind. Sometimes I hear the crashing at night, while I'm sleeping. I hear it in the daytime too ... it's just more muted. Does that sound weird?"

Mia didn't know what possessed her to reveal such information. Maybe it was the wine, maybe she just felt comfortable with Dee and Bob. They seemed to understand the pull of the ocean.

Bob looked at her for a while in silence with a faraway look in his eyes. He seemed to be contemplating something. Something just over the horizon. Then he took up the conversation, "Not weird at all. The ocean is powerful. Some of us just have that connection to it, in here" and he gestured to his heart. "It just sounds to me like you finally found your ground." He exchanged a gaze with his wife. "You've just found your ground is all."

"Found my *ground*?" Mia asked.

"Yeah. Your ground. My dad used to use that phrase. It means that it seems like you found your place, your home ... the place you belong."

"Found my ground," Mia repeated. "I like that."

And at that moment, despite the chill working its way up the back of her neck, it very much felt to Mia that she was in exactly the right place at exactly the right time. The waves in her mind agreed; she had found her ground.

Chapter Nine

CLAIRE

Claire and Trish were standing in a small cluster of people when Joe parked his car and rushed up the driveway. He recognized Diane Dixon and Mason Yardsleigh–all looking grim and wide-eyed–but not the two police officers dressed in navy blue jotting notes onto a clipboard.

"Joe," Claire called to him. "These are officers Pratt and Lackey, they specialize in missing persons." She wove her fingers with her husband's, needing to be touching him, needing someone else who could understand the measure of her sorrow. His hands were rough from the yard work he had done last weekend. Rough and warm.

Claire noticed Joe's deer-in-headlights expression when she uttered those words: missing persons. She herself could hardly believe that the missing person was their own little boy. She tried to push away the thoughts of little Jimmy; he must be scared out of his mind. She tried not to think of the terror he must be feeling, the panic; if she did, she would drown in sorrow and she knew how important it was that she fully attend to the task at hand: giving the detectives accurate information regarding the disappearance. Her husband shook the officers' hands as he joined in the conversation.

"So let me just make sure I have your statement, Mrs. Benicek. You were outside with Jimmy and Kyle while they played basketball in the driveway. You estimated the time at a bit after 4pm. Is that correct?"

"Yes," answered Claire.

"You did not notice any suspicious activity: unusual cars, people passing by. Nothing unusual whatsoever? Nothing is too small to mention."

"That's correct. I didn't notice anything." Claire scanned her memory one more time, just to make sure. "Nothing out of the ordinary at all. No cars, no people. It's a quiet street. I would have noticed something if there was something to notice. I'm sure of it."

Trish snorted at Claire's response.

Officer Lackey noticed the sound and asked, "Is there anything you want to add, Mrs. Yardsleigh?"

"No," Trish said, wiping at her eyes. "I just don't know if I trust Claire's judgment on this one. I mean, she left those boys alone outside. Doesn't sound to me like she was paying much attention to anything that was going on."

Claire paled at the harsh words. She noticed that Joe didn't come to her defense.

Lackey responded, "I understand you're upset, Mrs. Yardsleigh, but we must focus only on the task at hand at the moment. Let's save the blame for another time."

The officer continued, "You went downstairs to attend to the laundry and when you came back upstairs, you estimated the time at about 4:20 pm, the boys were gone."

Claire nodded her agreement.

"You heard no sounds of struggle–no yelling or crying–you heard no sounds whatsoever. No passing cars, no brakes, no sound of accelerators?"

"I heard absolutely nothing," Claire responded. "Nothing at all! It was quiet. How can that be? It seemed as though the boys up and vanished!"

"They did not vanish, Mrs. Benicek. The word we use in law enforcement is abduction, which is what all the evidence–or in this case the lack thereof–points to ... an abduction. A well-executed and well-planned abduction."

"Well-planned," Claire repeated. "Like someone planned to take our boys? Like someone planned to just take Jimmy?" Her voice was rising to a hysterical pitch, a pitch that she had tried to subdue in order to do what needed to be done. She felt her control slipping.

"We'll explore all options, Mrs. Benicek. But that's my guess."

"It just doesn't make sense," Trish uttered. "It just doesn't make any sense."

Ignoring Trish, the detectives continued talking to Claire, "You and Mrs. Yardsleigh have stated that, to your knowledge, there is no one you know who wishes harm upon your family or your sons in particular. Mr. Benicek, do you concur with your wife's assessment?"

Joe seemed to shake himself free of some spell, "Yes. Of course! Who would want to hurt Jimmy? He's just a little boy. Oh, God. He's just a little boy."

The detectives seemed unperturbed by Joe's reaction. Claire wondered how many times they have had to stand with shell-shocked parents and take statements and deal with tears of unfathomable grief and sorrow. What must it be like to bear witness to such horrors day after day? She did not envy them.

"Well, that's it. We'll put out an APB on the two boys matching the descriptions you gave and post officers in a 90-mile radius. We will also issue a BOLO bulletin and an AMBER alert to widen our reach. I'm going to call the station and have them file Missing Persons reports for both of the boys and enter them into the National Crime Information Center. They couldn't have gotten very far."

Claire had no idea what half those words even meant. She thought perhaps they were acronyms, but she desperately hoped the detectives were right. She glanced at her phone. It was 5:15–an hour, no ... almost an hour and a half since Jimmy and Kyle had vanished. In her mind, even though the detectives refused to use that word 'vanished,' that's what it felt like had happened. There was no evidence of their existence at all. No evidence except for that orange basketball still at rest on the other side of the street. It seemed as though they had disappeared into thin air, snapped out of existence.

"So now what?" Trish Yardsleigh asked the detective, her voice thick, tears falling freely; her emotions were bubbling over.

"Now, I need all of you to provide a list of friends, acquaintances, family members, anyone who might know something." The officer glanced at each parent in turn and continued. "Once I have all that, you let us do our job, Mrs. Yardsleigh. Someone will be by both of your houses later to take your lists, formal statements and to provide you with updates."

"But that's not good enough," Trish continued. Her husband was at her shoulder trying his best to calm her. "It's just not good enough. When will you find my boy? He's just a little boy. And he's all alone."

"Well, they have one another. Kyle and Jimmy are together, somewhere. And we will do our best to find them. But please. We need to go. Let us do our job," Detective Lackey responded with finality.

The two detectives walked back to their car and drove off up Maple Street.

"Oh, God," Trish uttered through tears. "Oh, God, Oh, God, Oh, God."

"Come, Trish," spoke her husband, Mason Yardsleigh. "It's time to go home. The police will find Kyle. They will bring him home."

It was obvious to Claire that Mason was trying to be strong. Whether or not he believed what he said, Claire couldn't quite know. But she admired his optimism.

Claire offered, "You can come inside, I'll make some coffee. We can wait it out together."

For the first time since that terrible realization that the boys were gone, Claire felt consumed by emotion. Her body had been running on autopilot, logic replacing emotion and now that there was nothing else to be done, that awful fear and unfathomable sadness were taking up residence in her very soul. She was winding down like a clock.

Trish nearly screamed at Claire, "I don't want to be anywhere near you ... you negligent ... you negligent bitch! How could you just leave two little boys alone outside? You were responsible to WATCH them! Not do your laundry. Get the hell away from us."

Claire flinched as though she had been slapped. She stared at Trish, who regarded her with hard, cold eyes. "I never should have allowed Kyle to come to your house. I should have known better." And Trish turned around and walked back towards her fancy, black SUV.

"Trish," Claire called to her back. "It was two minutes–less than two minutes. I swear–" Claire choked on the rest of the sentence. It *was* her fault. Trish didn't even turn around; she just kept walking towards her car.

Mason Yardsleigh turned back fleetingly with an apology in his eyes, but said nothing as he followed his wife down the driveway.

Claire and Joe remained in the driveway hand in hand, staring at the cars that raced away from their home. Curious neighbors, who had been peering out their windows when the police car rolled down the street and then stopped, began to emerge on their stoops. They looked around with wide eyes and puzzled faces, the gossip still hidden behind closed lips.

"I'll leave you too now," Mrs. Dixon said, giving Claire a final hug. "God will send Jimmy back. I just know it."

Claire wished that she had that same faith in God. She had stopped believing that prayer could save her long ago. But that was a story for another time.

"We should go inside now," Joe said, looking around at the neighbors' houses. It was the first thing he had said since his initial outburst with the detectives. "People are going to talk to us if we keep standing here. And that's the last thing I want right now. I can't stand the idea of even seeing anyone right now."

Joe removed his hand from Claire's grip and walked up the front stoop and into the house, leaving the door open for Claire. Claire cast one more searching look at that basketball across the street—the last thing Jimmy had touched—and followed her husband inside. She felt as though she were in a dream. Or if she was being accurate, a nightmare. This couldn't be real. This sort of thing didn't happen in real life, right? Just in the movies. This couldn't be happening. But it was.

Much to her mother's chagrin, she hadn't signed Jimmy up for Hebrew School yet. It was so time consuming, and the few times she made inquiries at the local temples, the tuition was exorbitant. It just didn't seem worth it. Also, Joe wasn't much for religion. He considered himself agnostic even though he was raised Catholic. He thought all religions were cults. She didn't necessarily agree with him on that one. Well, maybe she did. Claire didn't even know what she believed in anymore, but she rationalized with herself that she didn't really need to make a decision regarding Jimmy's religious instruction just yet. She had time. But in the face of such tragedy, Claire prayed to a God that she didn't even know if she believed in, because that was all she could think to do. *Please, God, bring him back.* She made deals and bargains on the absolute impossible chance that some higher power was listening. *Please, God. If you bring him home, I'll go to temple. I'll sign Jimmy up for Hebrew School. I'll fast for Yom Kippur. I'll do anything. Just please bring him home.*

She walked inside and saw Jimmy's discarded sweatshirt thrown in the middle of the hallway. How many times had she told him to put his dirty clothes in the laundry basket? Ten times? Twenty times? A hundred times? She picked it up and clutched it to her chest. It smelled like him. Like dirt and sweat and chocolate. Like little boys. Now the tears came, fierce and raw. A screaming sob wracked her body as she fell to the floor, clutching that old sweatshirt to her chest.

Claire's tears coursed rivulets down her cheeks as the lonely sun sank lower behind the horizon.

Chapter Ten

MIA

Mia left Dee and Bob's house much later than she had expected. After dinner the three of them made their way into the dimly-lit living room; Mia sat on their worn couch and listened to Dee and Bob tell stories about the past. Mia especially loved hearing how Bob first met Dee.

*"I was barbacking at Fenley's when I looked up and there she was."
An admiring glance in Dee's direction. "She was so beautiful, still
is beautiful, but she was wearing these tight blue denims and these
thingamajiggies on her wrist that jingled and sparkled when she
walked. God, I couldn't take my eyes off of her."*

"Bangles," Dee corrected with a laugh.

*"Silver bangles. Dee always looks good when she wears silver.
Anyhoo, I couldn't stop staring at her. I must have been pretty
obvious about it because she looked right at me and waved."*

*"You've never been known to be subtle, Bob," Dee said, giving
him an affectionate nudge on the arm.*

*"Yeah, I guess that's true. I couldn't wave back because my
hands were full with a huge bin of pint glasses just out of the wash.
I just stared at her with a goofy grin on my face."*

"I love that goofy grin of yours," Dee chuckled while taking a sip of her wine.

"And I'm grateful that you do, Dee. Well, I just kept on staring while she walked over to the jukebox. My boss at the time had to snap his fingers right in front of my eyes to get me moving again. I almost dropped the whole load of glasses right on my feet. That would have been a disaster. It took me hours to get up the nerve to ask her out. I was so worried that she would just leave and I would never see her again."

"Little did Bob know that I was kind of smitten with him too. He just looked so sweet."

Bob continued with his story, "Finally, I got up the nerve. I sputtered something stupid–"

Dee interrupted with a good-natured correction, "You asked if I liked to eat ... if I wanted to eat with you. I thought you were cute in a shy, clumsy way. I was happy to oblige. Never regretted it for a minute."

Bob took up the conversation again, "And that was it. I was hooked." He kissed her on the side of the head appreciatively. "I'm the luckiest guy in the world."

"I don't know I would say that. But we have been mostly happy ever since. Yeah, we've dealt with our share of hardships, but those are sadder stories, for another time. That was more than 40 years ago. We certainly have gotten old in the meantime. Ever notice how time always has its way? Even when you think you can avoid it, time always wins," Dee concluded the tale. She gave Bob another one of those pensive gazes that Mia noticed throughout dinner. Mia briefly wondered what that gaze meant, what emotion it contained.

As she watched them interact, their playful back-and-forth, Mia looked at them with admiration. More than forty years of togetherness had clearly not dulled their love for one another. Maybe there were some sad stories in their past. Even Bob had certainly hinted at one of them earlier while helping Mia unpack.

But they belonged together, that was for sure. Mia dimly hoped that she would one day find someone with whom she clicked ... her own Bob.

When Mia glanced at the clock it was past 11 o'clock. Her eyes felt heavy, so she got up to say her goodbyes. She had enjoyed spending the evening with Dee and Bob; they were comforting and welcoming ... albeit quiet and thoughtful at times. But Mia was never one to mind silence. In fact, she found it comforting. She hoped for more dinner invitations in the near future. She remembered something that Bob had said earlier that day, something about "finding her ground." Mia guessed that he was right. She certainly did feel at home and content in her new surroundings.

"Thanks so much for having me. Dinner was delicious and the conversation was even better."

"It was our pleasure, Mia. We are happy to have you upstairs. Enjoy your first night. Don't hesitate to knock if you need something," Dee responded.

With a laugh, Bob added, "Or stomp on the floor."

"Goodnight," Mia said as she walked out the front door.

Dee and Bob's silhouettes leaned together as the door closed, emblazoned by the warm light streaming from behind them. Dee rested her head on Bob's shoulder and Mia could faintly make out their whispers as she walked down the path towards the stairs leading up to her apartment. It almost looked as though they were conspiring; she briefly wondered what they were saying. Mia herself couldn't wait for the comfort of her bed.

The night had turned breezy and cool. She could hear those waves again. Was she really hearing them ... or were they just crashing on the shores of her mind? She couldn't be sure. But as she walked up the side staircase and into her new apartment, she thought that maybe the answer was both.

Her new apartment, though bare and scattered with cardboard boxes labeled 'kitchen,' 'clothes,' 'breakables,' etc, felt warm and comfortable. She opened up the box marked 'bedroom' and took out a clean fitted sheet, a pillow, and her plaid comforter. She would unpack the rest tomorrow. Her bare twin-sized mattress was on the floor in the bedroom—luckily it fit in the U-haul or she would have been sleeping on the floor tonight. She looked at the white rectangle and thought that it was probably time for her to treat herself to an adult-sized bed. A queen-sized bed without a large frame would fit nicely in her new bedroom. Tomorrow she would ask Dee where would be the best place to buy some new furniture, but for now, she hastily made up a make-shift bed and crawled inside the comfortable cocoon of warmth. The comforter smelled of home, but her hair had taken on the unmistakable briny scent of the sea. Mia drifted to sleep with the sound of the waves crashing through her subconscious.

Chapter Eleven

TRISH YARDSLEIGH

When Trish pulled her SUV up the paved driveway of her home, the sun had already dipped below the horizon. The windows were dark and despite the grandeur of her home, the whole structure emanated a foreboding and gloom. Probably because it was empty. Kyle wasn't there. His bed would remain empty tonight. No dinner-time, where she would have to coax him to at least take a few bites of the chicken cutlets that were currently defrosting on her counter, no bath-time where she would make sure that he actually used soap to wash himself, no story-time where Kyle would snuggle up against her and she could smell his clean, wet hair. No bedtime ... nothing. The sadness was crushing. It sat on her chest with a palpable weight taking her breath away.

She followed her husband up the walkway and into the house. Mason immediately pulled his cell phone out of his pocket and started making phone calls. He was a powerful man and had many business connections; it seemed like he always knew all of the important people: the mayor, the congressman ... the owners of most of the local stores. He had recently told her that he was thinking of running for assemblyman next term ... and he would probably get elected. Everyone loved Mason Yardsleigh with his affable smile and sincere eyes. Hopefully some of his connections could help bring home Kyle. Could help bring home her boy. Mason closed himself into his office; Trish could make out the rise and swell of his animated conversation. She herself felt no such animation. Only despair. Bottomless, empty, soul-crushing despair.

She sat down on the bottom step of the polished staircase to remove her shoes. Such beautiful shoes. Only throughout the past 2 or 3 years—now that Mason made partner at his law firm—had she allowed herself such extravagance. Designer pumps, handbags, sunglasses. Jeez, her closet was definitely a far cry from that of her childhood, which mostly consisted of hand-me-downs and gems found at the local Salvation Army. When Trish met her husband, she knew that he was her ticket out of the middle-lower class, blue-collar life in which she had grown up. She didn't have a terrible upbringing, but she had always wanted more. She had been adopted into her family ... and often wished for more of a "little orphan Annie" story. Her adoptive parents were far from Daddy Warbucks, but they loved her. Growing up, Trish often envisioned the truth of her biological parents. Who were they? Why did they give her up? Was she defective in some way? She guessed that much of her present life was geared towards making up for those feelings of insecurity, of inadequacy. She had asked her parents, a few times, about these mysterious people who had created her, but they were closed off about it—vague. A weird light would creep into her mother's eyes each time the topic was mentioned. So Trish eventually stopped asking and accepted her fate. Yet, the questions remained in her mind.

Aside from the fact that Mason Yardsleigh was definitely going places, he was kind, and handsome, and amazing in the bedroom, making the thought of a life with him even more appealing. She fell for him and fell hard. He was on the up-and-up, and he brought Trish up with him. They were a good pair ... a power couple. Beautiful, likable and newly rich.

Trish herself didn't have to work, but she busied herself with

PTA and charity events, along with daily spin and yoga classes to keep up her fit appearance. She adored the way people seemed impressed by her, the way people seemed to hang on her words–like she mattered. She basked in the male attention she received, the casual glances at her legs, her breasts ... after all, she expended quite a bit of energy on her appearance. Yet now, none of that mattered, did it?

Mason had always dreamed of a large family and Trish was on board, yet they had a hard time conceiving a child. When the typical methods didn't work, two years of daily IVF treatments finally did the trick. Trish got pregnant with Kyle and their life seemed complete, whole, perfect. And Kyle *was* perfect. Adorable, smart, and charismatic, he could light up a room. His teachers and friends adored him, and so did Trish. God, she spoiled that boy. About a year ago, once Mason was established in his career, they started discussing trying for another one. Kyle would be such an amazing big brother. Only two weeks ago had Trish contacted the IVF clinic for the second time in her life. She was finally ready to go through the hell of those treatments again. It would be worth it in the end of course (especially if the next one came out like Kyle), but she wasn't looking forward to the process.

Now a bitter resentment started to take hold of her and a crushing sense of anger. She had worked so hard to sculpt this life. This perfect, beautiful life. Those feelings of shame over her past had finally crept back to the edge of her consciousness–barely perceptible. For the first time in her life, she finally felt like she could breathe, like the other shoe wasn't about to drop. She had her son, her husband, her home ... a life. And now all that was slipping away, slipping away like grains of sand slip through the cracks of your fingers when you try to hold on too tightly. And maybe because it was too painful to think about Kyle right now, or maybe because she needed something tangible and nearby to latch onto, all her emotions at this moment narrowed into a single blade of throbbing rage–and that rage was focused on Claire. How could she have trusted Claire to watch her precious Kyle?

Claire could barely take care of herself. Working hours on end, barely scraping by. Always rushing around. Never able to even make an appearance at the PTA events. Claire was an unfit mother. How had she never realized this before? Unfit and negligent. Going to do laundry while she had two little boys in front of her house! Doesn't she know that she is supposed to actually *watch* the children that come over to her house to play? Claire would pay for this. Oh, yes. Trish would make sure of that.

She wiped the tears from her eyes, not even caring about the streak marks her mascara certainly left on her cheeks. She fished around in her Louis Vuitton purse and closed her fingers around her phone ... a potent weapon in our current society. She scrolled through her text chains, finally settling on the 150 member PTA thread. She started to type.

Mia tumbled headlong into a deep sleep as soon as her head touched her pillow. The magnitude of the day finally brought her to the brink of exhaustion. Leaving home, driving to Long Island, moving into a new, unfamiliar place, dinner with the landlords ... all of it left her mind tired and numb. The wine she had consumed also helped. She couldn't remember a time when she had felt this exhausted, this spent. She thought fleetingly of the fact that she hadn't called her mom back. She got home so late ... there just wasn't time. Home. That elusive word. As a kid, she used to watch in awe the scene in *The Wizard of Oz* where Dorothy Gale in her blue gingham dress clicked the heels of her ruby slippers together uttering the mantra, "There's no place like home. There's no place like home." How those shoes had sparkled in the blazing light of cinematic color. But what happens when a person gets older? When the word 'home' is no longer such a simple, given fact? She turned over in bed, pulling the covers up to her chin. Mia guessed that was what this place was now, home–even though it didn't quite feel like it yet. She would call her mom tomorrow.

In her dreams, Mia stood naked at the shoreline. She was in complete silence, not even the waves that greedily lapped up against her ankles, nor the gulls that flew overhead, emanated any noise. She looked down and noticed that her birthmark, the unsightly blemish on her hip that she always made sure to conceal, was moving, undulating, pulsing, mimicking the crashing waves. She descended into the expanse before her until she was fully submerged. The current pulled at her, egging her on. Daring her to go deeper. She did. And then there was noise. The silence was broken by a deep echoing in her ears, her soul. The pounding of her heart was almost deafening as she realized that she was being dragged under, the daylight barely perceptible through the glimmering surface overhead. Suddenly, Mia was a child again at the Jersey shore struggling to reach the surface. She tried to breathe, to cry for help, but the salty water filled her mouth, her throat, her lungs, drowning her. This time her mother wasn't there to drag her to the surface. She was alone.

Gasping, Mia was startled out of her nightmare. She sat bolt upright in bed as the sound of the waves came to her through the open window. It was cold in her bedroom, bare and empty. The boxes cast sinister shadows in the moonlight. With a trembling hand, she flipped the light switch. She took a few deep breaths to still her hammering heart. *It was just a dream. A nightmare. It wasn't real. I'm ok.* Eventually, the specific details of the reverie faded as her pulse returned to normal.

Chapter Thirteen

CLAIRE

The detectives had just left Claire's house for the second time that day. They took down an official statement in careful script on a large white legal pad and asked Claire and Joe for their list of contacts. They also outlined their course of action which included interviewing neighbors, viewing neighborhood surveillance cameras (which apparently exist), Ring cameras, and traffic cameras, contacting the surrounding police departments for assistance, and adding Jimmy's case to the missing children databases. A whole database ... no, not just one—*databases* ... plural ... with an 's,' dedicated to missing children. Claire couldn't think of anything more hopeless and sad than files upon files of innocent boys and girls deemed "missing." Claire also handed over a small photograph of her beautiful boy. His latest school picture, his toothy smile shining on the glossy paper, hair gelled and styled with such care and precision. When she ordered the photo package, she couldn't imagine what she would do with eight identical wallet-sized images. Now she was grateful for the extras. Looking at her son's photograph secured in the detective's clipboard reminded her of those faces that used to stare at her from the backs of milk cartons when she was a child. She used to read the descriptions of those kids with tears in her eyes while eating her Frosted Flakes at the kitchen table. The thought of kids wandering around without their parents was horrifying to her. Now her own son was one of them. Lost. Parentless. Missing. When did the milk companies stop putting those sad photos on their products? Perhaps if Jimmy's picture was on a milk carton, someone would know where he was. Perhaps someone would be able to help.

She and her husband were informed that there were no new developments in Jimmy's case, and Claire worried that she noted a trace of genuine concern in Sergeant Lackey's demeanor. He had seemed so confident earlier this afternoon, so sure of himself. But now, with the lack of any apparent evidence or updates, his comforting tone had changed. He had become more methodical, insistent. Now he was asking for medical and dental reports ... Claire didn't want to think about the why behind those requests. And he was putting together a search party. They would start canvassing the area tonight.

The sergeant also cautioned her about receiving phone calls. He didn't know if this would be a ransom or extortion situation, but they had to be prepared. The Beniceks were advised to keep a pen and pad around in case they needed to take down information. All phones would be tapped and monitored in case the kidnappers tried to contact them. *Kidnappers.* Claire thought that she would only hear that word in the movies, not in real life. Certainly not in *her* life. The word conjured up images of gangly masked men dressed in black and white prison stripes who carried off helpless children in burlap sacks. Was that what happened to Jimmy and Kyle? She felt like throwing up.

"But what can we do," Claire had implored the officer. "I can't just sit here while Jimmy is ... while Jimmy is ... gone. I have to find him. I have to do something. I have to help find my son!"

The officer had been patient and business-like, assuring Claire that, "The most important thing you can do right now is give us the information we need and let us take care of it. I know how desperately you want to help with the search, but it's just not the

best use of your energy. The first 48 hours are the most important, and we need to make sure we have the most accurate
information."

And before Claire could protest further, the officer had left
and the house was quiet. Claire paced around looking at all of this
stuff that she had accumulated over the years. She had so carefully
picked out those dusty rose throw pillows, that wooden sign that
says, *Welcome Home*, that ceramic vase on the dining room table
with the burlap ribbon tied around the neck containing silk
sunflowers, those vanilla musk candles from Bath and Body
Works–they filled the whole house with their fragrant aroma. All
this stuff. A houseful of pointless stuff. Junk. All of it. Who cared
about any of this shit? It was all so useless. What did anything
matter if Jimmy wasn't here?

Despite her exhaustion and absolute bone-crushing sadness,
Claire glanced at her phone and was greeted by a well-meaning
text from her friend, Joanne Doherty:

> Claire, Oh my God, I just heard. Trish
> Yardsleigh sent out a mass text to the entire
> PTA committee about it. What can I do to
> help?

Claire sighed. She hadn't even let her own family know. She
couldn't even bear to utter the truth to her loved ones just yet. If
she told them, then it meant that this nightmare was real. Her
plan was to tell her parents only after Jimmy was returned. Or
maybe not even tell them. No reason for her to leave herself open
to additional words of criticism from her increasingly judgy mom,
right? She knew that he would be home soon; why worry anyone?
These thoughts were what Claire told herself ... she tried to make
herself believe them. How else would she survive this? Apparently
Trish had a different reaction.

With a sigh, Claire texted back,

> I wish there was something you could do. Just send us all the hope, prayers, and positivity you can muster.

An immediate reply:

> Of course! Thinking about you. Poor Jimmy.
> Can't even imagine what you're going
> through.

You definitely can't imagine, Claire thought. Tears welled from her eyes. She was shocked she had any tears left at all. There must be hidden reservoirs inside of us, stored up for such occasions.

Another Ping. *Here's Joanne again,* Claire thought.

> I don't even know if I should tell you this or
> not, but Trish is bashing you on our PTA
> thread. She's always been kind of nuts, but
> she's blaming you … saying you are negligent
> and unfit to be a mother. Lots of people are
> agreeing with her.

Claire remembered that nasty look Trish had shot her before she made her hasty exit, the harsh comment she had made to the detective when he asked his questions. Claire sighed heavily. She supposed she couldn't begrudge Trish her anger. Everyone has a different way of dealing with grief … and Claire *had* left the boys alone. No amount of justification was going to change that one immutable fact. She was already beginning to feel that crushing guilt creep up alongside her sorrow. But this was a different kind of guilt than she usually endured–the daily feeling of inadequacy that often accompanies the working mom was common to Claire, ordinary and expected. But this guilt … this guilt was suffocating. She wished Joanne hadn't felt the need to share this tidbit of information. Even though the thought nagged a bit at her, she couldn't quite bring herself to care too much. There were so many other, more important thoughts crowding her brain—starting with getting Jimmy and Kyle back. What was Trish's anger towards her in the face of that?

She sent a final text back to Joanne:

> Well. My focus is on getting the boys back.
> That's it.

Then she put her phone on silent and walked over to Joe who had sunk down on the living room couch with his head dropped low on his chest. She sat down next to him and put her hand on his thigh. He didn't move.

For a second, she thought he might be sleeping, but then he uttered, "Shit, Claire, what are we going to do? I don't think I can survive this world without Jimmy right there next to me."

The desperation in his voice, the sadness brought a fresh wave of tears to her eyes. Joe was the strong one, the eternal optimist. It was devastating to see him like this.

"They're going to find him, Joe. I know it."

"You can't know that, Claire."

Claire searched his face, his averted eyes and repeated again, "They're going to find him, Joe. I feel it. Joe, look at me."

Joe's hazel eyes flickered up, they were the exact replicas of Jimmy's eyes. It was almost uncanny. He met Claire's steady gaze. Aside from the unfathomable sadness, Claire saw a hardness in that gaze, an unfamiliar coldness. She almost didn't recognize him. He had never looked upon her with anything other than love, even when they argued, which wasn't often, and the look that was emanating from him now was definitely not that.

"How could you let this happen?" he said. "How could you let our boy get abducted right before your eyes?"

Claire didn't know what to say or how to respond. It was a witch hunt, and she was the culprit. It felt like a noose had already been placed around her neck ... a noose that was getting tighter by the minute. Or maybe a witch hunt wasn't the right metaphor. Weren't witches innocent people? Claire wasn't innocent. Maybe she was a witch ... a real one. Maybe the noose was exactly what she deserved. She couldn't breathe. The accusation and blame in her husband's comments clamped onto her like a steel vise grip.

"I'm sorry," Claire squeaked through a throat that was raw with emotion and desperation. "I'm sorry, Joe. Trish already blames me, please tell me that you don't also."

Claire gripped his hand, held it in both of hers as though holding onto a life raft. God, she needed him. She couldn't do this alone. Joe pulled his hand from her grip and stood up.

"Well, if it's not your fault, whose fault is it? Jesus, Claire, you were supposed to be watching them. Who cares about the fucking laundry?"

Joe turned away from her and walked downstairs to the basement. His footsteps heavy on the creaking wood. Aside from the rare occasion when Joe was away on business, it was their first night apart. What Claire didn't know at the time was that this wouldn't be the last.

Instinct brought Claire's hand up to her throat for the comforting feel of the metal against her thumb; she had forgotten that the locket wasn't there. She groped around down her shirt, maybe she hadn't really checked thoroughly before. After all, before she had been totally shaken ... not that she wasn't shaken right now. Maybe it had come unhooked in the chaos of the day, but it wasn't there. It was gone. Another thing missing. Another dear thing. The tears came again and this time, they didn't stop. Only her own salt water kept her company through the night.

Chapter Fourteen

MIA

Mia found herself at the water's edge the following night. It had been a long day of cleaning and unpacking. She wasn't even close to done. She had at least gotten the kitchen organized. Her pots, pans, plates, cups, forks, knives, all taking up so many boxes in the U-Haul, barely occupied even half of the cabinets ... nothing like the jam-packed shelves of the cabinets back in Sparta, that she had to search through on her hands and knees sometimes, just to find what she was looking for. Here, there was so much empty space.

She had done her first food shopping at the local Key Food down the block, and stocked up on milk, eggs, canned soups, cold cuts, bread, flour, olive oil and all the other essentials needed when starting from scratch. Like the kitchen items, the groceries nearly spilled out of the shopping cart, but once put away in the refrigerator and cabinets, barely lined the shelves. Even though she had compiled a solid list of items to purchase, she had forgotten so much. Salt. How could she forget salt? Or coffee? Sometimes when you get so used to just having something, you forget that you actually need it. She would have to go back to the store again tomorrow.

Also, she needed to start job hunting. The grocery bill alone totaled almost $300. She definitely didn't have unlimited funds, even though her parents had given her some extra cash to help her establish herself. She wanted to feel independent, complete, like she could do this herself, which was why she declined further money from her father. This was also why Mia declined her mother's offer to come help her move in. For as long as she could remember, her mother had done everything for her. Even her laundry. Now, Mia needed to do this alone. She needed to feel competent and able. She had been struggling to feel like an adult, especially cooped up in her childhood bedroom—another reason why she knew it was time to move out.

All of these thoughts swam around her head as she stood with her feet immersed in the frigid waters of the Atlantic Ocean. Did she feel more like an adult now? No, she didn't think she did. She still felt very much like a child. Mia looked down at the blurred image of her feet in the water. She imagined that one day her poor ankles would be as numb to the cold as Bob and Dee's were; they were able to stand on the icy pavement completely nonplussed. But right now, Mia's teeth chattered in the biting late winter air. She didn't bother with her sneakers this time, and her flip flops lay discarded near the wooden plank stairs leading over the dunes. Pulling her knitted winter hat down over her ears, she nestled her chin and nose deep within her scarf. It smelled like home. Well, not her home anymore.

The night was clear and the stars blazed with a fiery intensity in the sky above. What was it about the water that so called to her? The ebb and flow of the tide drew her even closer, and she had to resist the physical urge to submerge herself further into the depth spread out before her. The waves echoed in the still night and also in her cluttered mind. They called to her. Their whispers muted, but there. She didn't know what they wanted.

It was late and she had much to do tomorrow, so she stepped back—the hard packed sand becoming less and less dense as she retreated. But, before she turned around, she felt something solid brush up against the side of her bare foot, which was now almost numb from the cold. Reaching down, Mia closed her hand around the object in question and brought it up dripping to her face to get a better look. Even though she couldn't make out the intricacies of the item she held in her grasp, she was clearly looking at a silver locket–oval in shape at the end of a long, delicately linked chain. She couldn't make out the nuances of the pattern, but from the way its dull sheen reflected the dusky twilight, Mia could discern that the object was certainly expensive. Something that would be missed.

Shoving the necklace into her coat pocket, she hurried back to the walkway and back out onto Minnesota Avenue. She was tired and a bit overwhelmed. She thought a good night's sleep would clear her mind. Hopefully there would be no nightmares tonight.

Chapter Fifteen

JIMMY

Jimmy looked around. He didn't know where he was. He was shivering. And he was crying. Snot was running down his nose and touching his top lip. He didn't have a tissue or even a napkin. And he wasn't supposed to use his sleeve ... his mom always told him not to do that. She said that was gross and unsanitary. The people that brought him and Kyle here were gone. They just sat them down, tied them to chairs and told them not to move or talk because they would be back. They said if they were bad, they wouldn't get dinner.

Jimmy had gone to the bathroom in his pants. He had to go so bad and he was so scared that he just went. He hadn't done that since last year when he was too afraid to ask his Kindergarten teacher to use the bathroom. He was sent to the nurse's office to change into new clothes. And the new clothes were from a box and they were too big and they smelled funny. Mrs. Diggs put his old pee clothes in a plastic bag to take home to his mom. He was embarrassed to give them to her, but she wasn't mad at him at all. She just gave him a hug. She smelled so good, like flowers. And she always had tissues.

The walls looked old, that's all he knew. And he was cold. Cold and wet. Well, he wasn't all wet. Just the bottoms of his pants. From walking though all that water. And in his pants where his pee wasn't warm anymore. He was wet there too.

Jimmy could hear sloshing sounds hitting up against the outside of the wall. But it was dark where he sat. There weren't any lights here. He could see a bit of the sky through the slatted boards of the roof. It wasn't like a home, this place where he was. There wasn't a couch or a carpet or even, from what he could tell, a kitchen. There were tools. He had seen an old boat outside tied up to the dock, not like the newer one that took them here. There was an upside down canoe. Jimmy recognized the canoe because he and his dad went fishing on a canoe when they went camping last summer with the Boy Scouts. He had caught his first fish. Daddy had told him it was a rainbow trout, even though it didn't look rainbow to him. He couldn't wait to go fishing again. He was going to ask for a tackle box next Christmas. But this canoe was old, and there weren't any oars. How were you supposed to use a canoe without oars to help you paddle?

Kyle was sitting across from him. But he couldn't talk to Kyle. He had something around his mouth. Something that tasted bad. And his hands too. Something held his hands together in front of him. Kyle also had something over his mouth and his hands were together in his lap too. He looked over at Kyle. Kyle was crying softly. Jimmy could see Kyle's shoulders shaking. Was he cold too? His pants were also wet. Was he scared like Jimmy was? Jimmy was so scared. Even more scared than when he watched that scary movie with his dad the night before Halloween. He had night-mares that night. He couldn't sleep. Jimmy didn't think he would sleep tonight either. This wasn't the same type of scared. This was real-life scared, which was different than movie-scared. He tried to stretch his foot out to tap Kyle, but he couldn't reach him.

Even though Jimmy's hands were tied in front of him, if he stretched out his fingers, he could reach inside his front pants pocket. He was searching for his mom's necklace. In his little boy's mind, he felt that touching it would be like touching his mom. And he wanted his mom right now, so badly. More than he had ever wanted anything. Even more than he wanted the Nintendo Switch. And he wanted that pretty bad. But he wanted his mom a hundred million thousand infinity times more. His mom always made things ok. He had found the necklace in the bathroom this morning. Knowing that Kyle was coming over after school, this would be their pirate treasure. They could hide it in the tree house next door and then go hunting for it. It would have been fun. He promised himself that he would put it back just where he found it when they were done with it. He knew his mom wore that necklace every day. She once told him that it was very special because daddy gave it to her when she became a mom. She said being a mom was the best present and this necklace helped her remember that. He loved opening it and closing it ... it made a soft, satisfying snap when he pressed both sides tight together. And there was a tiny picture of himself inside of it. He wondered how his mom got it so small. Did she have a shrink ray that he didn't know about? If he had a shrink ray, he could shrink himself and Kyle down so small that they could climb out of here through the cracks and go home. But he didn't have one. He thought that maybe those only existed in the movies.

But Jimmy's empty hands told him that there was no longer any necklace in his pocket. Jimmy's pocket was empty except for the lucky penny he found walking into school this morning. He was going to put it in his piggy bank, but he forgot to do that. The real treasure, his mom's necklace, was gone. Had it fallen out when he fell in the water getting out of the boat? He wasn't down for long before the man picked him up by his armpits and pushed him forward. He looked around the room frantically, the floor near his feet, but no luck. He checked his pockets again–turned them inside out–in vain hope, but it was gone. His mommy would be so mad at him that he lost such a special thing.

Without having something of comfort to grasp, Jimmy hung his head down and cried harder. His tears fell down and seeped through the floorboards, mixing with the ocean below.

Chapter Sixteen

TRISH

"I can't just let this go, Raymond. It's been four weeks. Four. That my boy has been missing. And aside from a few idiots who claimed to have seen him, there's nothing. No sign of him. How does a child just disappear without leaving a trace?"

"So those leads didn't pan out?" Raymond asked.

"No. They didn't. 51 reports came into the station ... 51 people claiming they saw Kyle. But not one of those 51 told us jack shit about anything. Just a waste of time."

"Trish–they're doing the best they can."

"Well their best isn't good enough, is it? And it's her fault. Claire. That negligent bitch left my boy *alone* outside. She's to blame, and she should be punished. I just can't accept that there are no legal avenues for me to pursue. There has to be something I can do. She shouldn't be allowed to get away with this. It's criminal!" Trish looked hungrily up at Raymond Stone, a man, a friend, that she had known for the past 15 years.

Raymond responded, "Trish, we've been through this on the phone already. In order to press negligence charges against Claire Benicek, there has to be solid proof that she—"

"But there *is* solid proof. I don't understand why you can't see that. Why nobody can see that. You're the fourth goddam lawyer I've met with. I didn't call you earlier because I didn't want to put this on you. But you're it, my last chance to nail Claire to the wall. I asked you here because you are a friend, you were in my wedding party for fuck's sake. Don't tell me there's nothing I can do here."

"Trish, the fact that your husband is my friend is the reason why I came out here. You have been through a terrible, terrible tragedy and I can't imagine how you've even survived this month. My advice, both as a lawyer and as a friend is to let go of this anger and deal with the fact that–"

"The fact that what ... ?" Trish spat back. "The fact that my baby boy was abducted in broad daylight, right under that bitch's nose? Accept the fact that he's probably dead already? The fact that whoever took him probably did something terrib–" Trish couldn't finish. The reality and probability of that situation was too dark, too hopeless to even utter aloud. "Well, I can't just accept that. I just can't. Will you help me, or not?"

"Trish, you're a smart woman. Again, I'm speaking as a friend. This anger you have boiling inside of you isn't helping anyone ... it's especially not helping you ... or Mason. It's unhealthy and consuming. And it's not going to bring your son back home."

Trish shuddered at the mention of her husband. Ever since the day that ... ever since the day IT happened, Mason had been a shell of himself. She wished that he would feel the anger that she did, the intense, bottomless rage burning in her stomach. She wished that he would feel *something*. Any emotion would be better than the nothingness that emanated from him. Maybe if he shared her anger, Trish would recognize him. She felt like she didn't even know him anymore. The fact that he was sitting up in his office right now, instead of down here with her, only amplified her temper.

"You clearly have no idea what would help me, or my husband. What I need right now ... what *we* need right now, is a lawyer, not a friend," Trish retorted.

"Well, I'm sorry to hear that, Trish," Raymond said without rancor. "When you're looking for a friend, I'm here. But as a lawyer, I'm going to leave now. I can't help you and I won't play a role in destroying another grieving mother's life. It's just not the right thing to do."

Raymond got up from the sofa, put on his coat and picked up his leather briefcase.

"Well, thanks for nothing, Raymond. Don't let the door hit you in the ass on your way out," Trish replied storming out of the living room and leaving her friend to let himself out.

She was raging as she paced back and forth. *What bullshit*, she thought to herself. *Stupid, stupid bullshit.* Well-meaning friends and family had provided her with unfailing support and encouragement over the past few weeks, helping her to maintain hope when deep down she knew that the situation was dire at best. But what did any of those well-wishes actually do? Absolutely nothing. They were useless. No one was able to do anything real to help her, not even the cops. And certainly not the blood-sucking lawyers. She was sick of them too. She was sick of all of them.

Shoving her hands in her pockets, she felt the business card for a local therapist that her best friend Maryellen had given her last week. It was wrinkled from being forgotten about and then from going through the washing machine. Why did everyone think that SHE was the one who had the problems? She didn't need therapy, she didn't have the "anger that accompanies the loss of a loved one," or whatever the 3rd stage of grief was that people were so fond of quoting to her. Screw that! How was it possible that Trish was the only person to see the clear fact here—that Claire Benicek was no better than a common criminal. She basically gave whoever took her boy the green light when she left them alone outside. What kind of adult does that?

Trish hadn't seen Claire since that day. She didn't think she could look at her without spitting in her face. Word around town was that Claire's husband, Joe, had moved out. *Good*, Trish thought. In Trish's mind, she wanted nothing less than this woman's total destruction. Trish couldn't even believe that at one point, she actually considered Claire a friend. What had she been thinking?

Trish had done an adequate job of gaining the support of the community and turning the local moms against Claire. Trish didn't even necessarily mean to do so at first, but the scathing Facebook posts and group text messages became a way that Trish could deflect her hurt, her worry, her pain and fear over her missing son into something more palpable and satisfying. So what if she had exaggerated a bit. So what if she let people believe that Claire had left the boys alone for an hour? Or that she had been drinking while Kyle and Jimmy were playing? She may as well have been. It's amazing how a story can morph and change after each re-telling. Trish could have corrected them, but why? It amounted to the same thing: her boy was gone. And that it was Claire's fault. That was the bottom line. All that mattered.

Even Claire's best friend, Joanne, had been joining in on the anti-Claire campaign–adding degrading comments to the threads that Trish had begun. The thought of this brought a tiny smile to Trish's face; it was the first time she'd smiled in weeks. *Forget them,* Trish thought–*forget those stupid lawyers, those moronic cops.* They don't know shit. How dare Raymond lecture her about the uselessness of anger. Her rage wasn't useless at all. In fact, Trish had come to believe that anger was more productive than sadness. Much more productive. Despair was what kept her in her room the first two weeks after Kyle was taken. Sobbing like a mess on her bed. Sadness is crushing and hopeless and idle. It wasn't until her hopeless melancholy turned into the first seeds of rage that she began to feel like herself again. Sadness didn't get her son back ... maybe anger wouldn't either–Raymond might have been right about that–but it was definitely better. It made her feel stronger. Powerful.

With that thought, Trish picked up the pad that she had left on her bedside table. On it was a phone number that she had written down and dismissed about a week ago. It was the phone number for *News12*, a local television network specializing in just that, local news. Maybe it was time to give them that interview they wanted. Maybe it was time for all of Long Island to know the truth about Claire Benicek.

Chapter Seventeen

MIA

Another nightmare. *They seem to be happening more and more frequently,* Mia thought to herself as she sprang awake in the dark. Her breaths came in deep, heaving gasps. Her pulse throbbed in her temples. Another dream about the ocean. In this one, she was again standing at the shore, the angry purple storm clouds huddled above her head. She could make out streaks of lightning shooting through them; the thunder roared, rippling through her. She felt the vibrations radiating through her ribcage and stomach. The waves crashed with ferocity against the sand. Her hair whipped around her face in the hazy, damp air. There seemed to be shapes swirling below the water, grotesque, distorted figures. She thought they were sharks, long dark shadows swimming just below, out of reach, but they weren't sharks. They were faces, gaping faces with gigantic open mouths screaming soundlessly up at her through the current. Then glancing down, an object glittered in her palm. The locket.

She was awake now; all signs of sleeplessness evaporated as she was jolted out of her nightmare and into her dark bedroom. The sound of the ocean waves tumbling softly through her open window were a stark comparison to the deafening sounds in her dream. She looked around; where was that damn thing? She had forgotten all about it until her subconscious reminded her of it. There it was, sitting on one of the three remaining boxes in the corner of her bedroom.

In the tumult of moving, she had forgotten all about this tiny treasure. It was cold in her palm as she inspected it up close. With a little silver polish, it would be a beautiful piece. Oval in shape with intricate filigree detail, Mia used her fingernail to pry open the tiny catch of the locket. As the clasp loosened, a bit of water that had been stored within seeped out into her palm along with a tiny scrap of paper … a fragment of a wet, miniature photograph. At least Mia assumed it was a photograph. What else belongs inside a locket? Due to the wet conditions in which it was found, the image was undecipherable; in fact it was bleached almost completely white, but upon further inspection, Mia could just make out a bit of glossiness along one edge, confirming her suspicion that it was indeed photo paper.

However, there was at least one element on the locket that remained fully legible. With the moonlight streaming through the window, Mia could perceive that, engraved on the inside front plate were the letters J.B. *Probably name initials*, Mia thought to herself as she ran her thumb over the tiny inscription. I wonder who it is? A mother, granddaughter, son, husband? So many possibilities. There must be a million J.B.s in the world. Who could this lovely piece of jewelry have belonged to? And how had it come to wash up at her feet?

As she gazed at the item, her mind wandered. The past few weeks were a blur to her. After many applications and introductions, she finally secured a job … a full-time receptionist gig at Long Beach Realty. She had even begun looking into what it would take to actually get her real estate license. The idea appealed to her. She loved looking at the homes around Long Beach, especially the charming old Tudors in the East End, that looked like they were right out of a fairy tale. With their intricate brickwork and antique lead-paned windows–some of which held squares of stained glass reflecting a soft ruby, sapphire, and emerald cast into the streets—her mind conjured up fantasy images of what they must look like inside. Were they as charming to those who lived in them as they were to the passersby? Even the single-story beach bungalows, with their cement facade—painted in various shades of tans, grays, and even pastel greens—and Spanish, terra-cotta, stucco roofs filled her with curiosity. Mia could visualize herself as a realtor, leading clients expertly around these structures and playing a small role in what would undoubtedly be a story with a happily-ever-after at the end.

For the first time in her life, Mia could admit that she was proud of herself. Even though she hadn't yet made any real friends (aside from Bob and Dee, and do landlords really count as friends?), her job was a step in the right direction. And it was the first time in her life that she actually had a plan for what would come next. In the past, Mia had been a fly-by-the-seat-of-your-pants kind of girl. The friends would come; Mia was sure of it. Hopefully, once the weather warmed up, there would be more young people around to socialize with.

She had spent a few more evenings with Bob and Dee, listening to their good-natured back and forth. Well, mostly good-natured. Despite her warm smile, Mia discovered that Dee wasn't always so easy-going. She sometimes picked at Bob ... and some-times Mia could discern raised voices from below. And Bob, too, had moments where he seemed absent. Moments where he would zone out with a frown on his face. Mia could almost hear the cogs of his mind turning as he stared off into the distance, maybe at some faraway memory—or perhaps he was conjuring up images of the sad moments in his life that were hinted at when Mia first moved in. She wondered what he was thinking about. What was he frowning at? You learn a great deal about people living directly above them, and Mia got to know their habits. She learned that oftentimes they went out on the boat for hours at a time carrying blankets and coolers. Even when the temperatures hovered near freezing, their boating excursions continued. Mia thought back to when she noticed their bare feet on the pavement on the day she moved in. She supposed their winter sailing was just another thing to which they had grown accustomed. She admired their desire to spend time together. Whenever Mia observed them returning from their trips, they held hands as they descended the walkway over the dunes. Bob, always careful to lead the way, making sure Dee didn't trip over the accumulated ice or frost on the path. When Mia saw them together like that, looking tenderly at one another, she imagined that the occasional discord she perceived was just the normal idiosyncrasy that happens over decades of marriage. Either way, Bob and Dee were good landlords. They respected Mia's privacy and didn't push too much into her life. She was lucky to have ended up living above them.

Snapping back to the moment, Mia returned her attention to the item in her hand, this lovely locket that had so carelessly washed up at her feet. She held it up; the moonlight reflected in its silver surface. Or was it careless? Why had her dream so clearly reminded her of this item? Maybe its appearance in her life wasn't as accidental as she thought. And then there were those waves; she could hear them even now flowing over the wrinkles in her mind, pushing thoughts to the surface, pushing ideas to the surface, ideas that didn't really make sense, that COULDN'T really make sense. She couldn't quite put words to those inklings, yes inklings–that was the word–that those waves seemed to arouse within her. But whether it was the waves or the fact that sometimes nighttime inspires intuitions that can be suppressed during the day, she started to get a feeling that maybe it wasn't mere coincidence. That maybe there was a purpose here, a purpose that remained hidden in the murky depths of her logical thoughts.

She gently placed the item back on top of the box. While her mind swam with possibilities, her eyes were getting heavy again with sleep. She turned off the light, and turned over in bed. The shushing of the waves against the shore lulled her to sleep and she passed the rest of the night time hours dreamlessly.

Chapter Eighteen

CLAIRE

Looking around, Claire couldn't believe what her life had become. She sat up, tangled in the cream-colored fleece throw blanket on the living room sofa, where she had spent the night. Glancing at her reflection in the gold-foil mirror on the opposite wall, she could see by the jagged red lines across her right cheek that her cellphone had left an imprint, as it did every night lately. After all, during the nighttime hours it rested right next to her on her pillow, snuggled up to her face like some robot lover. The thought of missing a call ... *the* call made her paranoid beyond end. She would never forgive herself if she failed to receive an important message regarding Jimmy's whereabouts. She would not fail him again. So, as a result, her phone was now a permanent fixture on Claire's body, like a hand or an ear–it came with her from room-to-room, accompanying her while she ate and while she attempted to watch television. She guessed that the lines on her cheek were at least proof that she had actually slept, because most nights sleep eluded her. Those minutes and seconds, filled with darkness and silence, dragged on endlessly–the moon, her only companion aside from her spinning mind. She would slip in and out of consciousness, making dreams indecipherable from reality. A few times, slumber allowed her to forget that

Jimmy was gone and for mere seconds, that weight on her chest had eased. But it only took mere seconds for her to realize the truth. The awful truth that her boy had been gone for a month. Well, almost a month. The one-month anniversary of her son's disappearance was two days from now. The word "anniversary" brought a bitter taste to her mouth. Wasn't an anniversary supposed to signify something happy and joyous? There certainly must be a better word to use when commemorating tragedy. When slashing yet another tally mark on the wall of devastation.

Claire took in her frazzled appearance. Heavy purple bruises had emerged beneath her eyes; badly in need of a trip to the salon, her gray roots were starting to show near her scalp, and her once manicured nails were overgrown and jagged. She looked old, almost unrecognizable. She had been wearing the same gray sweatpants for the past three days. Look how they hung on her hips. They didn't always fit that way. When had she lost so much weight?

Papers, barely eaten plates of food, and crumpled Poland Spring water bottles crowded almost every surface of the living room. Claire hadn't been able to bring herself to clean much the past few weeks, so her home, a place in which she had previously taken immense pride and care, was a wreck. And she didn't care. There was no more order in her life. No more joy. All of that flew out the window when Jimmy disappeared.

The past few weeks felt interminable to Claire. In the beginning, the searching, the filling out of paperwork, the interviews with the well-meaning police officers, the acquisition of medical and dental records, all of the busy work occupied her time. There had been a reason to get dressed, to wake up in the morning, to leave the house, to talk to people. She had felt productive. Useful. But once all that protocol was done and over with, and there was still no sign of Jimmy, despite all the false sightings—no clues to his disappearance, no extortion attempts, ransom, nothing—Claire's day-to-day routine became a succession of idle hours all jammed together. Idle hours spent on the couch. Idle hours spent staring at her phone. Idle hours hoping against hope that she would receive the news that Jimmy had been found and was ok and alive. But that news hadn't come. Her hope, along with the phone calls from the police department had dwindled. Even the local media, which had harassed Claire with the same lurking intensity that vultures stalk their unknowing prey, had gradually faded from the picture. No longer were the news vans in front of her home, no longer were there reporters with their pristine red lipstick, stiletto pumps, and tight skirt suits hounding her for updates and interviews. Her story had lost its luster. It had soured and spoiled right before her eyes.

In her heart, Claire didn't think that Jimmy was dead. She believed that she would feel it if he were. She believed that she would know if her beautiful boy was no longer on this Earth. But if what her heart said was true, then where was he? The thought of him being held somewhere was almost too much for Claire. Was he scared? Was he cold? Was he hungry? Those questions almost broke her. She could actually feel herself fragmenting. Losing Jimmy was like losing a limb, losing a part of herself. Worse than that. She would have gladly sacrificed anything ... an eye, her fingers, hell–her very existence to have him back, to know that he was safe and unharmed.

His birthday was last week. He was 8. She had pre-ordered him the newest Nintendo Switch about 2 months ago in preparation; there had been a sale at Target. She remembered cringing at the extravagant price tag as she checked out at the register. It was obscene, spending over $300 on a video game system ... for an 8 year old. Could she afford this? Now, Claire would have drained her bank accounts, given away every single penny, her pension, every investment she possessed, just to have him back. What did money matter in the grand scheme of life? Isn't the purpose of making money to spend it on things that will make your loved ones happy? Jimmy would have loved that Switch ... it would have made him so happy; he had been asking for it for close to a year. Claire could almost see him tearing through the wrapping paper, his eyes brightening as he beheld this coveted treasure. Now, the gift remained in her closet, never opened, never played with, collecting dust. Useless.

As Claire took in the scattered remnants of her life, she felt Joe's absence intensely. She didn't even know who he was living with this week. Maybe Greg from the office. Even though he tried to swallow the resentment he had towards Claire, he couldn't quite seem to do it. He couldn't forgive her for leaving the boys outside alone, and he couldn't suppress the blame that seeped from his skin in her presence. Instead of leaning on one another, the bitterness and accusation crept between them and ruined them. The disintegration was quick and complete. Claire wished that things had been different. Claire wished for a lot of things.

Looking down at the glowing phone screen, she saw that she had a text from Joe. Speak of the devil. It read:

> Claire, it's time. I need closure

He was referring to the Celebration of Life that his therapist suggested would help him move on and grieve. Joe wanted to organize a memorial ceremony to commemorate Jimmy.

Claire responded quickly:

> I'm not on board for that, Joe. I already told you. I won't have a funeral for my son when he's not dead.

Then the phone rang. She didn't think a text would suffice, and she was right. With a sigh, Claire answered. "Hey, Joe."

"Claire. I've been asking you only as a courtesy. Ultimately, I can do what I want. I need this. I don't need your permission. He was my son too."

"*Was* your son, Joe? He's not anymore? How can you have a funeral when you don't even know that he's gone?"

"It's not a funeral, Claire. It's a memorial. There's a difference. I don't understand how you can deny me this. We can't live like this forever. We have to go through all the stages of grief–"

Claire stopped listening. She recognized some of Joe's phrases from her own therapist, Dr. Kimler. The idea was that Claire had to allow her body to go through the steps of grief in order to rejoin the living. But Claire wasn't ready to do that. She wasn't ready to accept the falsehood that Jimmy was gone for good. And she didn't want to live a life without him. If she didn't hold out hope, who would? Certainly not Joe. She didn't begrudge Joe his own process. But she simply didn't feel that having a Ceremony of Life was the right move. Not yet anyway. Maybe not ever.

With a sigh, she ended the conversation with Joe. They weren't going to see eye to eye on this. They probably weren't going to see eye to eye on anything ever again. This separation, though not finalized with official divorce papers, was definitely headed in that direction. How could a marriage survive such a tragedy? Could "for better or worse" possibly include this unthinkable disaster? There are certain things that marriage vows simply couldn't cover. This was one of them. The thought brought a fresh wave of tears to Claire's tired eyes. Things had been good. Things had been so good. They had been happy once, although that seemed so far in the past. Who said, "Nothing gold can stay"? Was it Frost? Damn, was he right!

The bills that had accumulated on the coffee table made Claire think again about the email she had received from her boss a few days ago asking her when she was returning to work. Jane Wood had been patient and her email read like a tactful and sympathetic inquiry, but Claire knew the subtext. She was needed back at the office. And if she wasn't coming back, Jane would hire someone else. Claire had discovered firsthand that one person's grief doesn't mean that the whole world stops, even though maybe it should. In Claire's mind, the sun didn't even have a right to shine, yet it still did. Claire pulled out her laptop and hit the 'Reply' button. She needed the money; yet, going back to work after this leave felt like moving on. And she wasn't ready to move on, not without Jimmy. But again, she needed the money ... she couldn't deny that. And, Jimmy needed a home to return to. So Claire's reply to her boss read, "Hi, Jane. Thanks for the email. I will return to the office next week. Thanks for your patience. Sincerely, Claire."

After she hit the 'Send' button, Claire thought without rancor about the fact that her local friends had barely reached out after the first week. She didn't expect to hear from Trish, especially after their harrowing exchange on the afternoon of the disappearance, but what about everyone else? These people who she thought she had connected with at Little League games and at soccer practices, at birthday parties had become phantoms, barely even occupying the periphery of her life. She wasn't dumb to the fact that Trish had "gotten to them first." Claire saw her passive-aggressive Facebook posts–before Trish had blocked her–and imagined there was much more that she didn't see ... probably text chains and PTA events centered around the abduction, but she didn't really care. How could she care about something as trivial as public opinion when her son no longer slept in his bed? Claire had earned the title of Oceanside Pariah without even knowing it. Without even really caring.

Her parents tried to help ... after all, they too were grieving for their grandchild. They even offered for Claire to come live with them in Boca Raton. They were too elderly to fly here, especially now that her father's arthritis had progressed, both in his hands and in his knees. The warm Florida weather was supposed to help, but it didn't seem to be doing much to slow the degeneration. And her mom had never been quite the same since she recovered from that severe bout of Covid last year. But Claire wouldn't think about leaving Oceanside. Not while Jimmy was still out there somewhere.

Claire flipped on the television. *News12* was the default channel, and she absently stared at the screen as the weatherman reported the forecast. *Who fucking cares what the temperature today will be?* Claire thought to herself. However, the next headline did catch her attention and made her sit up straight on the couch, "Tune in this Friday at 5pm as Trish Yardsleigh opens up about the heart-breaking case of her son's abduction. *News12. Local as local news gets.*"

Claire let out a sigh and an audible groan. *I guess Trish is ready to talk to the media*, Claire thought to herself. She didn't know yet if she would indeed "tune in this Friday," but something told Claire that this wasn't good. No, it wasn't good at all.

Chapter Nineteen

TRISH

Trish felt nervous sitting in the small dressing room–an emotion she didn't often feel. The stylist had just left, and Trish admired the soft curls and eyelash extensions in the back-lit rectangular mirror before her. In her burgundy, fitted dress–bought explicitly for this purpose from Bloomingdale's–and simple black pumps, she looked as she always did: put-together. The professionals added an extra bit of polish to her overall appearance, but Trish prided herself on looking good ... always–even when she went to Pilates or took her bi-weekly classes at Spin City...hell, even when she went to the grocery store. The Tory Burch studs and matching necklace added the final touch and glittered in the harsh overhead lights.

She had gone through two interviews and a mock dress-rehearsal to prepare for this television appearance. And not only was she scheduled to appear on *New12* today, but next week, *FOX News* wanted her. National coverage for her story. As PTA president, Trish was used to the spotlight. She loved being in front of people. She was born to be seen and heard and admired. But she had to admit, to herself only, that this was a bit out of her comfort zone. And despite the fact that she did enjoy publicity, relished it in fact, the thought that this time, Kyle's disappearance was the event that prompted it, made her heart flutter. She had gone over the questions that she would be asked in front of the rolling cameras–practiced her answers in front of her bathroom mirror at home. Questions that were so personal and intimate. Questions not only about what actually happened, but about how she *felt*. Those were the questions that weighed upon her now. She couldn't wait for the parts in which she would get to publicly expose Claire's negligence. That fucking bitch deserved some accountability for what she did. The thought of that brought a smirk to Trish's face–that was the main purpose of agreeing to do this. But, the other parts, where she would have to talk about Kyle. Where she would have to talk about the inner emotions that bubbled within her just below the surface ... she didn't look forward to those parts. Not at all.

Over the course of the past two weeks, Trish hadn't talked much about the abduction of her boy, her Kyle, unless she had to. Unless she absolutely could not avoid it. It was too hard. And Trish wasn't one for public displays of emotion. She liked to come off as confident, sure of herself. Those moms who cried over every little thing, quite frankly, made her sick. But now, a public display of emotion was exactly what was expected of her ... and it wouldn't even be just for show. It was real. Kyle's disappearance had rocked her world in a way that took her breath away. Trish had cried more tears in those first two weeks than she had ever cried in her life ... seemingly endless tears. They cracked her flaw-less veneer wide open–exposed her vulnerability. To her horror, she had even cried at the fundraiser put together by her Oceanside moms, even though she had sworn to herself that she wouldn't. But that was the last time she had revealed her emotions so overtly. She promised herself that from here on out, she would hold it together. She hoped she didn't have to break that promise today.

An opening door interrupted her thoughts.

"They're ready for you, Mrs. Yardsleigh," said a young thin woman wearing black slacks and a headset.

Trish took a deep breath, stood up and smoothed down her hair and the front of her dress.

"I'm ready," Trish said as she followed the young woman out the door and into the blinding lights of the news set.

And she was.

Chapter Twenty

MIA

Mia walked home from the office feeling lighter than she had felt since moving to the West End of Long Beach last month. It was her first full day of work, and even though she was in the training phase, she truly enjoyed her time spent shadowing the current receptionist with her bulging belly.

"My official last day is Friday, but I'm not due until next month," Randi had said. "And then no more work for me. I'll be home with the baby from there on out. It's crazy to think how my life is gonna change."

"Congratulations. You must be so excited," Mia had responded. Even though she herself would have felt far less than enthusiastic had the tables been turned. Mia never understood how women could just leave their jobs, their independence, hell, their whole identities behind to take on the full-time role of motherhood. Maybe she felt this way simply because she had no kids of her own, nor any prospects of marriage, or maybe Mia just wasn't meant to be a mom. She didn't really know the answer, but the thought of having little ones clinging to her metaphoric skirts wasn't appealing in the least to Mia. Motherhood was a hell of a respectable job ... probably the hardest one that exists. But it wasn't for her.

"I'm really excited, but a little nervous too," Randi had answered in response. "I just hope this little guy turns around in there." She rubbed a hand absently along the curve of her abdomen. "I'm really hoping to avoid a C-section. It's been my dream to experience natural childbirth."

Mia had given Randi the appropriate nod and look of understanding compassion, but she didn't really know what a C-section entailed, nor could she really understand the concept of birth on anything deeper than a scientific level ... or why any sane woman would *dream* of pushing a human being out of her vagina. Nope. The thought just didn't sound appealing to her. She and Randi were lightyears apart. Randi was starting a family. Mia had just moved away from hers. Randi was ending a career and Mia was beginning one.

Randi had shown Mia the tasks for which she would be responsible once Randi was officially out on maternity leave, which included keeping track of the four in-house realtors' many showings and appointments, managing relationships with the company's real-estate law firm, and typing up contracts, just to name a few. While the list of her duties seemed extensive, Mia was up for the task. She was good with computers and with people and looked forward to the time when the reception area would be all her own, even though it would have been nice to have Randi and her friendly smile sitting at a desk opposite her.

April had hatched, but despite a few warmer days, the cold hadn't yet left Long Beach. The frigid breeze still blew off the ocean and up Minnesota Avenue, not quite ready to let go of its stronghold. It was past six o'clock and the days were starting to get longer—the one whisper of summer. It was still light out when Mia walked up the stairs to her apartment. Dee had asked Mia to stop in on her way home to tell her all about her first day, but the dark windows told her that they weren't home. Probably still out on the boat. As usual.

Her apartment felt more like home now. The tan microfiber couch she bought on clearance was soft and cozy, framed pictures of her mom, dad, and sister smiled at her from their place on her dresser, and yesterday she had finally gotten around to hanging up those prints she bought from Sea Glass, the local home decor store down the street. Even though they were a bit expensive, the black and white images of the Long Beach shoreline captured her eye from the window. She just had to have them.

Throwing the leftover pizza in the oven, Mia flipped on the television as she went about filling her glass with water and taking a plate out of the kitchen cabinet. She had barely watched anything these past few weeks. Too busy. She had always been a Netflix girl, but moving and unpacking and finding a job had occupied almost every waking minute and even though she had finally finished up the last few episodes of *Wednesday,* her screen remained mostly black.

But now, feeling like she had earned some relaxation time, Mia took her plate of pizza, sat down on the couch and clicked on the television, the Boob Tube as Bob so fondly called it. She was about to select the button on the remote that changed the input from Cable to Netflix, but the woman on the screen caught her attention and she stopped.

The woman on the screen was sobbing while the host of the program gently rubbed her back and spoke sympathetically.

"Mrs. Yardsleigh, what would you most like viewers to know about your story?" the host asked the bawling woman.

Mrs. Yardsleigh pulled herself together and used a crumpled up tissue to blot under her eyes in an attempt to keep her eye make-up intact. She took a shaky breath and then looked directly at the camera. Her stare pierced through Mia and definitely added the touch of drama that the network was clearly going for.

"I'd like to tell the viewers to be careful about who they entrust their children to. Kids are our most precious commodity. My sweet boy would still be here with me right now if I had listened to my gut and kept him home instead of sending him on that playdate. Everything would have been different ... for both me and for him."

"Powerful message. Thank you, Mrs. Yardsleigh. Thank you for coming on our show and telling your story. That takes a lot of courage. Everyone here at the studio is praying for your son's safe return."

Then the screen switched, revealing two photographs side-by-side. The voiceover said, "On the left is a picture of Kyle Yardsleigh and on the right is a picture of Jimmy Benicek. Both boys are currently missing. If you or anyone else you know have any information whatsoever regarding their disappearance, we urge you to please call CRIMESTOPPERS or contact your local precinct immediately. No detail is too small. Let's all help get these kids back where they belong."

Mia, nearly choking on a bite of pizza, scrambled for the remote and pressed 'Pause.'

On the left, was a solo picture of a boy, a school photograph, but on the right, the other boy's image had been cropped from what was clearly a family photograph. His parents were obviously the ones standing behind him; the viewer could see hands on the boy's shoulders, but everything above their shoulders was cut out, to keep the focus on the missing child. But Mia's eyes were drawn to the woman–probably the mother–behind the missing boy. More specifically, her eyes were drawn to the portion of the woman's neck that hadn't been cropped out of the photo. A familiar shape caught Mia's attention. Blurry and far away, but familiar all the same.

Throwing her plate down on the couch next to her, Mia raced to her bedroom and picked up the locket that lay discarded on top of the final few boxes of unpacked clothing. She brought it back to the living room and held it up in front of her. It couldn't be. It was hard to tell whether the exact necklace in the photograph was the necklace that was in her hands at that moment, but it COULD be. And what did the host say the boy's name was? Mia rewinded a minute and listened again "...a picture of Jimmy Benicek..." Mia glanced back down at the letters inscribed in the silver surface. *J.B.*, Mia thought. Jimmy Benicek. And the locket in the picture looked so much like this one. What are the odds? And what did it mean? That necklace had washed up on the shore weeks ago. How did it get there? Then a thought crept up at the edge of her consciousness. Did the locket choose her? Such a silly idea. That thought felt odd and paranoid to Mia as she considered it. Yet ... Yet, she remembered how when she first lifted it, dripping out of the foamy surf, she had thought that maybe there was a purpose behind its appearance, a reason why it had materialized. Now that thought resonated through her more vividly than before. It was like a siren was going off in her mind. She let the thought settle. It felt right, somehow. She couldn't convey why it felt right, or what made it feel right. But it did. OR was she simply being crazy? Her father always told her that she had a big imagination. Was this simply an unspooling of that creativity pent up inside of her? Unspooling like a ball of yarn? Or was this feeling that swam around in her gut real? And if it was, what did it all mean?

Mia couldn't answer any of these questions as her eyes traveled back and forth between the image on the television and the locket she held in her palm, trying to make herself believe that it wasn't the same one, it couldn't be. But the more and more she studied the item in question, the more sure she became that there was a reason why it came into her possession. What should she do as a result? That answer eluded her. But she had to do something.

Chapter Twenty-One

JIMMY

He had been here a long time. He didn't know how long. But it felt long. *Is my mom looking for me?* Jimmy wondered, *What about my dad? We were supposed to go to the Knicks game. Did he go without me? He told me we had the good kind of seats in the middle of the court.* Jimmy perceived enough to know that his parents couldn't drive here. There were no cars or roads, only water and tall, tall grass. They had to take a boat here. There was no other way.

Jimmy didn't cry anymore. They told him that if he cried they would tie up his hands again. And if they cried, neither one of them would get dinner. And he didn't want that.

He wasn't in the same place as Kyle anymore either. Kyle was behind that door. And there was a lock on it. In the beginning, Jimmy tried to open it anyway, but he couldn't. He wished that he could pick locks like that detective guy in *The Pink Panther* movie his dad had shown him. But he couldn't. Actually, he would have taken any superpower right now. If he was the Hulk, he could Hulk-Smash his way out of here.

Even though he wasn't in the same room as Kyle, he could still talk to him. At least that was good. When they put Kyle in there, he asked why they couldn't stay together. They told them that they couldn't be trusted together and they might try to leave. Jimmy and Kyle would talk through the door until they fell asleep at night. They didn't have much to talk about anymore, so sometimes they just made up silly songs to make one another laugh. There wasn't a TV or anything for them to watch.

They weren't as scary anymore either, the people keeping them here. They brought Kyle and Jimmy blankets and food. Yesterday he got McDonald's WITH a milkshake. It was vanilla and Jimmy liked chocolate better, but that was ok. It was still yummy and cold. They let him use the bathroom every morning and every night ... and sometimes during the day ... only if they were there. He had to hold it in between those times. He could just go in the corner of the room, but he felt weird doing that. Or he could go in his pants like last time. Jimmy didn't want that to happen again. The bathroom wasn't a real bathroom and the door was also locked. Yesterday or last week or last month, Jimmy tried to open the door when they weren't there because his tummy hurt and he needed to go to the bathroom. The door wouldn't open. He had to hold it even though it made his whole body cramp up. His belly felt like someone was squeezing it. Finally the people came back and let him go. There wasn't a sink though and this bathroom was definitely a bathroom that when you use it you should wash your hands. The toilet wasn't like a regular toilet and the water in it looked like a mud puddle. Jimmy missed his bathroom at home. It always smelled like lemons and he had superhero bath toys and crayons that you could use to write on the walls. He wasn't allowed to write on the walls with other crayons, though, and definitely not anywhere else but in the bathroom. He once wrote on the kitchen wall a long time ago, and mom got so mad. He got sent to his room. And his dad had to paint the whole kitchen again to cover up what he had done. He still felt sorry about it.

There were locks everywhere. On every door ... just like the bathroom. Even on the inside of the front door. That was weird to Jimmy. They couldn't go outside. UNDER ANY

CIRCUMSTANCES, the man had said. That was one of the rules. There were lots of rules. Don't go outside. Don't go near the windows. Don't open the doors–not that he could open the doors with all those locks. If they didn't follow the rules, the man said that they would be tied up again. Jimmy definitely did not want that to happen.

Even though this place wasn't as scary anymore, Jimmy was still cold and the wood walls made creaking sounds when the wind blew. It kinda reminded him of the club house next door in Mr. Rich and Miss Jeannie's backyard swing set. The wood looked the same. And the ceiling was made out of wood too. He could see some light come in through the cracks. And just like that clubhouse, this place was one big room–except for the small room in the back that Kyle was in–without too much in it. Just a couch and that old canoe. There was a counter on the other side with a sink that water only came out of when the man pumped his foot on the pedal. There weren't even any real lights. The man usually brought a lantern that looked like the one his dad took when they went camping.

It was dangerous here too. He got a big splinter in his hand, and he had to bite it out. It still oozed with blood and green goo. Jimmy wished they had the stuff that his dad used at home to fix his booboos–and a Band-Aid. Even the man got hurt once. The man tried to fix the front door and his shirt got stuck on a nail sticking out of the wall. It got so stuck that he had to pull so hard. Some of his sleeve ripped off. At least the bottom part did, the part where there is a button by his hand. The man was mad that that happened. He said the F-word and threw his sleeve so far away from him. It fell through the floorboards. Jimmy thought that his mom could probably fix it because he once ripped his pants and his mom had sewn them back together. But his mom wasn't here right now. He told the man that his mom could fix his shirt, and the man told him to shut up. His face looked really angry and got all red when he said it too. Jimmy almost cried when the man yelled at him.

Almost ... but he didn't. He acted brave. Jimmy was just trying to help.

He hoped his mom was ok. The people said that he might not see her again. But he hoped they were just joking. Adults joke too sometimes. They said that he would get a new family if he was lucky and that he would like his new family even better than he liked his old one. But he didn't want a new family. He wanted his old family. His mom and dad ... his house ... his bedroom ... his school. He almost cried again, but he stopped. He was getting hungry and the people said that he wouldn't get dinner if he cried. He asked Kyle if he was hungry and he was too. He wondered what they would bring them tonight. He would like McDonald's again. Or maybe pizza.

And unfortunately, as happens in many cases, Jimmy began to look forward to his kidnappers' return.

Chapter Twenty-Two

MIA

Mia typed the name into her phone: Jimmy Benicek. She had to consult the television screen to ensure she had the spelling right. B-E-N-I-C-H ... wait ... delete ... no H. Instantly a barrage of news stories and photographs bombarded her screen. She clicked on the first image, which was the same one she had seen moments ago on the television screen. Using her thumb and forefinger, she enlarged the picture as much as she could. It wasn't totally clear. When she zoomed in too closely, the image of the locket became pixelated and blurred, but even from afar, there wasn't a doubt in Mia's mind that it was the same one that now lay on the wooden coffee table in front of her. How odd.

The next picture was a school photograph of the boy in question ... of Jimmy Benicek. She remembered back to her own Picture Days in elementary school. Her mom used to style her hair so carefully and iron her best outfit on the kitchen counter the night before. One time her mom even allowed her to wear her favorite jean jacket, the one with the pink rhinestones and lace outlining the pockets. She used to sit so still in class until it was her time to have her picture taken, so she didn't mess up her hair or outfit. A week or two later, Mia was always excited to get the proofs back from her teachers and tuck them into her homework folder to bring home to proudly present to her parents. Each year, her mom would allow her to choose whichever background she liked best. There were so many options. A blue sky, tropical palm trees, a sunset, colored dots–each had its own appeal to Mia over the years. She would agonize over her choice. Her mom kept each year's photograph lined up in a school bus-shaped frame on the wall, which had allotted spaces for Kindergarten through 8th grade. It seemed to Mia that it filled up so fast. And Mia would often stop to admire her changing appearance, how her grin went from jagged and toothy, to metal-filled with braces, to finally boasting smooth straight teeth in 8th grade. Those wallet-sized images all in a row were proof that Mia was growing, changing. The baby fat from her cheeks faded away, as did the wildness of her hair. If only adults kept photographs of themselves each year, lined up like a baseball card collection on display. The thought made her feel nostalgic and homesick for the first time.

In his school photo, Jimmy Benicek could have been any 8 year old. He wore a buttoned-down gray dress shirt with the outlines of blue sharks swimming across the chest–fitting for a kid growing up in a town called Oceanside. His smile was bright and his hair was carefully styled and looked freshly trimmed. He was adorable. A pang of sadness struck Mia; how could someone just take this beautiful little boy? What kind of cruelty was the human heart capable of?

She clicked out of the photograph and moved on to the first link that came up on her feed. It was a news article titled, "Oceanside Abductions" and dated 6 weeks ago. It read:

Today, tragedy struck the quiet Long Island suburb of Oceanside when two young boys were abducted in plain sight. Kyle Yardsleigh (8) and Jimmy - James Benicek (7) were reportedly outside playing basketball at 4pm on Friday afternoon when the incident occurred. Claire Benicek, Jimmy's mother, reports, "One minute they were here. The next, they were gone. It's like they disap-

peared." Local police are conducting a full search and are canvassing the area to find any evidence to help them find the boys and facilitate their safe return. If you or anyone you know have any information–

Those boys have been missing for 6 weeks? Mia thought to herself. *How is this the first time I'm hearing about it? God, I must be living under a rock.* Mia couldn't be too angry with herself though. Her life over the course of the past weeks had been busy. And she had never been one to pay much attention to the news, as terrible as that sounded. Her college friends used to make fun of her for her lack of knowledge regarding the current events that most others drank up like juice. She was embarrassed to admit that usually, she didn't even know the names of the politicians running for office until late in the game. It wasn't that Mia didn't care about what was going on around her; it was just that she would much rather bury her nose in a book or a good television show than the awful tragedies that unwound around her. She always thought of the news as the Bad News, and she simply didn't want such negativity to take up too much space in her world. Life was hard enough.

She thought about the brief mention of Jimmy Benicek's mother. She scanned the article again to find her name. Claire. That's it. Claire Benicek. *Jeez, what that poor woman must be dealing with right now. It's unimaginable.*

Mia clicked on another article, this one dated two days ago:

Unfortunately, not much progress has been made regarding the abduction of Kyle Yardsleigh and James Benicek who were taken from the Benicek residence last month. While the authorities continue with their search, the community mourns. Today, Joseph Benicek, Jimmy's father, has invited friends, family, and Oceanside residents to attend a Ceremony of Life in honor of Kyle and his son, Jimmy. It will be held at Robert Moses Elementary School at 6pm this evening–

A Ceremony of Life? thought Mia. *That sounds a lot like a funeral. Are they assuming the boys are dead? How could they just give up hope like that?* Mia put a halt to this judgment. She wasn't Jimmy's mom or his dad. Heck, she had no idea what they were going through. The devastation, the overwhelming sense of loneliness they must be feeling, it must be staggering. It is so easy to pass judgment in our world today. Mia thought that maybe if people judged less and listened more, the world might be a better place. And after all, the boys had been missing for over a month. That didn't sound promising. At some point, wouldn't the parents want closure? She didn't know the answer to that question, nor at what point parents of missing children must come face to face with reality, no matter how bleak. But at some point, don't parents need to mourn? To move on? She supposed that everyone was different and decided that she wouldn't begrudge a grieving family its own process.

Mia skimmed through a few more articles. One was a scathing editorial, published in an Oceanside newsletter titled *The Atlantic* and was written by the same woman she saw on television just a little while ago. From the little section that Mia read, she could almost feel the woman seething. She seemed more focused on retaliation than on locating her son. She claimed that Claire Benicek was negligent and unfit and blamed her for the abduction. *Wow*, thought Mia. *Doesn't she know that Claire Benicek lost her child too?* Mia could understand that Mrs. Yardsleigh must be feeling extreme emotions, but it seemed counterproductive to her to point fingers. Especially when you were pointing at someone who had experienced the same tragedy. Shouldn't hardships bring people together? Not drive them to hatred? Again, Mia harnessed her judgment. What did she know? She probably would have been angry, had she sent her child to a friend's home, and he then disappeared. But Mia also believed that she wouldn't place blame on the other mother. But again, Mia had no children and couldn't possibly put herself in the Oceanside woman's shoes.

Being new to the area, Mia did a quick search on her phone to pinpoint Oceanside on the map in relation to Long Beach. She was surprised to learn that Oceanside was essentially the town next to her. She was also surprised to know that, despite its name, Oceanside wasn't technically on the ocean at all. But regardless of that, it was close to Long Beach. So close. Just over the small bridge near the Mobil gas station where she had filled up her tank a few days ago. Maybe 15 minutes away ... if you considered all the traffic lights.

Mia put her phone down and brought the locket up to her face. It couldn't be a coincidence. Could it? Even if it was, she had to at least try to make sense of it. Maybe it was important. Mia certainly felt like it was. The cold, metal chain vibrated in her hand like a talisman of some sort. At that moment the wind outside picked up, and with it, she could make out the sound of the waves down the street, the loud crashing assuring her that she was on the right path, that something had to be done, that SHE needed to do something. But what? What could she possibly do?

After dismissing many possibilities in her mind, she decided upon a course of action. And it was only once she had a plan in mind that the ocean settled down; then she could hear the water no more.

Chapter Twenty-Three

JOE BENICEK

It was a tough day. No. That was an understatement. It was the most brutal, heart-wrenching, soul crushing day he had ever experienced in his life. When Joe finally walked in the door of Greg's apartment after the Ceremony of Life, he was utterly exhausted. He had never been one for big displays of emotion, but that was before. Before his boy went missing. Before his life shattered to pieces right before his eyes. Now, he cried at the drop of a hat. Hell, he cried yesterday over a State Farm Insurance commercial. It was pathetic. And he had just spent the last three hours sobbing on the shoulders of friends and strangers alike standing outside Robert Moses Elementary. The outpouring of love and support from his Oceanside community had been staggering. There were over 1500 people at the event, all bearing flowers and stuffed teddy bears that now lay strewn against the far south side of the brick building. He wondered what would happen to them once the predicted rain arrived. Would they wilt and spoil? Would the mementos turn mildewy? Would the flowers wither away? Would it all rot, like his hope was rotting with each passing hour, each passing minute, each passing second without his son?

He released his grip from the 4 foot by 2 foot enlarged picture of Jimmy that he had been steadfastly holding and allowed it to rest at an angle against the entryway wall. He gazed into the face of his son and wondered where he was. Was he safe? Was he long dead and buried? Had his body been dumped somewhere like those poor victims of the Gilgo Beach Murders? That thought made him physically ill. The darkest of scenarios unwound in his mind, like a kite string continuing to support its diamond- shaped burden as it drifted further and further away. So many possibilities. Too many.

He collapsed onto the couch, hands entwined in his thick dark hair. It had been kind of Greg to allow him to stay here with him; after all they were new friends, office buddies. They didn't have much history together. But Greg was going through a divorce and had some empty space; he was also grateful for the help with the rent. Over a few beers last week, Greg had confided in Joe how much alimony he had to pay each month to his soon-to-be ex-wife ... it was staggering. And so, he said that Joe could stay as long as he needed to. Joe gazed around; it was quiet here, peaceful. But the apartment looked like a college dorm room. Nothing hanging on the walls–none of those little touches that he used to tease Claire about. Claire used to go to Home Goods and come back with countless trinkets that she claimed made their house look stylish ... comfortably cluttered. Joe thought that 'shabby chic' was the aesthetic his wife had gone for ... well, shabby-chic, but on a budget. Yet, in the absence of such possessions, Greg's place looked bare. There were a few pictures of Greg's 15-year-old daughter around, but they were either taped to the refrigerator or thumb-tacked to the small bulletin board resting against the formica backsplash in the kitchen. An aroma of dirty socks clung to the couch. Unwashed glasses stood like sentinels in the sink. But did that really matter? Not really. Not in his current situation. Joe knew he couldn't remain here forever. He would need his own place. He needed to start his life over again, even though the thought of that seemed impossible.

He missed his house. His bed. He missed the cool comfort of

his basement office where he had displayed his favorite Mets autographs and his posters of Nirvana and Metallica that had hung in his high school bedroom once upon a time. Claire wouldn't think of letting him hang these artifacts in the upstairs living room, so the small alcove next to the washing machine had become his sanctuary over the past few years. Despite the spider crickets ... and the laundry. But most of all, he missed his son: his little boy. This person who came into his life by storm one day and changed everything. This boy who had given him a purpose ... who had made him a father.

And even though he wouldn't admit it anywhere else but in his own scrambled brain, he missed Claire too. The way she smelled and the way she snuggled up next to him in bed. The way she always made him feel appreciated, even for the simple tasks he performed around the house. The day before Jimmy disappeared, she had asked him to change the lightbulb in the fixture hanging from the eave of the portico. He had forgotten to do so. He wondered if she did it herself, or was the front of their home still swathed in darkness. Should he go check? He loved Claire, or at least he did before this nightmare. This love for his wife was a simple, uncomplicated fact. Now, his emotions were much more complex. Because he hated her too. Hated her for allowing this to happen. He had to blame someone for what happened. For the disaster that befell his life. And that someone was his wife. Did she deserve it? Joe crushed that thought as he leaned back and absently flipped on the television. He couldn't think anymore about who *deserved* what. Did Jimmy *deserve* to be taken? Did he himself *deserve* to be the father of a missing child? Certainly not. Life wasn't fair, or right, or just. Joe had come to learn that firsthand over the interminable weeks spent without his son.

Even though it was already close to 11 o'clock, there wasn't a chance that Joe was going to be able to sleep tonight. He replayed the past few hours in his mind. The Ceremony of Life sounded like such a good idea when his therapist had suggested it a few weeks ago. It had given him a purpose ... something to occupy his mind as the days ticked by relentlessly. The planning and the organizing and the writing of his speech had all seemed so important. Now that it had passed, he wasn't so sure–another thing he wouldn't have admitted out loud. Claire had railed against him when he first approached her with the idea. *It wasn't a funeral*, he had assured his wife ... he had assured himself. But it certainly felt like one. Droves of people wearing black, the flickering candles, the overpowering smell of lillies. That was certainly what funerals smelled like. Now that he reflected upon it, maybe it wasn't the right move. In the aftermath, he felt empty and hollow. More so than before.

Joe thought that possibly Claire would reconsider and attend the ceremony after all, no matter how much she had assured him that she wouldn't. She had specifically said that *she wouldn't attend such an event even if there was a gun pointed to her head*. Joe was convinced that she was bluffing ... being over-dramatic. But she didn't reconsider. And after his speech, Joe looked out at the upturned staring faces thinking his eyes would undoubtedly meet hers, but that didn't happen either. Something else he didn't think would happen was that he would actually care about her absence. But he did care. He cared very much.

When he approached Trish Yardsleigh at the event, she had been conversing with a few other PTA moms, heads bent together like conspirators. The loud *Shhhh* made it obvious that they were talking shit about Claire. Everyone was talking shit about Claire. Usually, people tried, out of deference to Joe, to do so out of his earshot. But not always. It had not escaped Joe that while he somehow managed to stay in the good graces of the community, Claire's public image had been shattered. He guessed it was because he hadn't been there when the boys disappeared. Claire had. It was an unforgivable offense in the mind of the local parents ... hell, it was unforgivable to him too. Looking guilty, Trish had turned around to offer Joe a peck on the side of the mouth and a quick hug.

"How you holding up, Joe?" Trish had said.

"Not too hot, Trish. I'm a mess."

"Yeah. Me too."

"Well, you look great," Joe had said, trying to manage a small smile.

And Trish Yardsleigh did look great. She looked polished, as she always did and was dressed to the nines. Probably wearing some designer label that cost a fortune. The Yardsleighs always had a lot of money to throw around.

"Did you see my *News12* appearance?" Trish asked.

"I saw it."

"What'd you think?"

"It was tough to watch. Emotional. I think you did great though. You were a little tough on Claire, but hopefully it will help bring back Jimmy and Kyle," Joe had replied.

"Tough on Claire? Jesus, Joe. She deserves it. I know she's technically still your wife. But this is on her. She's the one–"

Joe's conversation with Trish was thankfully interrupted by Jimmy's 1st grade teacher, who had been full of sympathy and tears. He hadn't gotten to speak to Trish again ... he hadn't really tried to either.

Joe trudged over to the refrigerator and grabbed a cool Coors Light. Standing in the blue glow, he popped open the tab and guzzled half of the contents in one long series of swallows. Getting blackout wasted seemed like a good idea. He didn't have anything else to do or anywhere else to go. Greg was in Boston for the weekend, not that Joe really wanted any company. At least when he was alone he didn't have to talk about his missing son. Maybe tonight the alcohol would assuage, if only for a little while, the blinding hurt he felt deep within his core. Well, even if it didn't, he sure could try. He chugged the rest of his beer, grabbed out another can, changed his mind and went over to the counter. Bourbon would do the job much more quickly. Joe helped himself to a healthy pour of Maker's Mark–not his favorite, but it would do just fine–and carried the glass and the bottle back to the living room. He took a big burning gulp and stared blankly at the screen in front of him. He tried to watch *The Price is Right*–God, Jimmy loved that stupid show–but couldn't focus. He picked up his phone and absently, almost as though his fingers were performing the task by rote, typed *Good Night, Claire. Love you* into the text box. Instead of pressing 'Send' he deleted the words letter by letter. What was he thinking? God, he was getting weepy again. Joe took another large swig and waited for the welcomed numbness to finally take him away.

Chapter Twenty-Four

MIA

Getting into the driver's seat of her CRV, Mia felt the first inkling of spring. The sun was shining without any sign of dusk, even at 5 o'clock in the evening. Tiny emerald buds had emerged from the rough, gray branches of the azalea bush next to her car; Mia wondered briefly what color the blooms would be. She hoped they would be lavender, the soft petals of her childhood; she would enjoy looking at them every day after work once they were in full flower. It seemed as though March had dissolved almost overnight, thawing the streets of Long Beach, thawing Mia's very bones, at least for today. Who knew what tomorrow would bring? The weather here seemed to be fickle and unpredictable. But for today, Mia relished the freshness in the air. For the first time since the move, she even heard a chirping bird overhead as opposed to the harsh caw of the beach gulls as they pounded over the shoreline. She had missed that feeling of warmth; she always did ... every winter. And this winter seemed particularly long and cold.

She had been in the office all morning, finishing her last day of training with Randi and hadn't had a chance to get lunch. She had given Randi a genuine hug as she left for the day and wished her well. Randi would make a great mother; Mia was sure of it.

Stomach growling, she wiggled free of her winter jacket and cracked open the window. It felt nice to not have to put on the heat. Her hunger would have to wait until later. She had business to take care of.

Instead of going directly home after work, as was her habit, today Mia had an errand. It was the knowledge of this errand that had finally eased her jumbled mind last night, allowing her to sleep. At 2 o'clock in the morning, Mia finally made the deal with herself that she would go to the Long Beach precinct tomorrow. She would tell someone about the necklace that had washed up and hope for the best. And now, she was on her way. She felt nervous on the short drive to the other end of town. She was actually grateful for the at least 15 traffic lights that separated her from the station. The constant stop and go gave her time to plan what she would say upon entering. Yet, she hadn't quite figured it out when she parked directly in front of the low, squat brick building and walked out into the late afternoon sunshine.

Clicking the lock button on her fob, Mia took a deep breath and headed up the stairs towards the glass double doors of the Long Beach precinct. She felt unprepared, but she knew that if she waited any longer, she might have talked herself out of it altogether. She wouldn't allow that to happen. She needed to do this. And who knew, maybe Claire Benicek needed it too. So with a final inhale-exhale and with all of the hope she could muster, Mia approached the large desk surrounded by a plexiglass shield at the far end of the waiting room.

Mia stood there for what seemed like an eternity while the woman seated in front of her typed frantically on the keyboard, balancing the phone between her ear and shoulder. Once the call ended and the woman still didn't address Mia, she finally said, "Excuse me. I'm looking to speak with someone regarding a missing person's case."

The woman, Officer Drummond, said the metal tag pinned to her lapel, said, "Name."

"Jimmy–James Benicek. He's about 8 years old—"

"*Your* name," Officer Drummond corrected.

"Oh, *my* name. I thought you were asking–Mia. Mia Rossi."

"Please have a seat, Miss Rossi. I will add your name to the waiting list."

"Ok. Thank you. Do you know about how long I'll have to wait? Who will I even be speaking with?" Mia responded, feeling flummoxed.

"Probably about a half an hour. And don't worry about that. I'll call your name when it's your turn and direct you on what to do."

Mia turned around, walked over to one of the few open seats in the room, and sat down, holding her purse on her lap. She opened the flap and took out the locket. Its dull shine reassured her that she was in the right place, that she was doing the right thing. She tried to read an article about wealth management in one of the magazines on the table next to her–she could certainly use some help in that department–but couldn't attend to it. So instead, she pulled out her cell, typed in the WIFI code displayed on the wall opposite her, and lost herself in the Boggle app on her phone.

Chapter Twenty-Five

MIA

Mia stormed out of the police department as fast as she could without breaking into a full-out run. Flustered, she thought to herself, *God, what did I think would happen? Did I think that the cops would just bow down in front of me? I must have sounded like a lunatic! Talking about premonitions and gut-feelings. What are those things in the face of cold, hard facts? What are those things in the face of that enormous Missing-Persons wall?* Mia didn't think she had ever seen anything sadder or more hopeless than that enormous wall of children deemed missing. Those glossy photographs thumb-tacked to that corkboard would surely haunt her dreams. *Great, another thought to give me nightmares,* she said to herself as she got into her car.

She drove back towards home with the windows open; the air had lost its winter chill and even though still quite cool, it felt refreshing on her warm face. *Now what?* Mia wasn't ready to give up. Not yet. Mia was convinced that she was part of this story, part of it all. It wasn't a coincidence; it couldn't be. It felt too real, too right. She was supposed to be here. Something had guided her here; perhaps it was the waves ... even though that thought sounded too much like crazy-people talk.

Even though car rides usually had a calming effect on Mia,

this one did the opposite. Her 15-minute drive from one end of Long Beach to the other (*those fucking traffic lights are ridiculous*) only spurred Mia's frustration, and when she finally pulled next to the curb in front of her apartment, she was restless with nervous energy and feelings of impotence. She knew that she was supposed to do *something*, help in some way, but she was at a standstill. She had nothing to do and nowhere to go, and all these boiling feelings inside her propelled her up the path towards the ocean. She ran up the stairs, not even bothering to remove her shoes this time and didn't stop until the toes of her leather wedge boots met the surf. It was getting dark now, and she kneeled down at the shoreline, not caring that her dress pants were getting wet, not caring that her hair was getting tangled together as the gentle breeze turned more into a steady wind. Leaning forward, her hands grabbed handfuls of the wet sand in front of her, trying to grasp the meaning of all this, trying to understand her purpose in the story of Claire and Jimmy Benicek. Was she going crazy? Maybe.

"What do you want from me?" she whispered. "What am I supposed to do?"

At that moment, Mia felt something soft rub up against her hand, she thought it was seaweed at first, but when she picked it up, it wasn't seaweed. It was cloth, a shirt. Well, not a whole shirt … just a piece of one. A piece of a sleeve–the bottom part. Red and black plaid, flannel … with a cuff button.

What is this? Garbage? Who loses a sleeve? But something told her that it wasn't garbage. And she curbed her angry impulse to hurl it back into the waves. The ocean had delivered that necklace to Mia, of that she was becoming more and more certain. Who cares what the cop thought? Was the ocean delivering this to her, as well? Was she going crazy? Maybe. She didn't quite know what to make of this scrap, but she thought it was somehow part of this. But what did it all mean? How did this torn remnant of a shirt factor into this puzzle? She didn't know, and it didn't ease her feelings of anxiety. She squeezed the material together in her hand, wringing out the excess water, and stood up.

She was going to find Claire Benicek. She had to. The necklace belonged to this woman, didn't it? She could at least return it to its owner. Maybe she could shed some light onto the meaning behind this tawdry piece of sleeve also. Or was she being stupid, delusional? Don't things wash up from the ocean all the time? Even though Mia felt as though she was on the right path, the logical part of her mind harbored doubt. Was she just allowing her imagination to get the best of her? The push and pull in Mia's mind was starting to drive her mad. She had to know for sure. Oceanside was only the town over. Maybe Claire Benicek would listen to her and would understand the purpose of all of this. No harm in trying, right? Or maybe the woman would throw her out of her house, would dismiss her as a crazy person. After all, Mia was a stranger. Yes, that was a possibility too. But Mia knew that she had to try.

Chapter Twenty-Six

CLAIRE

Even a week later, Claire couldn't get that television appearance out of her head nor the thought of the Ceremony of Life that Joe had held at Jimmy's elementary school, despite her wishes.

As for Trish's television debut, Claire didn't even know why she watched it. She didn't want to. But like a magnet drawn to its polar opposite, Claire sat in front of that screen as Trish Yardsleigh spoke to the world about what had happened to her, what had happened to them. Claire thought that on some level, this exposure was a good thing; maybe more people would now be looking for Jimmy and Kyle, but parts of it made her cringe. Mostly because she agreed with what Trish had to say. Claire *was* negligent; she *had* gone downstairs leaving two little boys alone in the front of her house. It *was* her fault. The indisputable fact remained that if Claire *had* been outside with the boys, where she was supposed to be, they never would have been taken. Jimmy would be home with her right now, so would her husband. Her life would be normal ... beautiful.

Claire couldn't hide anymore under the justification that well-meaning family members had offered her this past month. The justification that all parents sometimes leave their kids ... in their

112

cars to run into 7-11 and grab a coffee, at home to drive around the block to pick up a sibling from school, in the front yard to race downstairs to transfer laundry over to the drier. She had been told, "Don't beat yourself up about it. All parents do it." But just because all parents did do these things, did that make it right? To Claire, this line of thinking had become akin to someone trying to escape a red light ticket with the explanation that everyone runs that red light. Or trying to avoid a late fee for a library book with the excuse that no one ever returns their books on time. Or using the logic that everyone shares their Netflix and Hulu accounts so why should I have to pay the monthly subscription fee? These excuses don't hold water because if everyone jumped off the Brooklyn Bridge does that mean you would do it too? Of course it doesn't. *But that's different*, people had said. *Bullshit*, thought Claire. It's not different. We all justify our wrongdoing; we all rationalize away our minor transgressions, but she would not do that anymore. There *was* no justification in this case. It *was* Claire's fault. As simple as that. As real as the grass beneath her feet. And she couldn't blame Trish for agreeing with her. If she were Trish, she would hate her too.

But even though all this was true, it didn't do anything to assuage Claire's absolute bone-crushing melancholy. A lost reputation, lost friends, a lost husband, a lost son. What else was there to lose? Nothing. She had nothing left to give.

As for the Ceremony of Life ... Claire couldn't believe that Joe had actually gone through with it. He had called at least three times trying to convince her to attend. Not a chance. There was no fucking way Claire was going to attend a funeral for her son. He wasn't dead. Jimmy was out there, somewhere. And even though there were doubts that sometimes threatened to overwhelm her, that crawled over her consciousness like spiders looking for their prey, Claire wasn't going to give up. She wasn't going to move on. Not without her son. Aside from that, there was no way she was going to allow herself to be in such close proximity to Trish and her little toadies. No thanks.

A light tapping on the front door brought Claire to the present again. She ignored the knock the first few times thinking that it was probably the media wanting her statement after Trish's infamous news appearance. Or maybe they wanted to know why she hadn't attended Joe's Ceremony of Life. She didn't want to talk to the media. Hell, she didn't want to talk to anyone. Not that anyone wanted to talk to her either. But the knocking didn't stop and with a sigh, Claire rose from the couch and walked towards the front door, ready to send whoever was there away.

Chapter Twenty-Seven

CLAIRE

"I'm not interested in talking to anyone," Claire said, not even glancing at the individual on her front stoop. "Please go away."

As she was closing the door, the person spoke, "Claire ... Claire Benicek? I'm not the media. I'm just a person. I feel like I am part of your story ... please don't send me away. It took me a while to finally get the courage to come see you."

Claire glanced up, seeing this person, this girl for the first time. Well, maybe she wasn't a girl exactly, but she couldn't have been more than 25 years old. She was pretty. Her dark eyes were lined with thick lashes and had an earnestness about them, as did her torn jeans and black converse sneakers. Her curly dark hair blew in the breeze, and a tendril stuck into the girl's mouth. She looked unsure of herself, tentative. She certainly didn't have that same brazen appearance of the newscasters that had approached her these past weeks. Newscasters who had an air of righteous belonging and condescension. Who thought that Claire owed them something.

Claire didn't close the door. Something about this girl seemed innocent and pure.

"Well, what do you want?" It escaped Claire like a sigh.

In response, the girl dug around in the front pocket of her jeans and lifted something out. She held it out to Claire in her palm, like an offering. The object twinkled in the early spring sunshine and Claire recognized it immediately. Her locket. Her shaky breath caught in her throat as she took this treasure out of the woman's hand.

"How did you get this?" Claire asked, breathless.

"It's a long story, Mrs. Benicek–"

"Please call me Claire. Come in–I'm sorry. What's your name?"

"My name is Mia. Mia Rossi."

The two women entered, and Claire closed the door behind them.

Chapter Twenty-Eight

MIA

Sitting opposite Claire, sipping a cup of dark tea, Mia told Claire her story. All of it. How she ended up living in Long Beach, how the necklace had appeared in her life, how she made the connection only when she watched that *News12* segment, how she had been dismissed by the cops, and finally how she finally decided it was time to go find Claire.

"Why did you hesitate?" Claire asked, pressing her thumb against the back of the locket that she had just restored to its rightful place around her neck.

"Well, initially, I was so sure. But then, somehow it felt wrong coming to find you. You have been through so much. I actually got in my car three separate times over the past few days and then talked myself out of it. I don't know. I felt crazy, I guess. The cops thought I was crazy too. I felt like I wasn't sure if I should intrude on you ... what if I was wrong? What would you have thought of some crazy woman on your stoop raving about the waves and premonitions if the necklace wasn't actually yours?"

Claire didn't answer. The two women regarded each other silently as they sipped from steaming ceramic mugs.

After a few moments, Mia spoke again, "I can't imagine what

the past weeks have been like for you. I'm so deeply sorry for what you're going through."

Claire began to speak, but her emotions overwhelmed her and she reached for a tissue out of the box on the end table. "I wouldn't wish this on anyone," she finally said, her voice thick and heavy with emotion.

"What do you think of my story? Does it make sense to you? I feel like I'm missing something. Something big. I feel like I'm—Oh, I don't know what I feel. But I feel like I'm ... close. Close to something. I can't really tell what. But I think it involves you and your son. I just have this feeling–"

Mia took hold of Claire's hand and gazed into the eyes of this new person in her life, struggling to understand her role, her purpose. Struggling to find the connection between what she felt in her heart and the logical part of her brain. There was something there, but she couldn't put her finger on it. Kind of like when she walked into the kitchen yesterday with such purpose, but then couldn't remember why she was there. Like an unscratchable itch that no matter how you twist and turn, relief is simply an inch too far away ... a centimeter. Instead of being on the tip of her tongue it was on the edge of her consciousness, just out of reach, but frustratingly close.

Claire spoke, "Nothing makes sense to me anymore, Mia. But in my heart, I know my son is alive. I don't care what anyone says. I know it. I feel him. I feel his presence, I smell his skin. He feels close to me. I don't know how to explain it. And I can't explain why my necklace ended up at your feet. But I do believe you. I believe in your feelings, your story. I have to. Mia–you have given me more hope today than I've had in awhile now. Thank you for finding the courage to come here today."

"So what do we do now?" Mia asked. "What's next?"

"I wish I knew. I guess we just wait."

"Wait ... for what?"

"For a sign, for the cops, for–anything. Maybe whatever it is ...

whatever force or magic or–whatever it is that's inside of you–will guide you. I wish with all my heart that it will," Claire responded

"I hate waiting," Mia said with a sad laugh. "I've never been good at it."

"Me neither, Mia. But I've gotten pretty good at it the past few weeks. And now, I think I can wait a little bit longer ... I can do anything to bring me closer to finding Jimmy. Anything."

As Mia listened to Claire speak, she became more and more amazed by this woman. A woman who had been through unthinkable tragedy, yet still found within herself a nugget of strength and hope. A woman who could listen to a crazy story about waves and fate and otherworldly messages, yet still found it in her heart to believe. Mia wondered if it was too hasty to admit to herself that she felt a kinship with Claire ... even after just one conversation. She felt a friendship and a sisterhood that was both strong and pure. Looking at Claire, Mia felt as though she had known her all her life. Did Claire feel it too? Mia thought she did.

"One more question," Mia said, pulling out the now dry piece of torn shirt sleeve that had washed up on the shore. "Can you tell me anything about this?"

Claire took the item from Mia's grasp and rubbed it with her thumb. "Looks like a man's flannel shirt," Claire said.

"Yes. But–is it yours? Does it look familiar?"

"I can't say that it does. It's definitely a piece of a flannel shirt, probably a man's shirt–I mean, I guess a woman could own it, but it definitely looks like something from the men's section. Joe probably has some shirts like this, but I can't say that this partic-ular pattern looks familiar ... Why?"

Gently taking the remnant from Claire, Mia said, "This was something else that washed up on the shore at my feet. I feel like it's part of this ... somehow. I know it sounds weird. When I picked it up out of the water, it just felt like I had discovered something important. It felt meaningful."

"Unfortunately, nothing comes to mind for me," responded

Claire after considering the item for a few moments. It looked as though she was really searching her mind to find some explanation. "I'm sorry."

"Don't be," Mia said. "Maybe it is nothing. Not everything that washes up on the sand is some significant thing, right?"

But no matter how much Mia tried to dismiss this silly scrap of fabric, she couldn't. In fact, the notion that this was important somehow blared louder than before in her mind.

The women sat in comfortable conversation for the remainder of the evening. Claire showed Mia pictures of Jimmy and mementos from his short life, the pride evident in her shimmering eyes, which were flecked with gold and green. Here was Jimmy's game ball from his tee ball championship last Spring–he had hit the game-winning home run. Here was his favorite action figure–Spider-Man–with a missing hand and scratched chest plate. Here was the sweatshirt he always left on the floor. Here was his bedroom, just as he left it. Toys strewn about and the bed unmade so his Lightning McQueen bedsheets showed. It was obvious to Mia that Claire needed this. She needed someone to talk to, someone to listen to her. Someone to mourn with her. Mia was happy to be that person. Claire hadn't mentioned her husband, the other hand on Jimmy's shoulder in the picture that had started Mia on this journey. But Mia could sense his absence. Maybe that was a story for another time.

When Mia got up to leave, Claire hugged her long and tight, almost as if she were grasping onto a life raft. "Please come see me again. Call me anytime. Again, I can't tell you how much I appreciate you coming here tonight, returning my necklace, and sharing your story with me."

"I can't tell you how much I appreciate you listening to my story. I will definitely be in touch soon."

Mia walked into the cool night air and got into her car. She let out a long breath that she didn't even know she had been holding and rested her head for a minute on the headrest behind her. It was nice to be believed. But Mia wasn't fully at peace. The feeling of inaction nagged at her. And she was no closer to understanding her role in all of this than when she first arrived on Claire's front stoop. Yes, she may have gotten some validation telling her that she was on the right path, but there were so many parts of this that remained unsolved. How was she supposed to see the whole picture with so many missing puzzle pieces?

When she pulled her car down Minnesota Avenue, the night was quiet and calm around her. The houses looked snug and cozy tucked underneath the night sky with a thousand tiny stars blinking in the distance. The closing car door sounded loud and echoey in the stillness. Her house was dark, Dee and Bob not yet home, and Mia felt the pull of the ocean tug at her subconsciousness. Yet again she walked up that walkway, over those dunes and down to the ocean that looked black and jagged outstretched before her, the moonshine reflecting pale yellow highlights in the choppy surf.

As Mia walked along the shore, it seemed like eternity was laid out before her in the billions of grains of sand beneath her feet. Mia and her mother used to lovingly debate about who loved the other more. Mia's mom would say, "I love you to the moon and back." And Mia would respond, "I love you infinity times infinity." That's how many kernels of sand must have existed just within her vision at this moment, infinity times infinity. An endless, uncountable amount of matter.

As she walked, Mia gazed back at her disappearing footprints behind her, any evidence of her presence here being erased by the ebb and flow of the tide. Before she turned her head back around, something small caught her eye. Backtracking, she approached the item. A seashell, curved and beautiful in its simple, delicate perfection. No chips or cracks were perceptible at all as she turned it over in her hand. Cool and light in her cupped palm, it might have been pale pink or yellow or tan. It had darker stripes bending along its exterior, but in the dim cast of the moon, most of its nuances were lost.

Mia remembered her first trip to the Jersey Shore so many

years ago. How she and her sister had proudly presented a bucketful of seashells to their parents for inspection. In their little-girl eyes, they were mermaid treasures–dear things. They had argued over which of them would get to keep the largest of their booty. Their mother had told them that seashells were how the ocean communicates with us and if they put the open end of the shells up to their ears, they would hear the mermaids' songs. From then on, every time she found a seashell, that was her first instinct. Hearing the muffled sounds of the beach through the coolness of a shell's shadow never got old.

It was this memory that urged Mia to place the shell up to her ear as she stood at the edge of the world that star-studded night in April. She moved her hair to her right shoulder and with a small smile, listened to the whispering mermaid song. *Shhhhhh*, it said. *Shhhhhhhhhhhh*. Just echoes. Calm and comforting. But then, it was more than just echoes. *Ssssooooooo Cloooossseee*, she heard. Then again, clearer this time. *So Close*. For the first time in her life, Mia contemplated her sanity as she threw the seashell far away from her. It felt vile and slimy in her hands, as if she was recoiling from a maggot or slug. It wasn't real. It couldn't have been. Yet it felt real. Again she retraced her steps and approached the item once more. Fighting against the gorge rising within her, she placed the seashell up to her ear hoping both that she was imagining it all–which would mean that she actually was losing her mind–and that she would hear those words once again–which would mean something far more terrifying. *Sooo Closeeee. So Close*.

"So close? Where is he? Where is Jimmy Benicek?" Mia screamed out over the pounding sea. "So close to what?"

No answer. But she didn't really need an answer anymore. She knew. She didn't need the seashell nor the waves to confirm her suspicions. She was part of this ... as crazy as that sounded. She played a role in Claire and Jimmy Benicek's story. She didn't know if she would be able to find him, but she was sure as hell going to try. Try to find him and bring him home. Was it her destiny? Was this realistic? She was just a girl ... a woman. A nobody. But she was close. So very close. She could feel it in her bones ... in her heart. Close to something. She just wished she knew what that something was.

Chapter Twenty-Nine

CLAIRE

Claire woke up the next morning without that pit in the bottom of her stomach. She felt lighter somehow, purposeful and optimistic for the first time in well over a month. A new pocket had opened up right in front of her eyes. And that pocket was in the form of a young woman who showed up on her front stoop last night out of the blue. A young woman by the name of Mia Rossi.

Claire showered and blow-dried her hair–another first since Jimmy's disappearance–and dressed in a fresh pair of jeans and a long-sleeved henley. With a critical eye, she looked at the dirty laundry that had piled up in the corner of her bedroom, and gathering all the clothes in a large bundle, trudged down the stairs. She had been avoiding the basement since the disappearance. After all, this was where Claire had been when the boys were taken. This was the source of her shame and guilt. A place of egregious sin. The fact that she had come down here to transfer laundry over to the dryer when she should have been outside watching those precious boys–she couldn't get past it. Adding a cupful of Tide to the washing machine, Claire felt a bit of that crushing blame lift. It was just a bit, a tiny lightening, but the difference was palpable and welcome. Claire took a deep breath and wondered if this was how forgiveness happens. How one begins to heal. A little bit at a time.

Claire reflected on her conversation with Mia, and she felt as though a gift had been dropped in her life. Hope. What a beautiful thing. At this moment, Claire thought that it was the best thing. It eased some of the darkness and allowed her to look at her situation with new eyes. She had to do something. She needed to feel like she was helping to look for her son. This need for productivity brought Claire out her glass-paned front door and into her red Toyota parked in her black-topped driveway. This was the first time she had ventured out of the house, with the exception of going to work, since that fateful day.

Almost as if she were on autopilot, she drove in the direction of the police station thinking that she would check in. It had been days, weeks maybe since she had spoken with Detective Lackey, and it was high time for an in-person visit. She also wanted to give him a piece of her mind about how he dismissed Mia Rossi and how wrong he had been about the necklace that she had found. She drove with purpose and intention ... two words that had previously been missing from her life.

Parking in front of the Long Beach Police Station, a familiar figure caught her eye. Could it be? That familiar loping run, the back of a head so etched into her memory from the many visits to Kidz Styles for haircuts. Those sneakers, lovingly picked out from Kids Foot Locker in the Roosevelt Field Mall. That Pottery Barn backpack that Jimmy had received last year for his birthday. It had Spider-Man shooting his web embroidered in the canvas fabric. Jimmy. Her Jimmy. Getting caught in her seatbelt, she threw open the door of her car.

"Jimmy!" she screamed. "Jimmy!" Why wasn't he stopping?

She ran after him down the sidewalk, finally catching up, grasping his shoulders from behind, screaming his name. Heart pounding. Her boy. He was here all along. Turning him around, she kneeled down on the sidewalk, out of breath, heart hammering, tears rolling down her cheeks, arms poised to gather him in a firm embrace. But, the eyes, they were different, and where was the smattering of freckles across his nose? It wasn't him. Claire's whole being deflated. The boy started crying; he was afraid of her and Claire didn't notice the man, presumably the boy's father, rapidly approaching.

"Hey. What are you doing?" the man asked firmly, gripping the little boy's hand and pulling him protectively back.

"I'm ... I'm sorry. I thought–"

"Well, whatever you thought, you thought wrong, lady. Let's go, Henry."

"I thought he was someone else," Claire whispered to their backs.

Maybe this was why Claire found it too difficult to leave her house now that Jimmy was gone. Reminders were everywhere. Reminders of her boy, her sweet Jimmy. *Please God*, Claire thought to herself. *Bring him home. Please let Mia be right. Please send her a sign.* She still hadn't decided what she believed in regarding the inhabitant or maybe inhabitants (plural) of the heavens above ... but she was desperate.

Claire wiped her wet eyes with the back of her sleeves and stood up, slowly walking back towards the precinct. *It's ok*, she told herself. *It was an honest mistake.* She took a deep, steadying breath and walked into the same double doors that Mia had entered just days before. She was ready to find her son. Ready to fight. Ready to rejoin the world of the living once again. Jimmy needed her.

Chapter Thirty

MIA

The next morning, Dee popped her head out of the front door to retrieve the mail as Mia raced down the side staircase on her way to work. She hadn't slept well last night. Thoughts of Claire and Jimmy and the ocean tumbled together in her mind.

"Oh, hey, Dee. I hope I didn't wake you up. I forgot to hold off putting on my shoes this morning."

Mia had been trying to avoid putting on her shoes until she was just ready to leave the apartment. She hadn't gotten around to purchasing throw rugs, and she was sure that the tread of her boots echoed in Dee and Bob's apartment ... especially so early in the morning. And she didn't hear her landlords come home last night until almost 1 in the morning. She heard their door open and close and also heard their impassioned murmurs persist until past 2am. Mia wondered if they had been fighting. Judging by the rise and swell of their voices, it certainly sounded like it. Didn't old people go to bed earlier? But Bob and Dee didn't seem like the typical "old people." They seemed young and active, and they clearly had some adventure left in them, as evidenced by their date-night boating excursions as Mia had come to think of them.

But Dee was chipper as she answered, "Not at all, Mia. I don't sleep like I used to. But Bob ... he sleeps like the dead. It's his snoring that woke me this morning. Not your footsteps."

"Oh, good. I always feel like you can hear me up there."

"Not to worry. We've always had tenants. Got used to the noise," Dee responded.

"Well, if I'm ever disturbing you, definitely let me know."

"Will do," Dee said. "Mia, I feel like we have been so busy we haven't gotten to catch up lately. How's your job going? What have you been up to? Make any friends? Pretty soon young people will be everywhere around here."

"Unfortunately, I have no new friends to report," Mia answered lightly. "But work has actually been pretty great. I'm thinking about starting a certificate program to get my realtor license."

"Wonderful news. I see you're on the go. Maybe you'd like to come for dinner tomorrow to tell us more about it?"

"I'd like that," responded Mia.

Just as Mia reached her car, she turned back around. Maybe Dee would know what to do. After all, she had more experience with the ocean than Mia did. And she hadn't thought Mia was crazy when she mentioned the connection she felt or her reason for moving to Long Beach in the first place.

Tentatively, Mia said, "Actually, Dee, I have been pretty busy lately and I have met some new people. I don't have to be at work for another 40 minutes or so." Mia had planned to stop at the deli for a coffee and a buttered roll, but that could definitely wait. She continued, "Can I talk to you for a few minutes?"

"Of course. Come, I'll make you a cup of tea."

Mia followed Dee inside and sat down on Bob and Dee's worn-out living room sofa, mind racing.

Before Dee even had a chance to sit down, Mia began her story. The words spilled out of her mouth with relief. She hadn't realized how much she needed advice, guidance.

"So, I feel like I was put here–in Long Beach–for a purpose," Mia began. "I know that sounds crazy, but it started when I was a kid. I mentioned it to you and Bob at dinner the first night I came here. I wasn't just being metaphoric. I have felt the waves pulling at me since I was little."

She looked at Dee and found the woman nodding, no judgment in her eyes. So she continued. "I didn't know what the purpose was. But now I do. Or at least I think I do. On one of my first nights here, I went down to the beach. It was freezing ... there was actual ice on the sand. But I took off my shoes. I needed to feel the water on my feet, you know? It was like a magnet or something pulling me. And when my feet were so cold, almost numb, and I was about to leave, this necklace washed up. I couldn't really see it at the time so I threw it on top of a box in the bedroom and in the chaos of unpacking, I kind of just forgot about it. And then, weeks later, I was watching the news–" Mia didn't think she was making any sense at all; the words all coiled out of her so quickly. The story seemed so fantastic ... too fantastic, yet she was sure it was true and right.

"Whoa, Mia. Take a breath. Take a sip of tea," Dee interrupted with motherly concern.

"Ok. Sorry. I know how this must sound." Mia took a deep breath and began again, more slowly this time. "So the necklace washed ashore, and I didn't think about it for a while. And then, weeks later, I was watching *News12*, and I saw that necklace ... in a picture."

"You saw the necklace–the one from the ocean–on *News12*?" Dee asked, trying to follow along with Mia's impassioned speech.

"Yes. There was a picture of a boy on the news. A boy who had been missing. His name is Jimmy Benicek. The woman standing behind him was wearing that necklace."

Dee spoke, "Mia. That's quite a story. How can you even be sure it was the same necklace? The ocean gives and it takes away. Lots of trinkets wash up on the shore. Not all of them mean something. Heck, most of what washes up is simply discarded garbage–"

"Dee," Mia picked up the conversation. "When I went back

to look at the necklace, it had the initials J.B. engraved on the inside plate. And even though the Long Beach police department dismissed me—"

"Are you out of your mind?" Dee burst in. All the concern had been replaced with incredulity. "You went to the police about this? Mia. It's a coincidence. There are a million J.B.s in the world. It might not even be initials. The police are incredibly busy. How could you bother them with such nonsense?"

Although Mia was surprised by Dee's tone, she continued undeterred. She said, "I thought it was a long shot at first too, but then when I went to Jimmy–actually his real name is James–Benicek's house and spoke with his mother, Claire Benic–"

Dee interrupted again, "Tell me you did not go bother this poor woman with such insanity–"

"Dee ... it *was* her necklace. Claire confirmed it. She said that–"

"Mia, I am saying this because I care about you and think you're a sweet girl. This is a fool's errand. Do not involve yourself in the tragedy of others. I understand that you are lonely, but go out and make some real friends. Don't prey on strangers. Leave that woman to her suffering and–"

"I know how this sounds. And I know it's hard to believe. But I think I'm supposed to help them. To help Claire ... and Jimmy. I think that–"

"Let me give you some advice," Dee said, looking directly into Mia's eyes. Her tone was steely as she said, "Drop this foolishness. This is not your story, Mia. You are looking for connections that simply do not exist."

The harshness of Dee's voice stopped Mia's speech and once again made her consider whether or not her intuitions were accurate. Doubt, that unfriendly companion, crept in once more. *So what if I found Claire's necklace? What does that prove? Am I looking for connections that aren't there? Is Dee right? Am I causing more grief? Maybe this is unhealthy? Crazy? Should I just leave this alone? Dee is trying to protect me. And maybe I do need some protection ... from my own wild imagination.*

But then Mia latched onto the thought, *What about Claire? Claire believes me.* Another thought popped up to answer that one, *Why wouldn't she believe me? She would believe anything that she thought would bring her closer to her son. Wouldn't all mothers do that? Does Claire's belief really hold any water?* But regardless of the thoughts spinning around in Mia's mind, she realized one thing for certain: Dee was not the audience for such a tale. She had chosen the wrong person to confide in. She could contemplate the sanity of her story later, and her motives for involving herself in "the tragedy of others," as Dee had framed it, but right now, she needed to get out of here. She needed to smooth things over with Dee–she didn't want Dee to worry about her, nor to argue with her. And it was time to head over to the office; she couldn't be late.

"Maybe you're right," Mia said with feigned sincerity. "Maybe I am just looking for ways to occupy my mind. Making up stories because I have nothing better to do."

"I *am* right, Mia. I've been around the block a few times to know when someone is headed down the wrong path," Dee responded with finality. "Put this out of your mind. It won't lead you anywhere. It's for your own good. You don't need to take on this woman's grief. And you don't need to cause her any more grief. I may not be a mother. But I know that."

After a pause, Mia said, "Well. Thanks for hearing me out. Now that I said it out loud, it does sound kind of nuts." Did Mia believe those words? Maybe she did.

Dee still looked doubtful as she walked Mia to the front door. "Mia," she said again. "I know you think you are doing the right thing here, but you're not. I'm a friend, kind of like your Long Beach surrogate mother in a way. I feel like it's my duty to look out for you. And I'm telling you not to dwell on this darkness. It's not healthy ... for you or that woman."

"Claire Benicek," Mia corrected. "Her name is Claire. And

maybe you're right." And this time, Mia wasn't lying. Despite her earlier confidence, Dee had planted a seed of uncertainty, and that seed was threatening to grow into a weed. To consume her.

"I know I'm right, Mia," Dee said. "Oh, and don't forget—dinner tomorrow." Dee smiled at Mia, but it didn't quite reach her eyes and there were creases on the bridge of her nose.

She's worried about me, thought Mia to herself. She felt guilty for even bringing this to Dee and causing her unneeded stress and concern.

"I won't forget. I love your cooking. Thanks, Dee."

Feeling the weight of Dee's stare on her, Mia got into her car, more skeptical and uneasy than she had ever felt before. On one hand, Dee was right. What was she doing befriending Claire, involving herself with the cops and plopping herself right in the middle of this kidnapping story she saw on the news? She wasn't Cam Jansen—that detective in those chapter books she used to read as a kid ... the one with the photographic memory. And Dee had been so kind and supportive of Mia. If someone as open and honest as Dee thought her story sounded crazy, maybe it was.

But—on the other hand—it all felt so right, like rotating the focus knob on a blurry image. The picture was becoming more and more clear as the days progressed. She still couldn't make out the final image, but she was getting closer. She could sense it somehow. And what about that bond that she felt with Claire Benicek? Could she be making that up too? Looking for a friend and preying on the weaknesses of a grieving mother? When she put it that way, it sounded downright despicable.

All these thoughts left Mia feeling jittery on her ride to work, unsettled and anxious. She didn't know what to believe nor what to think. She tried to push these feelings from her mind as she sat down at her desk, but they gathered around her like storm clouds, ominous and dark.

The buzzing in her back pocket brought Mia back down to Earth. Glancing down at the phone screen, she saw that Claire was calling. She felt a chill race down her spine. Was she wrong to have given this woman hope? Was she indeed on a "fool's errand," as Dee had put it? Despite her desire to talk to her and her curiosity about what she might want, Mia pressed the "end" button. She couldn't possibly have a conversation with Claire at this moment. She was too confused.

Switching her phone to silent mode, Mia put it in her bag–out of sight, out of mind, right? The stacks of paperwork next to her allowed her to lose herself in her job, for a little while at least. And Mia was grateful for the relief.

Chapter Thirty-One

CLAIRE

"How have you been this week, Claire? Sleeping any better?" Dr. Kimler asked at the start of their weekly therapy session.

Claire really liked Dr. Kimler. Her soft voice and thoughtful eyes gave Claire a sense of peace–like Claire was being heard and validated. She was grateful to find a confidant in Dr. Kimler, someone who looked at her without judgment or scorn. Truthfully, Claire didn't think she would have survived the first 2 weeks of Jimmy's disappearance without her. She had had some really dark nights in the beginning ... nights where terrible and hurtful thoughts raced through her mind. Nights where the allure of hurting herself, ending it all, whispered in her ear, almost too tempting to ignore. Dr. Kimler was the only one to whom Claire admitted these horrors; this office was the only place where she felt safe enough to be that honest. She was doubly thankful that her insurance was accepted; otherwise, she definitely could not afford the doctor's exorbitant fee.

"Actually, I *have* been sleeping better this past week," Claire responded truthfully.

Claire felt nervous as hell the first time she came for therapy ... she wasn't sure why. Possibly it was because she had actually been fearful for herself ... fearful that she would do something terrible because she simply couldn't resist the impulse. Fearful that Dr. Kimler wouldn't really be able to help her after all and she would be chained to this misery for the rest of her life. Or maybe it was the thought of sharing herself with someone else ... she had never been one to unload her personal baggage on others. Offering comfort was her specialty, not accepting it. But now, as she looked around at Dr. Kimler's framed degrees and the silk sunflowers displayed in a crystal vase on the bookshelf, she had to admit that she felt comfortable here. The neutral furnishings and the smell of lavender essential oils made her feel calmer somehow, focused. Claire would never have thought that she could find solace in a psychiatrist, but that is exactly what this place and this person had been for her over the past few weeks.

"I'm really glad to hear that. That's a positive sign. Have you given any more thought to beginning a medication regimen to help alleviate some of the anxiety and depression you have been experiencing?"

Dr. Kimler had suggested that Claire begin taking a low dose of Zoloft. She said it would help with the crushing melancholy she felt. But Claire wasn't sold on the idea. Somehow, in her mind, she felt that easing the pain meant erasing the memory of her son. The pain was a reminder of him, and it was her job to bear it. It was all she had at the moment. And she was *supposed* to have pain. Her son was missing. She didn't want to get rid of it.

"I think I've decided against that. I don't want to rely on anything to help me cope. I have actually been feeling more positive and hopeful," responded Claire. Even though the fact that Mia still hadn't returned her call was eating at her.

"Really? I'm so happy to hear that," Dr. Kimler responded. "Have you been practicing the mindfulness exercises I gave you?"

"Honestly, no. They didn't really work for me."

"Well, it does take some practice. The idea is that once you have mastered the techniques, you can apply them in times of anxiety and stress." Dr. Kimler was an advocate of mindful meditation and tried to convince Claire to adopt these practices as well.

"Yeah. Maybe I haven't given them a solid try," Claire responded. "I saved the videos on my phone, for future reference."

"So Claire, what has brought about this optimism? You even look brighter," Dr. Kimler inquired.

"Well, I met someone. Her name is Mia. She gave me back my necklace." Claire gestured at the silver pendant at her throat.

"I remember how upset you were about its disappearance," the doctor responded. "How did this Mia find it?"

Claire told Dr. Kimler the strange story that Mia had told her, leaving out the bits that might have sounded really weird ... like the parts about the waves and the premonitions. Claire didn't think that Dr. Kimler was a woman who gave much weight to gut-feelings and omens.

When the story was complete, Claire looked at her therapist with an open smile and said, "I don't know, but I really think that Mia can help me find my son. It almost feels like she's part of my family, a long-lost daughter or something."

Dr. Kimler didn't speak for a moment; she just gave Claire a curious look, like she was trying to process what she had been told. So Claire continued, "Well? What do you think? I know it sounds a little bit off the wall. But I feel lighter somehow ... you even noticed it. I feel optimistic again. The cops haven't been able to find him, but I really think Mia is on the right path."

Looking like she was choosing her words with care, Dr. Kimler finally spoke, "Claire. I understand that acceptance is a difficult thing–nearly impossible in a case such as yours when you have been denied the necessary closure–but this story is, at best, simply a distraction."

Claire expected some resistance from the therapist, but she didn't expect outright dismissal. "If at best this is a distraction, what is it at worst?" she asked.

"Well, at worst, it is a delusion," Dr. Kimler answered slowly.

She continued, "Claire, you are a smart woman. Tap into your logic for a minute. You can't possibly believe that some woman, someone who doesn't know you or your son, someone who is in no way affiliated with the law, can possibly be your savior just because your necklace happened to wash up at her feet."

"Not just the necklace," Claire tried to explain. "A piece of fabric as well–well, who knows if that's part of it. But a feeling and a knowledge too. It can't be coincidence. I can't accept that."

"It is natural for parents in your situation to experience denial, but I thought you were past that, Claire. I think I overestimated your progress. I think that we should go back to bi-weekly sessions. My secretary can help you contact your insurance company to discuss coverage–"

"I don't understand," Claire responded. "I thought you said that it was important to remain hopeful and optimistic?"

"Hopeful and optimistic about *your* grief, *your* future. You are more than your tragedy and are entitled to live a full and productive life in spite of such a loss. But looking for answers in unhealthy avenues will not help you go through the stages of mourning," Dr. Kimler explained. "Despite it all, Claire, rationality and logic are crucial steps towards acceptance and healing."

Claire picked up the conversation, "And you feel that believing in this woman is the opposite of rationality and logic?"

"Yes. I do. And I don't mean to sound cold, but if you take the emotion out of the situation, you will see it too. It is my job to give you my honesty; you deserve that, and that's what you pay me for. I'm happy you got your necklace back, but that's all this is. Nothing more."

Crestfallen, Claire didn't say anything. She didn't know what to say or what to feel. She respected Dr. Kimler, trusted her, and on some level, Claire understood that the connection between her and Mia did sound crazy, foolish, illogical. And yet. And yet she believed in Mia Rossi. She believed that she would be reunited with her son. Sitting in Dr. Kimler's office, Claire felt the pangs associated with feeling torn between two worlds. Torn between what was logical and awful and what was illogical and bright. She wasn't ready to dismiss Mia's appearance in her life; she wasn't ready to give up hope. She couldn't. Mia's presence had been a life raft that she desperately needed ... in more ways than one.

When the session with Dr. Kimler came to an end, Claire exited the room no closer to knowing how to view her life. But she made the choice to remain hopeful. She made the choice to believe in Mia Rossi, no matter how illogical it sounded. And this choice allowed her to feel peace on her drive home.

Chapter Thirty-Two

MIA

"Mom?" Mia said, getting out of her car and approaching the side stairs leading up to her apartment.

Her mother's bright orange cardigan was visible from all the way down the street. She had been sitting on the bottom step of the wooden stairwell on the side of Dee and Bob's house.

"There's my girl," Mia's mom said, standing up.

Even though Mia perceived that there was something off with her mom–maybe it was her tilted smile–it felt good to envelop herself in her arms. She hadn't realized how much she had missed her, and even though they spoke almost every day, a phone conversation is no substitute for the real thing. Mia inhaled the familiar clean scent of her mother's hair mixed with her smoky vanilla hand cream.

Shifting her bag to the other shoulder, Mia asked, "What are you doing here? Wait ... that sounded bad ... I mean, it's so good to see you ... I was going to invite you, Dad, and Gabby down once I was fully unpacked."

"Show me your apartment, and we can catch up," Mia's mom responded. "I want to hear all about what you've been up to and about your job. I'm so proud of my girl."

139

Arm in arm the two women ascended the stairs.

Mia took off her shoes, put her work bag down on an empty kitchen chair, and went into the living room where her mom was walking around admiring the cozy space her daughter had created for herself.

"Those pictures are lovely," commented Mia's mom.

"Yeah. I love them," Mia replied. "I splurged on them. They were taken by a local photographer. They're from a little store down the road. You would love it there ... maybe later we can take a walk over. I'd love to show you the town. Their stuff is kind of expensive, but so beautiful."

"Mia, you know we are happy to give you some money. Didn't Dad offer–"

"He did mom ... and I know. But I want to do this on my own," Mia responded.

"I understand, my love. But the offer is always open. We miss you so much. And we are so proud of you."

Mia went on to tell her mom all about her new job and how she had finally submitted her paperwork for the realtor coursework she was going to begin.

"Wow. A realtor. I think you'll be great. Aunt Judy is looking to sell her home ... maybe you can help her," Mia's mom responded.

"Oh, really? I'll give her a call. And thanks for the encouragement. It's not what I would've pictured for myself ... well, maybe it is. I didn't really have much in mind in terms of future career plans. But I'm excited about it."

"And I'm excited for *you*. I just can't believe you're all grown up. Gabby can't wait for you to take her to the beach this summer."

"I can't wait to take her," Mia said cheerfully. She missed her little sister and couldn't wait for the summer to arrive. She hoped that Gabby would come stay with her quite often when there was no school to occupy her days.

When conversation tapered off, Mia couldn't help feeling as

though her mom was skirting around an elephant in the room. She knew her mom and all of her little habits and facial expressions too well to miss the cues: the raised eyebrows, the slight squint in her eyes ... something was up.

Taking the bull by the horns, Mia said, "So. Again, I'm so happy you're here. But I feel like there's something you're not telling me, Mom. What's really up? Is everything ok?"

Mia's mind was brought immediately to her father, who suffered from migraines and high blood pressure. She always worried about his health, and after each of his doctor's appointments, Mia had always waited with bated breath to hear that he had received an "all clear" in terms of his health. Was her dad ok?

Mia's mom answered quickly, "Oh, yes. We are all fine. Nothing like that. Your father is as healthy as a horse ... he's not going anywhere. He's too stubborn."

"Ok," Mia said. "Then you just decided to take the three-hour trip from Sparta to Long Beach to say hi?"

Her mom replied, "Well ... not exactly. To be truthful Mia, even though I have been dying to see you and hug you, there is another reason why I showed up today." Mia's mom tucked a tendril of hair behind her daughter's ear and after a pause, "Your landlord called me."

"Bob?"

"No, his wife. Dee. She's worried about you."

"Really? That's weird. Why?"

Mia replayed her last interaction with Dee over in her mind. Yes, she did have that awkward conversation with her before work earlier this week. But Mia had gone over to her landlord's house for dinner the following night and everything was fine. They hadn't even discussed the Beniceks. And she had seen them one additional time after that. Could that be why Dee had called her mom? How did Dee even get the number? *She must have used the "Emergency Contact" section from her lease agreement. That was a little forward of her,* Mia thought to herself.

"Well, it was an odd conversation," her mom replied.

"What did she say?" Mia asked.

"She said quite a bit, Mia. She said that you were poking around in some missing child case? That you went to the police? That you actually went to go see the woman whose child has been abducted? Mia, tell me this isn't true."

"It's not like that, Mom. I know how it sounds," Mia pleaded. "But the case came to me. Not the other way around–"

"In what way did the case come to you? Why haven't you spoken to me about this? Have you been hiding it?"

"Mom, I understand that this sounds crazy, alright. I get it, I really do. But this woman's necklace washed up at my feet when I was down by the ocean. I saw that same necklace on the news and put it all together. I'm part of this."

"Dee told me that as well. It *is* wild that this necklace that washed up just happened to belong to this poor mother. And I *am* sympathetic to her situation. God, if I were her, I don't know what I would do if you or your sister were abducted. I don't think I could survive it. But, Mia ... it's just a coincidence. A fluke. A freak thing. You have to see that. It's not divine intervention. I didn't even think you believed in such things. You didn't move away from home to embroil yourself in a news story, no matter how compelling."

"I didn't go looking for this. I don't even know how to begin to tell you, but it didn't start when I moved to Long Beach. It started years ago ... remember that family trip we once took to the Jersey Shore? Mom–I have wanted to live near the water for so many years. I can't explain it. It just–calls to me. And I feel like I am here for a purpose. Dee thought I was crazy too ... which is why she probably called you–"

"She's worried about you, Mia. And I am grateful that you have her to look out for you. I'm worried about you too. I am very, very worried that this is how you have been spending your time. It's morbid. And unhealthy ... and possibly harmful ... to you, to that woman–"

"Claire, Mom. Her name is Claire Benicek. And she is distraught. Beside herself. Her son is gone ... her 8-year-old son. And what if I can help–"

"Mia, I wish I had known this was going on. How could you possibly help? How could you possibly know how to find her son? You're not a cop."

"It has something to do with the ocean," Mia said with finality. She thought about mentioning the shirt and the seashell, but she didn't think that would help her convince her mother that she was connected to Claire Benicek. Despite how crazy it sounded, she *was* connected and part of this. Yes, there have been times when she doubted it ... like during her conversation with the detective, and with Dee ... but the surety had crept back in. It was weird; she could admit that. But just because it was weird, did that mean it wasn't true? Weird things happen all the time in this world. Sometimes the truth is stranger than fiction.

"Mia, I know that I cannot force you to stop this, to give it up, to focus on yourself ... but if I could, I would ... I might even insist that you move back–"

"I'm *not* moving back home, Mom. I moved here to gain some independence, to grow up ... I adore you and Dad and Gabby ... but I couldn't be anything but a child in that house and–"

"I get it, Mia. I do. And I respect you for it. But this–this situation. It isn't helping you find that independence."

Mia didn't know how to respond, how to make her mother understand. And she couldn't help but feel a bit betrayed by Dee. Maybe Dee did have her best interests at heart, but it seemed sneaky to call up her mother and tell on her. Dee could have at least given Mia the heads-up that her mom was coming down. And of course, Dee and Bob weren't even home to witness this ... out on the boat, as always. Was this why landlords ask for character references? So they can rat out their tenants if need be? Tell their moms on them? Mia knew that her anger was misguided.

Dee had called her mother because she cared about Mia ... she was looking out for her. Yet despite that knowledge, defiance bloomed in Mia. She would not give this up ... but she did need to assure her mother that she was sane and ok. So, for the first time ever, Mia told her mom what she wanted to hear ... even if it wasn't the truth.

"Ok, Mom. Maybe you're right." Mia couldn't be sure, but she thought that her mother sensed her deceit.

"Mia, I love you. I want what's best for you. I just don't see how involving yourself in this tragedy helps anyone ... most importantly *you*." Her mother's tone was careful and measured. "Maybe I should have insisted on coming down here with you. Help get you settled. But I wanted to respect your privacy and I wanted to respect the fact that you are trying to prove something to yourself by doing all this alone–"

"I'm not trying to prove anything to anyone," Mia responded, trying to calm her trembling anger. "I'm just trying to grow up."

"Mia, do you want me to stay with you for a few days? Make sure you're–"

"No, Mom." Mia corrected herself and curbed her tone, "That is such a kind offer. But I'm ok. Really. I will step back from this. You're right. Dee's right ... so are the cops. This is silly." Mia gave her mother the sweetest smile she could muster and hoped that it would be believed.

"Ok. I'm so glad your landlord called. That was so kind of her to take such an interest in you. She really likes you. I think she likes having someone to take care of."

"Yeah, Dee and Bob mean well," Mia said. And she did believe that too. No matter how frustrated she was ... Bob and Dee did mean well. So did her mother.

"So let's put all this behind us. Let's grab dinner ... my treat, I insist. Take me somewhere delicious."

Mia and her mother walked arm in arm up Minnesota Avenue and away from the ocean. Even though the food at Cafe Laguna was delicious–the sauce on the rigatoni savory and the steak perfectly cooked–Mia couldn't relax or enjoy her mother's company. She was too conscious of feigning happiness and ease when inside her soul was trembling.

Most of the businesses in Long Beach close early during the week, especially before the rush of summer, so Mia did not get to show her mother the tiny shop where she had purchased the prints of the ocean. Instead, the two women walked back towards her apartment–Mia's mother chatting amiably away and Mia herself trying to pay attention and add the appropriate responses to assuage any remaining worry that her mother might have possessed.

Walking her mother to her car, Mia said, "Drive carefully, Mom. It's so late to drive so far."

"Don't worry about me, my girl," Mia's mom responded, wrapping her arms around her daughter in a long embrace. "I have a book on Audible that I need to finish before the library takes it back. Plus, that cappuccino I drank after dinner will keep me awake. I probably won't even be able to sleep tonight ... caffeine always gives me the jitters, but it was worth it. That place is delicious! Your father would love it."

"You, Dad, and Gabby should come down in a few weeks. We can go back," Mia responded.

"Let's talk tomorrow and put a date in the calendar," said Mia's mom as she settled herself in the driver's seat of her car.

"Ok, Mom. Love you."

"I love you too, my sweet girl," Mia's mom said, giving her daughter a kiss on the forehead through the open window. "And please, remember what we talked about earlier. Leave this whole unpleasant business behind you. You are on the up and up ... don't let this tragedy bring you down."

"I won't let it bring me down, Mom."

"Promise me you will focus on yourself ... you're a budding realtor. Not a private eye."

"I promise, Mom. Drive safely."

Aside from the typical childhood dishonesties, that was the

first time in her adult life that Mia ever lied to her mother, and as she watched her car pull away from the curb, and as she watched the taillights recede down Minnesota Avenue, Mia felt wretched about it. The effort of pretending brought on a tension headache as thoughts slammed and ricocheted off the inside of her mind. The cops ... Claire ... Dee ... her mother ... She needed relief. The ocean could give it to her.

She raced over that wooden plank walkway, down the sandy expanse of beach and right down to where the waves lapped greedily up on the shore. She sat there, on the cool sand, for quite sometime ... her heart slowing to the beat of the tide. Just being here calmed her turbulent soul and quieted her careening mind. What should she do? What was her role? Should she continue down this path when everyone in her life was telling her to stop? Everyone except Claire? The image of Claire's face came to Mia's mind ... her sad eyes. The way she had shown Mia her son's room with such glowing pride and reverence. The way she had gazed at Mia with such hope ... such desperation. She couldn't abandon this woman. She just couldn't. Mia knew that to be true as she regarded the glistening ocean spread out before her in the approaching darkness. Maybe she could help her ... or maybe she couldn't. Mia didn't know. But she *could* be her friend. She *could* be open and honest with Claire about her doubt, about her worry, about her fear of giving false hope. She could do that.

She pulled her phone out of her back pocket. Some grains of sand had lodged themselves in the crevices of the screen, but Mia didn't mind. She texted Claire:

> I'm sorry it took me so long to respond

An immediate ping. Claire responded:

> That's ok, Mia. I'm just glad that you did.

Mia smiled softly to herself.

> Are you around to meet for coffee sometime soon?

> Just tell me when and where.

Mia didn't know if this was all a curse or a gift, but she owed it to Claire, to the waves that crashed through her mind, and to herself to see it through.

Chapter Thirty-Three

TRISH YARDSLEIGH

In the aftermath of her news appearances, and in the aftermath of the Ceremony of Life that Joe Benicek had organized, Trish felt as though time was endless as it spread out before her. She struggled to fill the weeks, days, hours, minutes of her life. Previously, so much of her energy had gone into being a mom–the PTA meetings, doctor appointments, tee ball games, school pick-ups and drop-offs, playdates, holiday parties, barbecues; there never seemed to be *enough* time, enough hours in the day. But now, there were too many ... too much space. Her schedule went from jam-packed, to empty.

People stopped asking her to organize events or go out to dinner. They didn't think she would want to do any of it–she must be too busy mourning, people assumed. They felt as though they would be intruding upon her grief, so instead they avoided her ... all under the guise of compassion of course: under the guise of giving her some space. They tiptoed around her, treated her as if a stiff breeze could knock her right off her feet ... and instead of this making her feel better, it made her feel desperately alone. Like an outsider.

People never know how to react to another's grief or trauma. In an attempt to be respectful, most people isolate themselves.

And no one wants that continual reminder–the reminder that awful things can and do happen, and that awful things can and do happen to anyone ... it could even be them. It's inevitable that at some point in life, we will all get the short-end of fate's metaphorical stick. But people tend to forget that immutable fact when fortune runs in their favor. And right now, Trish's grief was unfathomable. To those around her, it wasn't *their* burden ... at least not yet. They might one day be on the receiving end, but at this moment, Trish's friends, family, community members all remained blissfully ignorant. At some point, the person who has experienced tragedy becomes just another burden on others ... a compulsory phone call to be made, a weekly stop to visit–a chore. All Trish wanted was a sense of normalcy ... to be able to talk to her friends and family without that veil of sympathy and pity clouding their eyes. But Trish didn't think she would ever have normalcy again ... not without Kyle. She fleetingly thought about Claire ... another human who could truly understand the depth of her sorrow and isolation. Possibly the one other woman in her town, hell ... in the world who could provide a measure of comfort and companionship. But Trish had burned that bridge ... burned it intentionally, and she couldn't go back. Not now. And if Trish was being honest with herself, maybe she didn't want to adjust to this new life–this empty life. Kyle's abduction had left a gaping hole in her heart, and she didn't know how to fill it.

She continued to dutifully attend her various exercise classes, her hair appointments, nail appointments, but those only took up so much time. Instead of driving through Starbucks, Trish got in the habit of actually parking and waiting on the winding line in person. She had nothing better to do. Sometimes, she even remained in the cafe long after the barista called her name to indicate that her Nitro Cold Brew with almond milk was ready. She would sit in a firm leather armchair and scroll through her emails ... which had dwindled since Kyle's disappearance, or read *Newsday*, or gaze mindlessly at her Instagram feed. Anything to take up some time in her day. Anything to delay the inevitable return to a quiet, empty house.

Mason had gone back to work about a week after Kyle's disappearance. He was never one to do well with idle time, even in his 20s. Trish remembered how even on their honeymoon, while she herself was sleeping late in their beachfront hut in Tahiti after a night spent drinking mai-tais at the blue-tiled mosaic bar, Mason would wake up at the crack of dawn to go out golfing, or running, or he would swim laps in the Olympic-size swimming pool. Then, he would return to their room where he would make love to her with a fervor and zeal that took her breath away, left her screaming his name into the abyss of pleasure. She always admired his passion, his energy. He simply couldn't sit still. Then, Trish didn't care. She hadn't minded the quiet. She had enjoyed luxuriating in the king-sized bed all by herself, knowing that her husband would soon return hungry for her ... and breakfast. But now, she tried to not feel betrayed by his absence. Betrayed and jealous. By throwing himself into his work, Mason had found a way to cope with their son's absence, to numb the pain. Trish hadn't. This resentment had planted a rotten seed within her that festered with each passing moment without Kyle.

Trish still had that business card that her friend had given her with a psychiatrist's name on it ... a psychiatrist who supposedly specialized in grief counseling and trauma. She hadn't thrown it away. But once again, she dismissed the idea of therapy. She was far too proud to admit to another human that she wasn't ok–even if that human was a stranger sworn to confidentiality. She couldn't envision herself laying on some couch in some strange office listening to someone else counsel her on how to let go of her crushing sadness. What did anyone really know about what she was going through? Nothing. No one knew jack shit about the depth of her struggle. Pretending was the only thing that kept her whole, that stopped the walls that she had built up around herself from crumbling to a pile of rubble on the floor. If she admitted the truth about her emotional state, there would be nothing to stop the flow, no dam strong enough to stopper the onslaught of sadness, terror, shame that would undoubtedly gush powerfully forth. But pretending was becoming harder and harder with each passing day. Her walls had cracked ... and the spackle was no longer holding. She wondered if the decay was visible in her face.

She gazed at herself in the bathroom mirror—a mosquito trapped in amber. Frozen in time ... unable to move forward, wishing she could move backwards—through time, through space. Back to a moment when life was good and happy again. She tried to smile at herself, but the corners of her lips didn't pull up the way they used to, and her eyes remained hard and still—lifeless. No joy left in them anymore. Kyle was her joy, and now he was gone.

She opened the medicine cabinet. Lined up on the shelf was a box of Batman Band-Aids, a tube of Neosporin, a small bottle of children's chewable Tylenol—grape—and a half-full bottle of NyQuil she bought two years ago when she had COVID and couldn't sleep—probably expired. Finally, her eyes focused on what she was looking for. A small gold pill case with pink roses etched on the lid. Her friend Janine had brought this over weeks ago ... when Kyle first disappeared. "For emergencies," she had said. "I took a few of these when my mom died last year and they really helped me cope. It's Vicodin ... you just need half a tablet." Trish had unknowingly pocketed the container and found it again a month later when she was emptying her pockets to take her clothes to the dry cleaner. She just threw the container in the medicine cabinet because she didn't know what else to do with it. Maybe she should have flushed all those little pills down the toilet. But now, Trish picked out one tablet from the holder and held it in her palm—she thought about breaking it in half, but what tool would she use? A razor blade? She didn't have one of those handy. There was no perforated ridge that would have made it easy to snap it in two. The pill was so small anyway. Surely one tiny tablet couldn't do too much damage. Fuck it. She placed the pill between her lips—a light bitterness lingered on her tongue—and swallowed it down without water. It stuck a bit in her throat, but just a bit. She went to her bedroom and lay down in her perfectly made bed—Marisol had been here earlier to clean, which included changing the sheets. That fresh, cold scent clung to the down comforter, to the Egyptian cotton coverlet. Finally, the drug took her away. It was the first time she slept dreamlessly since Kyle had been taken.

Chapter Thirty-Four

CLAIRE

Claire sipped her coffee quietly as she scanned the entrance for any sign of Mia Rossi. They were supposed to meet at Beach Beans at 10am this morning, and Claire had arrived early ... very early. She wanted to make sure that she had secured one of the cafe's coveted back booths so they could talk without the watchful eyes of the other customers. Claire felt self-conscious about the stares she received from her community members; she had become a well-known fixture of the town—the woman with the kidnapped child ... a local celebrity—and found that the best course of action was to avoid eye contact, lest she be pulled into awkward conversation. She didn't really want to talk to anyone anyway ... with the exception of Mia.

It had been 3 weeks since Mia had arrived on her front stoop and imprinted her with the fresh stamp of hope. She had exchanged intermittent texts with Mia since then ... but sometimes it took her quite a while to respond, and Claire wondered if maybe Mia had decided to pull away. She hoped not. And that was one of the reasons Claire felt restless as she waited. She desperately hoped that Mia wouldn't stand her up. She didn't think she could cope with any more disappointment.

It was 10:06 when Mia walked into Beach Beans and got on line to place her order. Claire had to subdue a desperate urge to rush up to her and consume her in a bear hug. Instead, Claire waved her arm in the air to catch Mia's attention and waited while the barista poured the coffee and then waited again while Mia stirred in sugar and creamer and then replaced the plastic lid.

Mia slid into the opposite side of the booth with a warm smile that made Claire's trepidation and anxiety fade. Claire didn't have anything specific to discuss with Mia. Yes, she was curious if Mia had received any further signs, but more so, Claire was content to just be in her presence. Sharing a space with this young woman made her feel closer to Jimmy somehow. There was a comfort that Mia exuded, and Claire relished it.

Reaching across the table, Claire enveloped Mia's hands in her own.

"It's so good to see you, Mia. Thank you for meeting me today."

"Honestly, I was looking forward to it. I'm sorry if I've been distant these past few weeks. There's been a lot going on."

Claire felt guilty for not having asked about Mia's life. Tragedy can certainly make a person self-absorbed.

"How have you been, Mia? I should ask more about your life. I'm sorry if our conversation has been one-sided," Claire said.

"Don't be sorry," Mia said, giving Claire's hands a squeeze. "I talked to my landlord and my mom about you. They think I'm crazy. They think I'm giving you false hope. And maybe I am. Claire–I can't make any guarantees. I desperately want to do right by you–I don't want to mislead you into thinking that I'm some savior that can magically bring Jimmy back–"

Looking straight into her eyes, Claire responded, "Mia ... you have absolutely nothing to explain. I am the one who should be sorry. I never meant to put any pressure on you–"

"You didn't," responded Mia honestly. "You didn't put any pressure on me. I'm the one who showed up at your house talking about signs and intuitions. What if it's all just a coincidence? I don't think it is ... but I have to account for the fact that maybe—"

"Whatever this is," Claire began steadily. "...coincidence, fate, divine intervention, dumb luck ... I don't know. But I am humbly grateful that you have come into my life. Even if all this comes to nothing. I have gained you as a friend. You have brought me so much hope. And I know you can't work miracles. I don't expect that of you. And I know that Jimmy's disappearance does not rest upon your shoulders. But you gave me the courage to keep fighting. I was at the end of my rope before you came to find me. And, if nothing else ... I got my necklace back." Claire clutched at the locket that rested against her throat. "I am truly thankful that you found it."

Claire noticed that Mia looked lighter somehow; the crease line disappeared from between her eyebrows. *The poor girl,* thought Claire. *She's been carrying the weight of the world on her shoulders.* Mia removed the lid from the styrofoam cup and the steam floated around her face in a wispy halo as she took a deep sip.

"Damn, that's a good coffee," Mia said with a groan.

"It's my favorite place," Claire agreed. "Jimmy loves their chocolate croissant. We used to come here every Sunday."

Mia noticed that Claire spoke about her son in the present tense, "loves" instead of "loved." The woman still had hope. She admired that.

While there was sadness in her tone, and an aching nostalgia, Claire rose from the booth to approach the counter.

"I'll take two chocolate croissants," she said to the cashier. "And a refill please."

Claire brought her fresh cup of coffee and the pastries back to her seat and handed one over to Mia. Taking a bite, Claire's teeth sunk into the buttery flakiness of perfection. The chocolate, a perfect counterpart to the slightly salty coating.

"Yum," Mia said, eyes widening. "Thank you."

And the two women sat at that booth for two additional cups

of coffee and two additional croissants chatting like old friends. The melancholy seemed to rise up into the air, to lift. Claire knew that it would come back ... it always did. It would settle back on her like frost on the morning grass. But for those few hours, sitting across from Mia Rossi, she felt happy. And that was enough.

Chapter Thirty-Five

MIA

The air felt warm the next morning when Mia walked down the side steps. Early May had bloomed bright in Long Beach, and dressed in a tee shirt and jeans, she tied her sweatshirt around her waist instead of putting it on. Summer was on the horizon, and Mia felt hopeful and light as she approached her car. She needed to get some food shopping out of the way, but she planned to spend the Sunday afternoon at the beach curled up in her new Tommy Bahama beach chair with a coffee in the cup holder and a book in her lap. The air would be undoubtedly cooler near the water, but Mia didn't care. The thought made her smile. This was what she had been waiting for ever since she moved to Long Beach almost 2 months prior ... had it really been that long ago that she first made the pilgrimage here from Sparta? It felt like yesterday and forever ago at the same time. And while she did look forward to relaxing, she also hoped (as she did every day) for a sign.

Her parents and sister were coming down next weekend, and she was truly looking forward to seeing them. Although she still bristled at the memory of her mom's last visit–when she had lied about her future plans concerning Claire Benicek and Jimmy's disappearance–she had moved on ... so had her mom. Mia

157

supposed that false pretenses made it easier to let bygones be bygones. If her mother only knew that she continued to be in touch with Claire and that she remained hopeful that the ocean would give her another sign to help that poor family, she would be horrified. But she didn't know. And Mia didn't plan on telling her.

Something caught her eye as she breezed over to her car, and she shifted her gaze to the front lawn of the house. Right out front, planted into the grass next to the walkway to Dee and Bob's front door, was a wooden post with a 'For Sale' sign hung from the cross bar ... and it was being sold by Long Beach Realty–her own job! Mia blinked twice and it was still there, solid and intimidating. *It has to be a mistake*, Mia thought. *There's no way Bob and Dee would sell this place.*

Mia trotted up the path towards the house, and just as she was about to rap on the door, it swung in and open. Dee and Bob emerged in the rectangular space holding a red Igloo cooler and a large tote bag filled with towels and blankets, ready for yet another boating expedition.

"Oh, Mia. You scared me," chuckled Dee as she sidled past Mia.

"What's with the sign?" Mia asked immediately. "It's got to be a mistake, right?"

"Well, Mia," Bob chimed in. "We have put a lot of thought into it, and we have decided to head south. The winters are just too cold up here and–"

"You can't be serious. You love Long Beach ... and Dee grew up in this town. How can you just sell it?"

"We do love Long Beach ... but the world is wide. And there are lots of other oceans to explore. It's our time to go," answered Dee.

"But–" Mia began.

"Don't worry, Mia. The house has been listed as a mother-daughter, and I put in the notes that a tenant is currently living here. Usually new buyers account for renters. You'll probably be able to keep the apartment, that's my guess. And hey. Maybe the new buyers will renovate. Maybe you'll get an updated kitchen or bathroom. That apartment can definitely use some improvement," Bob said breezily.

"It's just—so sudden. I had no idea. I'm shocked," Mia said after a moment. "Why didn't you tell me?"

"I'm sorry. We should have told you. We were going to wait until fall to put it up, but the broker said that now is a good time. Lots of people are looking to buy something before the summer. We could probably get over the asking price for the place ... especially being so close to the water," Dee explained.

Based upon the look Dee and Bob exchanged, Mia suspected that there was more to the story, but she wasn't going to pry. Money troubles perhaps? She was sad though ... she had come to enjoy Dee and Bob, even though Dee had told on her and called her mom. But she had meant well. Mia didn't love the idea of getting new landlords, or the uncertainty it inspired within her. What was that phrase her dad always used? *The devil you know is better than the devil you don't*? Except that didn't work in this case, because Bob and Dee were far from devils.

Would she even be able to remain here? Dee seemed confident that she would, but Mia wasn't so sure. Things happen. What if the buyer decided to knock down the whole structure and build one of those mini-mansions that had been springing up all over the West End of Long Beach since Hurricane Sandy hit a few years back? Mia did work in a realtor office, and she had progressed in her coursework to become a certified realtor herself, so she supposed if need be she could find another apartment ... *if* it came to that. But she liked it here ... being so close to the water. She was comfortable. And settled.

"Well, I'm going to miss you guys. I mean ... good luck and everything. But it won't be the same here without you," Mia said truthfully.

"Aw, sweetie," Dee said. "We will miss you too. But it's just our time to go."

"I guess there's still some time," Mia said. "I mean, it just went up on the market, right?" She had learned a great deal already about real estate and the process of selling and buying a home. And it definitely is a process.

"Well, yes and no," answered Bob. "Our realtor has been doing some background work, and there's a guy coming tomorrow to take a look."

"A potential buyer," Dee chimed in.

"Really? That's fast," Mia said.

"Yeah, like we said ... it's a good time to sell. Everyone wants to move to Long Beach in the spring," Bob amended. "This guy will probably want to see your apartment. We have an extra key. I hope you don't mind if we show him around if you aren't home."

"No. I don't mind," Mia answered.

"Thank you, Mia," Dee said.

The confusion on Mia's face prompted Dee to say, "Mia. We have to run out now, but why don't you come for dinner later on? We can cut our boat trip short and talk about it more tonight over some tacos. Sound good?"

"Yeah. That sounds good," Mia responded, not feeling very "good" at all.

Again, Mia noticed Bob and Dee exchanging an odd glance. She didn't know exactly what it meant, but it didn't ease the feeling that spiders were skittering up her back. This was not how she envisioned her day would go. All the lightness that she had felt just minutes earlier had turned stale and sour. *How odd*, Mia thought to herself. She was still trying to process what she had been told and the implications it had on her life and future.

"Well, I guess I'll see you later," Mia said as she turned around towards her car.

"Bye, Mia," Bob responded. "See you soon."

The turmoil that Mia felt weighed heavily upon her as she meandered around Key Food. She barely glanced at the items that she had absently placed in the cart. Something just felt weird to her ... off, in an intangible way. She tried to sort out whether she was being selfish or not. Surely, Dee and Bob were entitled to lead the life they wanted, right? ... regardless of what it meant for their tenant. But, the fact that they hadn't mentioned anything about it previously nagged at her. And why would they put the place up for rent in the first place if they were just planning on selling? They did say that they had been talking about moving down south for awhile. Maybe it was just talk. Maybe the opportunity had just arisen and they decided to act quickly. Sometimes life just happens without plan or convenience.

As Mia placed her groceries on the belt and paid the bill, that feeling of loneliness crept up on her. She wanted to call home, but she couldn't tell her mom about this yet ... not without having all of the information and a proper course of action. It would just cause her to worry. And aside from workplace acquaintances, Mia hadn't made any real friends yet. Well, actually, that wasn't true. There was someone she could talk to about all of this.

Even driving to Claire's house alleviated some of the weight that pressed on Mia's shoulders. Maybe Claire wouldn't have any advice, but she would listen. And that was all Mia really needed.

Chapter Thirty-Six

CLAIRE

Claire had forgotten her purse in her car after her trip to the deli this morning, and as she walked out the front door of her house to retrieve it, she saw Mia's car pull up and park against the curb. Although she was happy to see her, Claire wondered if something was wrong; it wasn't like Mia to show up unannounced ... well, since her first visit of course.

"Hi, Claire," Mia called as she emerged from her CRV.

"Mia! Hi. How are you? I'm surprised to see you here."

"I'm sorry for just showing up here ... again," Mia responded with a small chuckle. "I needed a friend. And right now, you're really the only one I have."

"Well, come on in. Let's chat," Claire said, quickly grabbing her purse from the passenger side floor and closing the door.

Claire held the front door open for Mia, but as she pulled the door in, she noticed a blur out of the corner of her eye and an inkling that she was being watched crept upon her, making the hairs on the back of her arms stand at attention. An unfamiliar car was parked on the other side of the street and down a ways–in front of Ted and Jackie Trenton's house. She couldn't make out the model ... it was a small sedan, silver in color, nondescript; Claire had never been one to pay much attention to car brands.

The driver's face was obscured by large sunglasses and a baseball cap pulled down low over the forehead, and the sun was almost blinding as it reflected off the windows, but the mirrored shades were directed towards Claire. Just as Claire walked down the stoop again, hopefully to offer directions to a lost driver, the car zoomed away. *Weird*, thought Claire. *Maybe I should have looked at the license plate.* Claire had developed a paranoia since Jimmy had been taken, and she had fallen into the regrettable habit of suspecting the worst, of seeing trouble in innocent situations. No one could fault her for that, could they? She had a right to be suspicious. *Stop it, Claire, you're being paranoid*, she said in her head. *It's nothing.*

She remained outside for one more minute, just to make sure the car didn't return, until she heard Mia call from within, "Claire? Are you coming in?"

Claire shook her head to clear the gathering storm clouds from her mind and called back, "Yup. Coming."

She walked back up the stoop and into her living room. The nerves cleared when she saw Mia perched on the side of the couch.

"Is someone out there?" Mia asked.

"Nope." A brief pause. Then, "Now, let's talk about you. What brings you to this side of town?" Claire responded lightly. She was already starting to forget the car, the weird way the light reflected off the driver's sunglasses.

"I don't even know where to start," Mia said. "Ever feel like the world is conspiring against you–?" Mia stopped herself. Of course Claire could understand that. She had experienced it first-hand when her son was taken.

"Every day of my life," Claire responded honestly. "Tell me. What's been going on."

"Well ... I've been lying to my mom about you. I never told you this because I didn't want you to feel bad. You know how I mentioned that mom thinks it's a bad idea for me to be spending time with you? How she thinks I'm giving you false hope?"

"I remember you telling me that over coffee," Claire answered.

"Yeah, well, she doesn't want to see me spending so much time immersed in a tragedy ... thinks it's unhealthy or something. I told her that I would remove myself from you ... from your son."

"I see," said Claire.

"But I don't want to. For the first time in my life, I feel like I'm in the right place at the right time."

"I feel that way too," Claire responded with a smile.

"It just seems like no one else does. My mom ... the cops. Even my landlord agrees with my mom. And I'm worried that they're right. Even though when we met for coffee you assured me that I wasn't giving you false hope, I haven't been able to shake that thought. And now on top of all that, I found out that my land-lords, Dee and Bob, are selling their house ... just like that. They didn't even tell me about it. A potential buyer is coming to take a look at it. What if he levels the place? I guess I can find another apartment, but I feel settled there. It's all so weird ... and rushed. Dee grew up in Long Beach, they seem so attached to the town ... I don't understand how they could just sell it. And why would they have put the apartment up for rent if they were just going to sell the whole house?"

"That does sound like a lot to take in," Claire offered.

"And ... I haven't gotten any more signs or offerings or intu-itions to clue me into your son's location–and I'm so incredibly sorry that I haven't been able to offer more. I just thought my life was on the up and up ... now I'm not so sure."

Mia seemed to run out of breath, like a worn-out steam train huffing along the tracks, and Claire could see the turmoil behind those deep brown eyes.

"Well, not that I'm one to give advice, but in my life, I've learned to take things one at a time. So let's start with your worry that you're giving me false hope," began Claire. "Hope is a beau-tiful thing. A thing that I have been missing since Jimmy disap-peared and a thing that you brought back into my life. And even though I wish that finding Jimmy was as simple as waiting for some otherworldly sign to whisper in your ear, I do know that's not the case. Your story, Mia, inspired me to stay hopeful. And whether your gift is what brings Jimmy home, or the cops find him, or whatever … you made me realize that I can't give up. He's out there somewhere. I know he will come home."

"A gift," Mia repeated. "I never thought of this-thing that I have as a gift. It's always sort of scared me."

"I can see that," Claire responded. "But try to look for the positive."

"Maybe you're right," Mia said.

"And the next thing that's stressing you out is the fact that you haven't been honest with your mom, right?"

"Yeah," Mia sighed. "I've never really lied to her. And I feel awful about it."

"That's a tough one, Mia. Maybe try talking to her again. You have to do what you feel is right. You're an adult now, living on your own. Your mom will come around. She loves you and wants what's best. I think that if I was in her position, I'd feel the same way."

"My whole family is coming down to visit soon. Maybe I will try to bring it up again," Mia said with a sigh. "But, I just know that she won't approve."

"All you can do is try to make her understand," Claire offered.

"You're right. The lying is making me feel uneasy."

"And regarding the apartment. I can understand why you're upset. You came all the way here, settled in, made yourself a new home, and now you're worried the rug is being pulled out from underneath you. But you'll land on your feet. I know it. There are plenty of rentals in Long Beach, if it comes to that … and you work in a realtor's office-you'll have first dibs! And I'm here to help, if you need to move again. I'm good at organizing," Claire said.

"Wow, Claire. That's really kind of you. Thank you."

Tragedy had brought these two women together, and mutual understanding and respect gave them friendship. Claire thought that she was too old to make new friends, too tired and over-worked to carve out the time needed to tend to a blooming relationship, but as she listened to Mia unload the thoughts plaguing her mind, she felt only gratitude for this new pocket that she had discovered in the face of such immeasurable sadness.

"I'm here for you, Mia. Always," Claire said.

Claire realized that those words suggested a certain level of intimacy—a level of friendship that hinted at years of shared experience. Mia had just come into Claire's life; could she in good conscience use the word "always" with someone she had known for only a short time? Claire quickly dispelled this thought. She meant it. She *would* always be there for Mia; there was a kinship between them that couldn't be ignored. And Claire could sense that Mia could feel it too, that she knew that Claire was telling the truth.

"Ok," Mia said, exhaling a long breath. "You made me feel a lot better. Don't sell yourself short, Claire. You're an amazing advice-giver."

"Maybe therapy is rubbing off on me. I'm glad I could make you feel better," responded Claire.

"Unfortunately, I can't stay long," Mia explained. "Bob and Dee invited me for dinner so we could talk more about the sale of the house. Maybe I'll get more insight into their reasons for moving and what that means for my apartment."

"Hopefully, you'll get more clarity into their decision. And you're welcome here any time," Claire said, walking Mia to the door.

Claire took a brief glance down the block and focused her eyes on the spot where that silver car had been parked when Mia had first arrived. Nothing. Just a quiet, tree-lined street. The birds chirruped in the late afternoon sunshine.

"Thanks, Claire. I really appreciate you listening to me today. I needed it."

Claire winked in response, and Mia climbed into the driver's seat of her CRV, hoping that the perishable items still in brown paper bags in her trunk from her trip to Key Food hadn't spoiled.

As Mia drove away, Claire felt that creeping sensation once again, that feeling that she was being watched. But there was no one there ... no strange cars, nothing. *Oh, give it up*, she said to herself. *Little Miss Paranoid at it again. Helicopter mom is never at ease.* But no matter how much she reassured herself, she still couldn't shake that feeling that eyes were crawling all over her. She hurried back up the front stoop and engaged her lock on the front door. She had been meaning to add one more, but hadn't gotten to Home Depot yet to buy one. Eventually, the feeling faded along with the setting sun.

Chapter Thirty-Seven

MIA

When Mia arrived back on Minnesota Avenue after her visit with Claire, Bob and Dee weren't home yet, so she unloaded her groceries from the trunk of her car–the task required two trips–and headed over the dunes towards the ocean. It was only 4pm ... there was still plenty of daylight left, and even though her plan for spending the whole afternoon folded up in a beach chair with a book in her lap hadn't worked out, she could certainly enjoy an hour or two of tranquility before her landlords expected her for dinner. It would do her good to lose herself in the harrowing plot of the latest Stephen King novel that she had ordered from Amazon last week. Anything to take her mind off the uncertainty of her reality.

Setting up her new beach chair–Mia hadn't yet even removed the plastic tags attached to the headrest–the unmistakable briny scent of the sea reached her nostrils. It was a warm smell, full of life and possibility. She took a deep breath, filling her lungs with the salty air and plopped herself down. The chair creaked under her weight; the taut canvas still needed to be broken in. Mia cracked the spine of her new novel, a habit her mother hated, and opened up to the first page. But, despite the fact that the premise was compelling, Mia couldn't quite immerse herself in the story. Whenever she met with Claire, she always came away thinking of Jimmy. Her eyes kept drifting out to the horizon and the blue expanse unrolling before her in choppy ridges. She sat there, staring out, silently begging for another sign ... something to point her in the right direction, anything to guide her on the correct path. While the surf crashed lightly, both on the shore and in her mind, nothing came to her. *Oh, sure. Now you're silent,* Mia thought to herself with grim humor. *Figures. Just when I really need you, you have nothing to say.* Mia closed her book. Why bother trying? She couldn't process anything she had just read; she would eventually need to start over. *Am I really talking to the ocean?* Mia asked herself. *Maybe I really have lost it.*

Mia sat there solemnly, studying the view before her as one might inspect a painting, noticing every nuance, every hypnotic ripple. A new chill permeated the air as the afternoon drifted on, reminding her that although summer was only a month or so away, it was certainly not here yet. Mia tucked her sweatshirt around her shoulders for warmth. The sound of the waves was so soothing, the cast of the sun so soft on her upturned face. Mia's eyes drifted closed.

Ping. Her eyes snapped open. She hadn't meant to fall asleep. How long had she been out? She looked at the time on her cell-phone: 6:10. And she had a missed text message. Two of them, actually. Both from Dee.

5:27pm:

> Mia, we're home. Come over when you're ready.

6:09pm:

> Are you still coming for dinner?

Oops, Mia thought to herself. She typed quickly back into the phone:

I'm coming. Lost track of time. Sorry!

Mia stood up and rubbed the sleep out of her eyes with the back of her hand. God, she was tired. She folded up her beach chair and tucked the novel into the pocket behind the headrest, and with her shoes in her hands, headed towards the stairs leading onto Minnesota Avenue.

It was almost 6:45 when she knocked on Bob and Dee's front door. She could smell the taco meat cooking as soon as she walked in, and her stomach growled. She had totally forgotten to eat lunch, which wasn't like her at all. Mia's mom used to joke around with her and say that she could never miss a meal.

"Hey, Mia," Bob said. "Hope you're hungry. I know I am."

"I'm starving," Mia replied. "I'm sorry I'm so late. I fell asleep on the beach and totally lost track of time."

"Sounds to me like you could use a good night's rest," Dee said entering the room with a platter piled with small bowls containing shredded cheese, lettuce, cilantro, and soft flour tortillas. "I tend to go for the 'make your own' style. Hope you don't mind."

"Not at all," said Mia, sitting down at the dining table opposite Bob.

Mia helped herself to two tacos piled high with fixings; Bob and Dee did the same.

When neither Bob nor Dee mentioned selling their home, Mia took the bull by the horns and said, "So, how do you feel about moving?"

They seemed to consider her question for a moment before Bob spoke, "Gee, Mia. I guess we are excited about starting fresh somewhere else. Dee found a place outside Tampa today on that Zilly website,"

"Zillow," corrected Dee. "It's a small one-story, but it'll suit us just fine."

"Why leave?" Mia inquired. "Won't you be sad to leave Long

Beach? And what about your boat? You love that thing. You're on it every day."

"I'm ready to move on," Dee said.

"...and who said anything about selling that boat? We'll find a place to store it until we can ship it down south," Bob added.

They exchanged another one of those pensive glances with one another that Mia could never quite interpret.

"Mia, don't worry about us. And as for yourself, I understand that you must be concerned, but take it one step at a time. Like I said earlier, most buyers want mother-daughter homes. They want the supplemental income. And the fact that we already have an established and responsible tenant ... well, I think that will actually be a draw for potential buyers."

"Well, good luck, I guess. I'll be sad to see you go."

"That's sweet. I'm sure we will keep in touch, Dee said vaguely. "Now tell us about you. What's been new? I feel like we haven't gotten to catch up."

"Yeah," added Bob. "How's that realty office treating you?"

"It's actually been really great," replied Mia. "I've started my certification coursework, and I finally feel settled there. The people are really nice and the job ... it's busy, but in a good way. If you were going to sell next year, I could probably be your realtor."

"That is too bad," responded Bob.

"While I'm here," Mia said. "I just wanted to clear the air about something. I know that you reached out to my mom about–"

"I had to Mia," Dee interrupted. "Someone has to look out for you here. And you were headed down a bad path."

"Yeah, I understand why you did it, Dee. But I wish you had told me. I had no idea my mom was going to come down. You caught me off guard," Mia said honestly.

"Yeah, we're sorry about that," Bob interjected. "We wanted to make sure that you knew how serious it was. You were wading in water that was way over your head. You have given up on all that–unpleasantness, right?"

Mia didn't respond. On one hand, she did want to be honest, but on the other ... she had no desire for her parents to hear the truth about her whereabouts from her landlords ... again. Especially since they were scheduled to visit soon.

"I have," Mia answered without meeting Bob's steady gaze.

"You haven't been in touch with– what's her name? Clara?" Dee repeated.

"Her name is Claire. And no. I haven't," Mia answered.

"Well, that's good, Mia. You're better off not having anything to do with such negativity," Dee said.

Mia didn't know if Bob and Dee believed her. Their slanted gaze told her that they probably didn't, but the subject was not brought up again that evening and the three of them enjoyed their meal in quiet company.

Before she left, and after a dessert of store-bought apple pie, the two landlords exchanged a cryptic glance and then Bob said, "Mia. Why don't you come out on the boat with us this week? We've been wanting to invite you out with us now for a few weeks, and we just haven't had the chance. What do you say?"

"Actually ... I would love that!" Mia answered.

The thought of being out there on the water with the sun shining on her shoulders made Mia feel lighter somehow. After all, that was why she moved to Long Beach in the first place–to get as close to the ocean as possible. Could there be a place closer than on a boat skittering across the vast surface of the Atlantic?

"Great! Let's look at the weather this week and see what day looks the best," said Dee.

"Sounds like a plan," Mia said in response. "And let me know if someone needs to look at the apartment."

"Will do," said Bob.

Mia thanked Dee and Bob for their hospitality and for the invitation out on the boat and left. She walked up the side stairwell leading to her apartment in the darkness, feeling utterly exhausted. *So much for a relaxing day*, Mia thought to herself as she leaned against the kitchen wall to remove her shoes. She had tried to brush the sand off before she went into Bob and Dee's house, but there were still tiny grains stuck in the crevices of her sneakers. Mia had learned that part of living in Long Beach meant living with the sand that got everywhere; despite her best efforts, she even found it in her bed. She didn't mind though. She felt it was a small price to pay for living by the beach.

Just as Mia was about to turn out the lights and head into her bedroom to get some sleep, the shades covering the kitchen window began to clatter and crash against the frame. Thud, Bang. Thud, Bang. Thud, Bang. Thud, Bang. Mia couldn't remember leaving the window open, but she walked over to the sink to pull down the leaded pane. Leaning over to adjust the pull strings of the blinds to give herself a better angle–with many coats of paint, the window often stuck–she caught a glimpse of the ocean that lay unobstructed before her. The moon hung huge and low in the sky; she could see its cratered face as it illuminated the heaving surface of the Atlantic. *There must be a storm coming*, Mia thought to herself, arms poised on the window frame. She had never seen the ocean so turbulent, so unsettled. It's restlessness permeated her mind, her thoughts. Suddenly the crashing was deafening ... nothing like the muted ebb and flow that typically trickled through her mind. This was a booming, reverberating through her ears, her brain, her soul.

"Stop!" she called out. Her voice smothered by the full-throated cacophony that threatened to overtake her.

Like a gaping mouth, the window was stuck open. The veins in Mia's neck stood out as she strained, climbing up on the counter to give herself better leverage. But it wouldn't budge. The relentless howling of the waves shattered her thoughts, and all Mia could do was slither down from the counter and curl up in a huddled ball against the cabinets, hands over her ears, trying in vain to drown out that thunderous sound that had invaded her senses.

She tried again, all thoughts of feeling foolish fleeing from her,

"What do you want from me? I'm trying dammit. Give me another sign!"

But this *was* a sign. Despite the pounding, her mind vaguely recognized it as such. She *was* getting closer somehow. Closer. *So close. So close.* She perceived the phrases in white hot flashes searing through her mind. Much more insistent than the whisper from the seashell. *So close So close soclose soclose soclose SO CLOSE.*

"So close to what? Where is he? I need more!" she shouted back.

But the ocean didn't give her anymore. Maybe it couldn't. She didn't know how this all worked. Maybe nobody did. In the face of the gripping fear that Mia experienced at this moment, she needed this. She needed to know that she was not forgotten–that Jimmy and Claire were not forgotten. Mia was part of this ... their lives inextricably bound together like the links in a chain, like drops of water in the same sea. She had felt it before, but here, on the kitchen floor, with her hands pressed firmly over her throbbing ears, the sensation was stronger than ever.

All of a sudden, the window slammed shut and a heavy silence permeated the room. The message had been delivered. Slowly, the terror faded. Mia's heartbeat and breathing slowed. The panic transformed into a quiet relief. She still didn't know how to proceed–no, that was still a mystery. But she had gotten the reassurance she needed to keep trying. To keep herself open to the possibility of magic ... to the possibility that strange things do exist in the world, to the possibility that she could help locate Jimmy Benicek ... eventually.

# Chapter Thirty-Eight

JIMMY

It was almost over. The man told him that. He wouldn't have to stay here anymore ... neither would Kyle. They were going somewhere. He didn't know where, but he didn't think it was home. He wished it was though. He missed his home ... especially his bedroom and his toys.

But he missed his mom and dad more. His heart hurt when he thought about them. He didn't even know that a heart could hurt ... but his did. Sometimes it hurt so bad that it felt like he couldn't breathe. Like a big giant was sitting on his chest. An ogre as big as Shrek, but not as nice. It seemed like he hadn't seen his parents in so long. Years and years it seemed. Did they even remember him anymore? Were they still looking for him? Time went slow here. No television, no video games ... just hours and hours and days and days of the same thing. Sitting around. Playing with those Happy Meal toys with Kyle. Waiting for the people to come with food.

Jimmy even missed school, which he hated because math was just so so hard and his teacher was just so so so strict. He was supposed to be line leader ... but he never got to do that because he was here. That was the one classroom helper job that he had been looking forward to.

Kyle was sick. He was coughing real bad, and the man took him out of the back room because it was so drafty and now they were together again. The man didn't think it mattered anymore. The man said that they could be together now because it was almost over and there was nowhere for them to go. They were surrounded by water and grass.

Even though it was getting warmer, Kyle was always cold. Jimmy gave him his blanket, but it didn't help. He would pat him on the back when he would cough and Jimmy could feel his ribs through his shirt. Jimmy tried to tell the man that Kyle needed to go to the doctor, or maybe the walk-in place where his mom took him when he had ear infections. Jimmy used to get ear infections a lot, but not anymore. He almost had to get tubes put in when he was 2, whatever that meant. But the man just said that it wasn't his problem. He said that they would be someone else's problem pretty soon and that when they got where they were going, someone else could take Kyle to the doctor if they wanted to. Jimmy needed a doctor too, he thought. He got a splinter a while ago and his whole finger was now kind of gray. The cut didn't heal and it oozed green goo for awhile, but now it just looked scary and weird. It also hurt a lot when he touched it. And it felt really hot and stiff. His mom always told him not to pick at his booboos, so he tried not to pick at this one. But sometimes he couldn't help it.

Jimmy learned not to ask questions. He got yelled at when he asked too many. But he really wanted to know who would take care of them when they left here. And where they would go. Here, they got McDonald's sometimes and Taco Bell sometimes and Dunkin' Donuts sometimes and yesterday they got a Subway sandwich. Jimmy had never had Subway before, but he used to see the commercials when he watched Nickelodeon at home. It was pretty good. Jimmy even ate the green stuff because he was so hungry, and he hated green stuff. But it wasn't so bad. His mom would have been so surprised because he never wanted to eat vegetables at home—they were gross. He even told Kyle to try it, but Kyle didn't eat anything. Kyle wasn't hungry that much anymore. He tried to feed Kyle the other day; he got him to eat a few fries, but not enough. He said to Kyle, "Three more bites and then you could be done," just like Jimmy's mom sometimes said to him. But it didn't really work. Jimmy's mom used to never let him eat all this fast food. He was only allowed to get McDonald's once a month at home. One time, his mom got mad at his dad for taking him to Burger King. But now, he and Kyle had so many Happy Meal toys they didn't even know what to do with them all. Between the two of them, the boys had 5 of the same SpongeBob figurines. He never watched SpongeBob, but Jimmy knew who he was because he saw the huge SpongeBob balloon last year when he watched the Thanksgiving Day Parade on TV with his mom. His mom said that one day she would take him to see the parade in person. He wondered if that would still happen. It would be super cool to see those huge balloons in person. Jimmy wondered if the balloons ever lifted up the people that held them. Maybe if Jimmy had a balloon, he and Kyle could float away home.

Jimmy wondered how long he had been in this place. It felt like a long time. He tried to think about it in terms of food. They usually got Dunkin' Donuts for breakfast each morning. Jimmy could remember eating 7 chocolate chip muffins, 5 egg sandwiches ... a whole box of munchkins one day–that hurt his tummy so bad. Together, he and Kyle had 30 Happy Meal toys. Could that help him determine how many days they had been here?

Even though he loved McDonald's, Jimmy actually missed his mom's healthy food. A year ago he told his mom that he would rather eat McDonald's every day than her food. He even told her that the school cafeteria food was better than her cooking. That was mean. And now he realized that it wasn't true either.

Jimmy was bored a lot ... especially now since Kyle slept so much. They used to play with their Happy Meal toys. They made an army out of them and played Cops and Robbers. Jimmy would even keep score about whether the cops or robbers won each game. He wrote the tally marks on the back of a brown paper bag with a stub of pencil that the man had left there after he wrote down measurements for a new door.

He was starting to get worried about Kyle. This morning, the man even looked worried about Kyle. He walked over to him and put his hand on his forehead. The man muttered something, but when Jimmy said, "What?" the man told him to mind his own business. Jimmy didn't ask again.

He couldn't wait to get out of this place, but he was also worried. He wondered if he and Kyle would be together wherever they went next. He didn't know. Jimmy didn't have a brother, but if he did, it would be Kyle. He thought Kyle felt the same way. They had that in common. They both didn't have any brothers or sisters. But now they had each other. Jimmy tried to keep Kyle from shivering at night. He would hold him like his mommy used to cuddle with him at night–like spoons. But no matter how close Jimmy got, Kyle kept shivering. It was scary.

Jimmy sensed that things were changing. The cellphone rang a lot. He perceived that plans were being made. He just couldn't tell if things would be better or worse when they went to their next stop. Maybe his mom and dad would find them before they went somewhere else. He wished that all the time, but it hadn't happened yet. That was still possible, right? Things like that happen all the time in the movies. But, Jimmy was starting to realize that life was not very much like the movies. Not at all.

Chapter Thirty-Nine

MIA

It was the first week of June and Long Beach had transformed before Mia's eyes. Cars crowded the streets and twinkle lights emerged on the front porches of the bungalows that lined Minnesota Avenue. Some of them boasted signs like, "Welcome to our Porch" or "It's 5 o'clock Somewhere," or her favorite, "I'm Outdoorsy. I Drink Margaritas on the Porch." Mia giggled every time she passed that one.

People spilled out of the bars onto fenced-in tiled patios decorated with Wax Begonia and Devil's Ivy, drinking Bloody Marys in the morning and Moscow Mules in frosty copper mugs in the evenings. The local restaurants were jam-packed for every meal time (and in between meal times) with young tan people dressed in bikini tops and sarongs or board shorts, flanking the tables and high-topped pub chairs.

Sometimes Mia heard the echoes of late-night frolickers coming back from the beach way past midnight as she dozed in her bedroom with the sea air wafting through the open window. She didn't mind it one bit.

Mia had gone out to Happy Hour at the Saloon a few times with some of her co-workers; Hailey (one of the receptionists at the sister branch of her office–located in Point Lookout) might

179

prove to be an actual friend. They had made plans to go out for dinner and drinks next weekend, and Hailey had invited Mia to go to the beach with her after work on Thursday. Mia looked forward to both events with eager anticipation; after all, this was part of the reason why she had moved here in the first place. To meet new people.

Yet, despite the revelry surrounding her, part of Mia remained somber. She imagined it had to do with Claire, and the fact that Jimmy remained missing ... and that Mia herself, despite all of the confirmation that she was *so close,* hadn't been able to offer any real guidance or direction. She still spent time with Claire–grabbing breakfast at Beach Beans, or watching movies curled up on the couch in her living room, and she mourned with Claire. The sadness had crept into Claire's gaze again, huddled behind the cheerful greetings and pleasantries. Claire never pressured Mia for signs or intuitions, but the ache within her permeated through every fiber of her being. Not that Mia really minded; she had come to view Claire as a friend ... no, more than a friend. Family. Mia wished that she knew Jimmy, even though she felt as though she did; he was so present in her conversations with Claire. And his presence was felt so keenly in that house. She had come to also look forward to the time at which he would hopefully return. But that hadn't happened yet. So while summer bloomed outside, Claire remained in perpetual winter.

Unfortunately for Mia, Dee and Bob's home had sold rather quickly, and now the sign on the front lawn boasted an addition—a sticker that said "In Contract." When Mia snooped into the property notes on her work computer, she was surprised to see that the house went for $20,000 below asking price, which was odd considering that most places around here sold for over asking price. She guessed that Bob and Dee were in more of a rush to move than they had previously conveyed to her. And unfortunately again for Mia, the new buyer–as long as everything went smoothly in the real estate proceedings–planned to do major renovations to the property, essentially forcing her out of her beloved upstairs apartment. Even though Mia still had a few weeks to secure a new apartment, in her mind, it felt like a ticking clock. Her boss had kindly emailed her a few rentals, but none of them seemed right ... and none of them were as close to the water as Mia's current place.

Something else that ate at Mia was the fact that she had to cancel her parents' visit. She couldn't have them here amid the boxes and the packing and the uncertainty, and quite frankly, she missed them ... she especially missed her sister, who texted her constantly about visiting this summer. Also, she hadn't yet come clean to her mom about her continued friendship with Claire. Not that Mia outright lied to her, she just omitted the truth of who she was spending time with. But isn't that the same thing as lying?

All these facts vexed Mia, as she tried to rub out the tension in her neck and shoulders. Today was the day that Mia found herself on Bob and Dee's boat, finally. She refused to let worry dampen her mood.

"I'm sorry it took us so long to get you out here with us," Bob said as he expertly maneuvered the boat through the water.

Dee added, "I don't know where the time goes."

"Don't be sorry," Mia said; she had to raise her voice a bit to be heard over the motor. "I'm happy to be here now. What a beautiful day!"

"You can say that again," Dee responded. "Perfect weather."

And the weather truly was perfect. The early afternoon sun scattered a million shining rays across the water as the boat cascaded south, sending its wake trailing out behind them in white foamy ripples. Mia felt her spirits lift as they moved farther and farther away from the land and came to a stop, the boat bobbing slightly in the softly undulating surface.

Dee had packed a picnic lunch of small turkey sandwiches and pasta salad, laden with tomatoes and olives. A pitcher of pink lemonade completed the meal. She started to dole out the food onto white scalloped paper plates as Bob wove his way up front to sit at the prow with them.

"Thanks, Dee. This looks great," Mia said.

"Nothing like some sandwiches and some sea," Dee responded.

"I guess this will be your last few weeks out on these waters," Mia said, sipping her drink.

"Well, there will be other waters ... bluer waters from what I hear, down south," Dee responded.

Bob was oddly silent as he munched on his sandwich; Mia suspected that he might not be as enthusiastic about leaving these waterways as Dee. The last few times Mia saw him over the past week, he had a faraway look in his gaze, and Mia sensed turmoil behind those watery blue eyes.

"So, Mia. How are things? How's work been?" Dee asked.

"Things have been good. I finished my first realtor course and I'll be starting the next one in about 2 weeks. And I think I actually made a friend."

"That's good news, Mia. Not that Claire woman, right?" Dee asked, concern creasing her brow.

Mia averted her gaze out towards the horizon and said, "No, not Claire. Someone else. Her name is Hailey. We're supposed to go grab dinner soon."

"Well, that's good to hear," responded Dee, glancing over at her quiet husband.

Bob watched Mia and Dee exchange their friendly chatter without comment, so in order to draw him out of his mood, Mia said, "Hey Bob, is this the spot where you fish?"

After he swallowed a mouthful of sandwich he said, "Nah, that's down a ways. I'll take you there after we're done eating."

"Great. I'd love to see the spot," Mia responded.

So after they put their plates and napkins in a small garbage bag, Bob went back to his seat behind the wheel and angled the boat south.

Mia watched as the scenery changed. They were no longer out

in the middle of the Atlantic; they were in a narrower channel surrounded by marsh grass. Tiny houses, painted in bright teals and yellows and reds–some in muted shades of brown– stood out sporadically, propped up on stilts. Bob eased the boat to a slower speed.

"Wow. Look at those tiny houses," Mia observed. "They're adorable."

Her comment made Bob come alive a bit, "Those are the Reynold's Channel Bay Houses. Lots of history there."

"Do people live there?"

Bob continued, "No one lives there permanently, at least not that I know of. There aren't too many of them left anymore ... most of them got washed away by storms over the years. Hurricane Sandy took at least 10 of them out to sea a few years back."

As they rode past, some of them did look a bit run-down and dilapidated, but no less charming. Mia's curiosity was piqued by these structures that dotted the channel with a bit of color. They were far apart from one another ... only two that she saw were even remotely close together. They all were of similar construction and looked kind of like the house a child might draw on a scrap of paper: rectangular frame with a triangular roof, two windows flanking a front door. Each house had a private dock– some in better conditions than others–and one or two of them had boats parked out front, but most were empty.

"If they got destroyed, why not rebuild them?" Mia asked, eyes fixated on one particularly run-down bay house.

"There are a lot of laws surrounding those structures. There used to be over 300 of them ... now there's only about 28 left, maybe even less. And they can never be sold. They can only be transferred within family. As you can see, they can only be reached by boat ... making repairs damn near impossible. Getting supplies to them is a major headache. They date back to the 1700s ... originally used for collecting and selling salt hay to local farms; some of them were built by waterfowl hunters. Duck used to be a more fashionable menu item back then. Heck, most of them have long been forgotten about."

"If I owned one of those bay houses, I would never forget about it," Mia responded. "I would want to spend all my time there."

"Yeah, well ... families move on, time erases some of 'em. Those houses just kinda sit there. Reminders of a long ago era," Dee added.

"Bob, you know so much about these houses. Have you ever been in one of them?" Mia asked.

"Well, I own one of them, Mia."

Chapter Forty

CLAIRE

Summer had always been Claire Benicek's favorite season. Nothing unusual there; most people who live by the ocean share that proclivity. But while June shone brightly around her, Claire felt her hopelessness return full-force. She tried not to feel bitterness at the joy in the air, the promise of vacation on the breeze, the influx of tourists in the area, the twinklebells of sunshine reflecting off the cars, but she couldn't help it. Even though she knew it was a selfish thought, she wanted the whole world to stop and cry with her ... to feel her pain. Up until a few months ago, summer meant long days at the beach with her family, late night trips to Marvel–the best ice cream stand on the island–and long bike rides through the windy streets of Oceanside. But the carpet had been cruelly yanked from beneath her feet, and she had tumbled head-first into a nightmare. Claire didn't even want to think of what this rapidly approaching summer had in store for her. More time alone? More time without her son? Without her husband? It was too depressing to dwell on.

The one light spot in her life was Mia Rossi. This young woman who had become a constant and comforting figure for Claire, when there was precious little constancy nor comfort to be

185

found. Claire had come to value her time spent with Mia; even if they just rented a movie On Demand and relaxed at her house, those times were some of the few in which Claire was able to smile, where she felt like an actual person. Yes, it was disappointing that Mia hadn't been able to help her locate her son–no … disappointing was the wrong word. Crushing was more accurate–but she had helped in so many other ways. She helped her to mourn, to process, and to feel human, if only for short bursts of time. And if she was being honest with herself, Claire realized that this was her own burden, not Mia's. It would be wrong of her to put so much weight on her friend's shoulders. Claire knew that Mia felt that weight with or without her bringing up Jimmy's abduction.

Yet despite it all, Claire's hope prevailed–a stubborn weed growing wild in the depths of her mind. But the fact remained that her son had been missing for 3 months, one week, 2 days, and 16 hours. If she really looked at the clock, she could probably narrow the time down to the minutes. And each of those minutes, every second that Jimmy didn't return home, didn't sleep in his bed with the Lightning McQueen sheets, didn't ride his shiny blue Schwinn down the street ringing that silly metal bell on his left handlebar, they punched holes in Claire's soul. Her insides must look like Swiss cheese, she thought with dark humor. At some point, doesn't a person stop being a person? She felt like she was close to that. Living without her son hadn't gotten easier … no, not at all.

Aside from her growing depression, a deepening paranoia had begun to surround Claire. She often felt as though someone was watching her, and she had seen that same silver car–the one that was parked down the block from her when Mia was visiting that time–a few additional times since then. Oddly, she mostly noticed it when she was spending time with Mia. She hadn't mentioned it to her; what was it about Mia that made her paranoid? Made her want to protect her? Claire understood that she was probably making something out of nothing, but she just couldn't quite shake that uneasy feeling of unwanted eyes studying her.

She even texted Joe about it. Lately their interactions had been briefer then ever and she felt as though it was simply a matter of time before the divorce papers came in the mail.

Yesterday, she had texted him:

> Hey Joe. How have you been?

It took him a whole day to respond and when he finally did, all he wrote was:

> Fine. What's up?

Despite her annoyance at his delayed text, Claire wrote:

> I feel like someone has been following me. There's this silver car hanging around and whenever I try to approach the driver, the car drives away. It's weird.

To which Joe responded:

> You're being paranoid Claire. No one is following you.

With a huff, Claire tossed her phone aside. He was probably right. Why would someone be following her anyway? What in her life could possibly merit that? She briefly thought about going to the police, but she didn't even have a full license plate number. The car always took her unaware, and before she could pull out her phone to note the number, the car always drove quickly away. The only letters that stood out in her mind were the first two: BL. Claire promised herself that next time, she would be ready. If there was a next time.

Maybe she had been wrong to withhold this information from Mia. Especially since the car always seemed to appear when

Mia was around. Didn't Mia have a right to know? Claire thought perhaps that if she told Mia about the car, she would have more insight ... and less judgment. After all, Mia was the one with genuine intuition, but then again, she didn't want to worry the poor girl. Mia was worried enough about Claire ... that much was obvious by the concern hidden just under the surface of Mia's brown eyes whenever she looked at her.

Claire changed her mind. Why hide it? She reached over for her phone again and typed:

> Hey Mia. You around to chat?

Claire sat on the edge of the couch waiting for Mia's reply, which usually came relatively quickly if she wasn't at work ... and Mia wasn't at work right now. It was Sunday afternoon.

Chapter Forty-One

MIA

"You own one of these bay houses?" Mia asked, surprised. It seemed to her that this should have been the first tidbit of information that Bob shared with her as he recapped the history of the Long Island Bay Houses. The boat bobbed slowly in the water; the calm surface had given way to a choppy surf and Mia perceived her whole body rising and falling with the swelling tide. *When did that chill enter the air?* Mia thought to herself as she slipped on her light-weight sweatshirt. Judging from the sun, it was late afternoon already and the sea breeze had picked up; Mia wished she had brought something warmer to wear on the boat. She heard the faraway ping of an incoming text message, but her phone was tucked deep within her tote bag, which had been stored in the bench on which she was currently sitting, to ensure that it didn't fly into the water.

"Yes, Mia. I do own one of the bay houses," Bob said, his gaze suddenly intensifying.

Bob dropped the anchor into the waters of Reynold's Channel and leisurely walked over to join Mia and Dee, who were seated on the tan leather benches at the front of the boat. All of a sudden, Mia's teeth began to chatter. A thought was coming to her, coming to her ... no matter how hard she tried to push it

189

away. *So Close. So Close. Right Here.* The thought wasn't in words, more of a sensation, an urgent sensation prying into her locked mind, trying to wiggle its way in. Trying to make her understand. Was it the ocean? Was it intuition? Was it magic? Mia didn't know, but whatever force had invaded her mind, it lit a spark of utter fear within her.

Glancing across the small space of boat separating her from Dee and Bob—who sat before her with their hands intertwined—her eyes were drawn down to Bob's wrist. It took her a moment to process what she was seeing, but once she knew and understood what her eyes perceived, the realization struck her like lightning. It was right in front of her all this time. The answer. Downstairs. Just one layer of sheetrock away.

"Bob. What happened to your sleeve?" Mia asked through trembling lips even though she knew the answer.

There, by his right wrist, his flannel shirt ended in a ragged, uneven rip, as though the cuff had been torn off. Her mind flashed to that remnant of fabric that had washed up all those weeks ago. A realization was dawning, dawning on her ... rolling over her like the crashing waves. And in that moment, she knew it. She didn't know how she knew ... but there it was. A shimmering gem submerged beneath the murky waters of her thoughts. Blazingly obvious in its presence. Would he really still wear that shirt? With its incriminating imperfection? She thought briefly of her own grandfather, who wore his stained and ripped gray Champion sweatshirt every single day. The hair on the back of her neck stood up as gooseflesh emerged all over her body.

Time seemed sluggish. It was impossible ... well, not impossible. Improbable, yes. But not impossible. And ridiculous. And absurd. And yet ... and yet. It fit. It made sense. *So close. So close. Right Here. DANGER.* Thoughts flashed like neon signs all throughout her being. Piercing her consciousness with futile urgency.

"Well, you see, Mia, I seem to have torn my shirt while I was working on my bay house. See that old brown one over there?"

Mia's gaze followed his pointing finger. She did see it. A shrouded gloom emanated from the structure in the distance souring the beauty of the natural scene before her with bitterness. She could taste acidity in her mouth.

"That one is ours," Bob explained patiently.

A beat of silence.

"And that's where Jimmy and Kyle are ... aren't they," Mia said flatly. Mia announced this without any question in her tone. She knew it to be true. She felt it to be true. And once she made that connection in her head, the waves crashed in acknowledgement in her mind. Certainty. A feeling that had been evasive for Mia ... evasive that is, until this very moment.

"Well, that's quite an accusation," Dee responded.

"It's true though. Isn't it?" Mia said with a surety that she had never felt before. With a knowing that she had never experienced.

It all made sense. Images flashed in her mind ... the locket, the seashell, the 'For Sale' sign, the quick sale of the home—and for below asking price, the call to her mother–trying to thwart her in her pursuit of the truth, the piece of seemingly meaningless sleeve that had washed up ... the relentless rhythmic crashing. And Mia knew ... she knew what they planned to do to her here in the middle of Reynold's Channel. The knowledge was a gale force of wind that took her breath away. She had read enough murder-mysteries to know that this was the perfect place to make someone disappear. To make the nosy tenant insignificant. She had gone and become a book character without even realizing it. A literary cliché. Yet, despite the knowing, and despite the bitter terror that gripped her, something in her very core felt heavy, wet.

"You're a clever one ... a little liar," Bob said.

"A liar?" Mia repeated.

"Yes, ma'am. We've been following you. You told us you weren't in touch with Claire Benicek anymore. Not nice, Mia. Not nice at all. You were just getting too close. That's all. It's nothing personal. We liked you. You should have just minded your own business ... like we told you. Like your mom told you to do."

"But–"

"No buts anymore, Mia. The drugs should be starting to work now. Do you feel them?" Dee asked, her eyes shining with curiosity.

"Drugs?" Mia responded.

But as she said the word, she knew it to be true. She could already feel their presence in her muddled mind. The lemonade ... Bob and Dee hadn't drunk any. Or maybe they had. She was confused, jumbled. She tried to think of Claire ... and Jimmy. Of how she got here. Of how her life narrowed to this moment. This insane reality.

"But—why?" Mia sputtered out.

"Why? Well, there's a story worth telling. Dee ... wanna do the honors?"

"It'd be my pleasure, Bob."

And as the edges blurred around her with each passing minute, Mia listened as Dee told her story, her voice rising to a shrill pitch at some points, and fading to a near whisper in others.

Chapter Forty-Two

DEE'S STORY

The miscarriages started when I was 30 ... I remember I was pregnant on my birthday—a little backyard party, we had. Nothing too big. We had to start saving if we were gonna be parents, right? Bob planned the whole thing. Some baked ziti, salad, a few kegs of Bud. But only sparkling cider in my champagne glass; I didn't mind though. I was so excited. So completely happy. People always like to tell you about the bad stuff of motherhood. The sleepless nights, the crying, the soreness and stitches, but I wasn't afraid. I couldn't wait to be a mother; I was made for it.

Bob and I had been married for about 5 years already by that time and we finally had the money and wherewithal to start a family. I had 9 of them ... 9 miscarriages. First one about a month after my 30th birthday. I was pretty far along too. But we tried again ... same thing. And again. 9 miscarriages over the course of about 15 years, one after the other after the other after the next ... I never lost track. All of them ended in blood. And I mourned every single one. Do you even know what that does to a person? To a person's mind and body? It nearly broke me. And they weren't all clean affairs, where the bits and pieces of a would-be child get flushed down the toilet. No. Not for me. A lot of those pregnancies *ended up with me in a hospital bed getting scraped out by the very doctors that took all our money in the first place. Hurt like hell too. But the cramps were nothing compared to the heartache. The darkness. The emptiness.*

We tried fertility clinics, IVF–borrowed against every asset we had, cleared out our bank accounts. Nothing worked. Quack doctors with their shitty prescriptions. Not one of those physicians–with their fancy cars and their mini-mansions on the North Shore, with their degrees and accolades–knew a goddamn thing. They scammed me; they preyed on my hope and my innocence. I'm sure I personally helped fund their luxury vacations to Europe or the Caribbean, maybe even their own kids' college tuitions ... all those copays. All those appointments. Years of them. They made their promises and as long as my visits didn't go past the 15 minutes they allotted, they looked at me with their kind, sympathetic eyes. Giving me assurances. Poking and prodding and examining. Such indecency. We were cursed. I was cursed. My womb was poisoned ... and it poisoned me and our marriage after a while.

It wasn't until I was in my late 40s that we considered adoption. Yeah, maybe our own blood wouldn't be passed on, but that didn't mean we couldn't adopt an unfortunate soul that had been given up, abandoned. Lots of children need homes, right? Well, it turned out that our home wasn't good enough. We were too poor ... all that money spent on trying to have a baby ruined our chances for good. Ironic, isn't it. Filled out our first adoption application at a Christian organization in Manhattan. Denied. We thought that maybe we were denied because we weren't members of an active parish. So, we tried again at an agency in Queens. Denied. We said, Screw New York City, let's try somewhere else. Denied. Denied. Denied. Denied. We were too old. Too poor. We didn't have any parental experience. At least that's what they said. Hell, those miscarriages taught me more than I care to say about parental experience. But apparently we weren't good enough. We were tainted, Bob and I.

One agency suggested we try an organization that placed babies from Asian countries. I wasn't too keen on adopting a baby from overseas ... I wanted a child that looked as much as possible like me and Bob. Now, I didn't mean that in a racist way ... I have nothing against anyone else. We're all people ... no matter the skin or the shape of our features. But we said, To hell with it. *And we gave it a go.*

Things looked like they would work out, for a while at least. We even went to China. Stayed there for a whole month. A WHOLE MONTH! We had to take out a loan with a crazy interest rate to fund the trip. But, that was what the agency required. We had to go. The thinking was that we needed time to bond with a baby before we took it back to the States. And we had a beautiful match. A little girl. Li was her name. We were told that we could change it if we wanted to once the official paperwork was processed, but we thought it was just darling. We toyed with changing the spelling from L-i. to L-e-i-g-h, but we never got that far. At our exit meeting, the one where the head of the place got the final say about us, we got another big, fat, Denied. Again ... too old. Too unfit to make a good home for a baby. Too broke. That one hurt. We came to love that little girl after we spent all that time with her. She had the most beautiful face ... like a porcelain doll. I still think about her sometimes, wonder where she is now, if someone better came along. Someone younger. She would have been happy with us. We would have given her a good home. Would have loved her. I know that.

The rage and bitterness invaded me at that point. I hate to report this, but we tried another way to get Li out of there ... but the gentleman we hired to help us got caught. Another 5k down the drain ... 5k we didn't even have in the first place. And back Li went to that dirty orphanage where she had to share a crib with another child. Where she had only rice and soup to eat. Did that director honestly think that she was better off there than with us? Lucky for Bob and me, we never got caught. No one could prove our involvement and we were sent back home as opposed to a jail in China. Thank goodness for small blessings.

When we got back here, I locked myself in the house for weeks. I refused to come out. Everything good in my life turned to poison. I was devastated. Angry. Bitter. Couldn't even look at the young moms pushing their plastic strollers down the streets anymore, the little kids playing in the sand with their shovels and buckets. It was just so unfair. So cruel.

One time, about 5 months after we got back from China, I drank a fifth of whiskey and walked down to the ocean real late at night. I took off all my clothes and walked right in. I was going to end it all. Give myself to the ocean. If Bob hadn't dragged me out, I wouldn't be here right now. Bob saved my life that night.

You might not see it Mia, but we're just people. Same as you. Same as Claire Benicek. You might think we're monsters for what we've done. But we deserve our due. We've had our share of pain and suffering. We are owed some happiness too. And we're cashing in.

Chapter Forty-Three

MIA

Despite the bitter hatred that welled up in Mia's gut, she couldn't help but feel a slight pity for Dee. Listening to her tell her story through the dreamy spell the whiskey cast over her mind, part of Mia could perceive the well of grief that resided within her. So many failed attempts at motherhood. So many hopes dashed to the ground. Anyone could understand that such tragedy could direct a person down a dark path. But Mia's sympathy did not extend far enough to justify such a terrible, monstrous act. It was almost impossible for Mia to imagine that these people, her landlords that she thought she knew, could be capable of such atrocity, could orchestrate such pain within another human being. Within her friend.

But the longer she sat with the scathing truth, the longer she turned it all over in her brain, the more likely it all seemed. Her mind was rapid-firing connections too quickly for her to fully comprehend in her scrambled state. Her heart ached for Claire. Would she ever see this woman, who she had come to view as a sort of surrogate mother, reunited with her son? He was so close ... within Mia's eyesight. She tried to glance over to the structure, the decaying brown bay house, but found that her eye muscles weren't working as they should. This poor boy. One town over from his mom. So close, but so incredibly far away. If Claire could only know how close he was. Mia wished she had made the connection weeks ago. But she hadn't. And now, she was here. In the middle of nowhere. Drugged. Disoriented. Useless. A failure. She had missed the messages. Jumbled the signs. It was too late.

Even though Mia's mind felt woozy, she managed to spit out, "I wish the ocean had taken you that night. It would have been better off. Jimmy would be home right now, where he belongs ... with his mother."

"That's quite unkind of you Mia," Dee responded with a calm that sparked a fresh wave of terror within her.

Mia thought she knew where the story was going. Her eyelids felt so very heavy. She was so tempted to just close them, float away. Surrender. But she fought that urge; she had to. She owed it to Jimmy, to Claire ... to herself, to fight. To hold on for as long as she could.

Dee studied her with an expression of curiosity, "You must really be feeling those drugs by now."

Dee extended a hand and stroked Mia's hair; Mia tried to swat away her hand, but she was having trouble focusing. Mia fought with every ounce of her being to stay awake, just a little bit longer.

"Just give in, Mia. It will be so much easier that way," Bob added.

She tried to lunge, but her body wouldn't do what it was asked. In her mind, it seemed so clear, but all she managed was a feeble lurch, causing her to slump even farther down in her seat. A terrible pins-and-needles sensation coursed through her muscles. *Wake up,* she screamed at herself internally. *Wake the hell up!* But no amount of will could force sensation into her limbs.

Mia turned her eyes to Bob. God, they had fooled her, especially him. How gullible. All their fake concern about the negative impact involving herself in the Benicek case would have on her— just an elaborate facade.

"How could you?" Mia asked Bob. "You just figured that you would steal some local kids? Couldn't have your own, so you just took someone else's? And now you'll all go down to Florida like one happy family? Someone will find out. Those two boys have been plastered all over the news. You won't get away with it." Mia could hear a slight slur in her speech.

"You just think that you have it all figured out, don't you, Mia? We don't want *these* kids. We're trading 'em in for another," Bob responded.

"What? How?" Mia asked, although she wasn't sure that she really wanted to know.

"Young people now-a-days, they think they know everything. But you don't know anything about the possibilities in this world. What the right people with the right connections can do," Bob responded.

Mia focused all her concentration–she had to snap her eyes open twice–on Bob as he picked up where Dee had left off.

Chapter Forty-Four

BOB'S STORY

Now I see how you're lookin' at me, Mia. Like I'm crazy. Like we're crazy. Well, don't be so fast to cast judgment. And I know what you're thinking ... same as what all those adoption directors thought. That we're too old. Too frail. Too broke. Unfit. But we're not. Lots of old folks become parents ... and lots of old folks help to raise their own grandchildren. I suppose that's what we'll tell everyone. That the baby is our grandkid ... maybe that our own kid died, or went away somewhere. We'll figure all that out. No one will know. It's not these two kids we want. Jimmy and Kyle–no. They're just our barter material. We're gettin' a baby.

I couldn't stand to watch Dee suffer like that. Years and years of sadness. Those years changed her. I almost didn't recognize her. She lost so much weight. I thought I was gonna lose her. And I couldn't let that happen. She was all I had ... my soulmate. Ever since I saw her, my heart never belonged anywhere else.

Dee mentioned the ocean incident, but there was another time too. We don't like to talk about it. A time when I came home from work–it was a Wednesday night in winter–damn cold out too. My hands were so numb I could barely get the key in the lock to open the front door. But when I finally came in, I called her name. No *answer. I heard the shower running and knocked on the bathroom door. No answer again. I pushed open the door a crack and then rushed right in. I found her in the bathtub with an empty bottle of pills floating in the water next to her. There was no light in her eyes. She was lifeless. But she was still breathing. I wasn't too late.*

I pulled her outta that tub, wrapped her in a towel, and I shoved my fingers down her throat. All the pills came back up, some blood too because I had cut the roof of her mouth with the rough edge of my wedding band. But that didn't matter. I sat there with her, hugging her. She shivered in my arms on the bathroom floor, sobbing. I sobbed too. I'll never forget seeing her like that.

I mean, fatherhood was an important notion for me too, but not as important as it was for Dee. I made a promise to her, right then and there. I said, "Dee. I'll get us a child. I promise. There's other ways. Forget all these doctors. These stupid adoption directors. I promise Dee. I'll figure something out." I don't know if those were my exact words, but they're pretty close. And I was serious. I didn't know exactly how I was gonna do it, but I was pretty smart. I knew I could figure something out. It would come to me ... somehow. I just didn't know how. I wasn't gonna lose her.

By the time we got home from China, I'd been promoted to manager of Fenley's. Was making a decent salary too. The owner liked me. He was generous with me–probably more than I deserved. He even talked about passing the whole place over to me when he retired in a year or two. He had a few other places around the island and no kids of his own to help him. So he treated me well. So around the time that I made that promise to Dee, I was spending a lot of time there. And those late nights brought in some odd fish. I mean, I met people from all walks of life at that bar. The stories I could tell! Never knew there were so many different types of people in the world. Lots of 'em were trying to find some escape at the bottom of a pint glass or lookin' for answers that only booze can provide. But there was this one guy, let's call him Mr. M., used to come in every Thursday night at 1 in the morning, like clockwork. Bar was mostly empty at that

*time, especially during the week. Just the two of us usually, shootin'
the shit. You know. Talkin'. I guess you could say we became
friends. He never really mentioned what sort of work he was
involved in, but I could tell it wasn't the sort of thing he liked to
talk about. Whenever he would pay the tab, he would pull out this
wad of money rolled in a rubber band ... from my end, it looked
like mostly hundreds. Always tipped well. Always behaved himself
... no fighting or anything. Fenley's didn't have too many tussles,
but there had been a few in my time. One of them, Mc— Mr. M.
actually helped me break up. Two middle-aged drunk guys
fighting over God knows what. Rollin' around on the floor like a
bunch of teenagers.*

*But anyhow, I'm getting off topic here, hope you'll forgive me.
You're lookin' extra tired, Mia. I'll try to finish up quick. Where
was I, oh, yes ... got it now. The night after I pulled Dee out of the
bathtub, I was trying to be so strong, at least while I was at work,
but I was losing the battle, if you know what I mean. I just couldn't
get the image of that empty bottle of pills out of my head. It was just
me and Mr. M.; we had done a shot of Jack Daniels, which led to
another one. You know how that goes. And the emotions just
exploded outta me. Next thing I knew, I was bawling like a baby on
that bar. Mr. M. was sorta listening, patting my shoulder. Funny–
I was the bartender, usually folks spill their guts to me. But here I
was blubbering to him. I told him about the promise I made to Dee
and how I didn't know how to fulfill that promise. About how I
pulled her out of the bathtub. A whole bucketful of tears fell out of
me that night. I guess I needed it. A person can only keep things
bottled up for so long.*

*After a few minutes, I guess I was all dried up. I got myself
together. Stood up. And then, it was like the heavens smiled down
on me.*

*He said something like, "Bob, I think I can help you with that
promise."*

*And I looked up at him and said something stupid, something
like, "Oh, yeah. Don't suppose you got an extra baby hanging*

around that you could give to me?" I laughed about it too ... guess I was still feeling the booze in my system.

He just looked at me, all serious and said, "Something like that."

I don't know what I said after that, but Mr. M. went on and said something like, "Hey, Bob. We've been friends now for a while. And you never asked what it is that I do for a living. Well, I'm a people mover," he said. "And some of those people are babies."

Don't quote me on any of this. I can't remember the exact conversation, but I think I'm pretty close. It's not something a person forgets. But I basically asked him if he was serious. And he said that he was. But he said that he can't just give me a baby ... it's not that easy.

He said, "Babies are in high demand." That line I do remember word-for-word.

But he said that he could get us a baby ... and a valid birth certificate, with a social security number and everything. But he needed something in return. I told him that I didn't have the money to pay him nothing.

And he said, "Payment comes in lots of forms." That's something else I remember exactly.

So I asked, "So what would our payment be ... for something like this?" I was still only half serious when I said that. The whole thing was hard to process. The booze made it easier I guess, but it was still outta this world.

And Mr. M. answered, "How about two for the price of one?"

I wasn't sure what he meant by that. But he explained it. Said that if we didn't have money, we could get him two other people—kids ... had to be kids. And that the two kids would be our payment.

I asked him why kids. I asked him what would happen to them ... would they be ok? I was starting to sober up I guess.

And he said, "Oh, yeah. The kids will be fine. They go to rich people all over the world. And even though they're rich and you're not, in a lot of ways they are like yourself and Dee. People who want kids, but can't have them."

I thought about it for a bit. Turned it over and over in my mind. Sounded fair. I wouldn't only get a baby for me and Dee, but I could also help other people like us. People who couldn't have kids, but wanted them. Maybe other women who suffered through depression spells like my Dee did. People who have been sucked dry by doctors and so-called fertility specialists. Maybe I would even save someone else's life?

Don't look at me that way, Mia! Hell. I see people around here, how they treat their children. How they sit them in front of screens and send them to daycare centers … how they pay out the ass for babysitters because all they do is work all the time. They don't deserve kids. Kinda like the parents of these boys. I saw Kyle Yardsleigh with his mom once at the movies. What a witch. She just left him in the theater while she chatted away on her phone in the lobby. That's when I knew who we would use as trade material. And we've been keeping tabs on their whereabouts ever since. She doesn't deserve her son. And I'm sure the Benicek lady is just as bad … why else would she associate herself with Patricia Yardsleigh?

Jimmy and Kyle. They'll go to families that really want them … that really need them. And they'll be happy. They'll be thankful … eventually. They will realize what a gift they have been given.

And as for Dee and me … it's finally our time to make it happen. It took a real long time. It's not so easy to get babies. We also had to save up some moving money … which is why we rented out our apartment. Didn't know when it would happen. We hoped soon. We've been waiting a long time. But we've been patient. Haven't we, Dee? And now it's finally here. It's all set up. We make the trade soon … just waiting on the phone call. It's a good thing for us that we own that bay house. Can you think of a more perfect place to hide some kids? I can't. It's fate. I know it. Finally, things are looking up for us. We'll be headed down south as a family of three. Jimmy and Kyle … they'll be well cared for. And you, Mia … unfortunately for you … you won't be around to see any of it.

Chapter Forty-Five

MIA

That last line sent a chill down Mia's spine. She didn't even want to think about the implications behind it. Now that Bob had finished his tale, Mia vaguely noticed that his faraway gaze became more focused, and he peered at her with scrutiny. She noticed him glance at her drooping shoulders, sagging eyelids, the way her hair hung over her eyes in sweeping curtains. She was falling. Mia could see that Bob and Dee felt very much justified in what they were doing. In their minds, they were heroes, saviors–helping those who couldn't have children of their own ... giving Jimmy and Kyle a better life. There wasn't an inkling of guilt or remorse present within either of them ... Mia could sense their blind righteousness. But there was nothing that Mia could do. She was desperately gripping at her last shreds of conscious thought.

Before she could no longer fight the seductive power of sleep, Bob spoke with a rising temper. "The one thing I don't understand," Bob said. "..is how the hell you ended up living upstairs from us. Things would have been much easier if you had just moved somewhere else. Figures, we get the one tenant who could put all this together somehow."

205

"But I didn't put it together," Mia's slurred speech slipped out of her drooping lips.

"But you would have, Mia. You were just getting too close. The whole situation is quite the coincidence."

Mia wanted to say that it wasn't a coincidence at all. She wanted to scream it until it rang like deafening chimes in Bob and Dee's ears because she finally understood. Before her eyes closed, she thought back to the time when she was still living safe and sound in her childhood home in Sparta. The realtor had sent her those Long Beach listings. Was that only 5 months ago? It felt like a lifetime had passed since then. She remembered how she had initially dismissed that second story Minnesota apartment as being too old and too pricey. But something had made her reconsider. Her thumb hovered over that rental property ... something in her mind was frozen, forcing her to commit to it. It wasn't coincidence ... was it fate? Now, in her drugged state, she became quite certain that it was those waves in her mind that brought her here. Brought her directly upstairs from Dee and Bob. Brought her into Claire and Jimmy Benicek's life, even though Jimmy didn't know that she existed. Put her right in the path of this insane storm that threatened to blow her down. That was blowing her down as her respiration and heartbeat slowed to a faint crawl in her chest. She was part of the story. An integral part. But what was her role now? What good could she possibly do now? She was winding down like a music box, slower ... slower.

She could just perceive someone tying something around her ankles and wrists; she felt fingers working at her extremities, tugging. But she was fading, fading quickly now ... she could actually feel the drugs working their way through her system, like fingers tickling her in the most vulnerable, most hidden parts of her psyche. They were much more persistent now.

Then her mind slipped and she was gone. She didn't feel the cold waters of the Atlantic closing over her head, nor did she feel the burn of salt water in her nostrils. Tethered, Mia's body sunk slowly into the depths of the sea.

Chapter Forty-Six

TRISH

Peering into the pill case, Trish fished around for the last white tablet. *God, those went fast*, she thought to herself. She placed the small white circle directly onto her tongue. Taking a swig of her iced latte to wash it down, she said to herself, *Ok, that's the last one. And this time it's for real*. But who could blame her for needing Vicodin today? No one could. *Anyone in my situation would do the same thing*, she thought to herself as she fixed her lipstick in the rearview mirror of her new Escalade. Her lease was up last week, and in an attempt to brighten her spirits, Mason had come home with this gorgeous vehicle. It had a leather interior, massage seats, an enormous moonroof and every luxury feature one could want ... along with a price tag of almost 85k. But when Trish caught a glimpse of the backseat in the periphery of her reflection, it lacked one thing: a carseat. And that one thought, that one "but" brought Trish crashing back down to reality.

She wished there was one more pill left. Two of them made her feel much better than one, and it seemed like lately, almost any excuse was enough to justify needing a "little upper," which was what Trish called her growing habit in her mind. It was easier to accept and even easier to say ... although she never said it to anyone else, ever ... except herself and her friend, Janine, who supplied the pills. All she needed to do was text her friend and say, "I need some more of those 'little uppers,'" and within the next day or so, she would find the package in her mailbox. Her general practitioner would gladly medicate her, but it was just easier this way. No appointments necessary. If Trish saw the whole situation for what it really was ... that Janine had become a glorified drug dealer and that Trish herself was well on her way to becoming a junkie ... well, she just couldn't handle it. Even though in a dusty corner of her mind, Trish did know it to be true. And if Mason ever found out ... well, that couldn't happen either. *But he wouldn't find out*, Trish assured herself. After all, this was the last one. This would be the last time she would really need them. She wouldn't need to send any more of those degrading messages to Janine. Hell, she didn't even need Janine in her life. They weren't that close anyway. Trish pulled out her phone and deleted their text chain. She felt much better about herself after she did that.

She gave herself one final glance in the rearview mirror; she looked ok ... more than ok. She looked great, as she always did. Maybe her eyes were a little glassy, but the heavy concealer she applied this morning took care of the dark circles, and her new jeans and fashionably bulky cardigan hid the fact that she had lost some weight. Yeah, sure, it was June, but now that the schools have all been air-conditioned (thanks to her endless campaigning), the buildings were freezing.

The principal of Robert Moses Elementary School–Kyle's school–had called the other day, both to check in, and to ask Trish if she would like to pick up a box of Kyle's "things." She was immediately defensive; how dare they impose on her like this? And the message behind such a request was uncouth and insensitive ... Trish didn't miss that. Were they cleansing themselves of him? Was the assumption that Kyle would not be returning to school? But the principal assured Trish that this was not his intention and that he only thought that, now that the school year was almost over, Trish might want to see what Kyle had been working on in class along with his academic record. And, of course, it was June now. Kyle would no longer need the extra heavy sweatshirt, gloves, and hat that lingered in his cubby ... when he did return, of course.

Trish got out of her car and checked to make sure she did an ok parking job. Jeez, this car was even bigger than her last one. The size made it damn hard to park. Or maybe it was the Vicodin that made it hard to park. Whatever. Once she was satisfied that the car parked next to her was at least far enough away that upon entering, the driver wouldn't accidentally slam into her door, she pulled her bag up higher on her shoulder and walked towards the front entrance of Robert Moses Elementary School.

After showing her identification in the clear glass vestibule, Trish swung open the front door and was greeted immediately by the muted laughter of students enjoying Phys. Ed. ... the gym was directly to the right of the main lobby. The squeaking of sneakers on a gymnasium floor always reminded Trish of her own brief foray into the sport of basketball when she was younger. Kyle used to be one of those kids in there ... laughing. Did his class-mates still think about him? Or does life just move on, unfazed ... making room for the little tragedies that happen and then adjusting accordingly? If it wasn't for the Vicodin, that thought would have brought tears to Trish's eyes.

She entered the Main Office and was greeted by the sympa-thetic eyes of Principal Gavin–God she hated that look. She felt her face burn crimson as the secretaries seated in desks behind the large wooden counter turned to ogle her ... the woman with the kidnapped child.

"Mrs. Yardsleigh," Principal Gavin began. "It's very good to see you." His voice dripped with concern and emotion.

"You too," Trish offered back.

"Everyone here at Robert Moses thinks about you and Kyle every day. We pray for his return," he continued.

This was what she needed to hear. They haven't written him off ... forgotten about him.

"Thank you, Principal Gavin. My husband and I appreciate that."

"Well, I know you're a busy woman. And I myself have to go read to Ms. Johnson's Kindergarten class in a few minutes, but I wanted to give you this box of Kyle's belongings. You'll see his 3rd marking period report card in there. He did quite well, especially in reading. And also his art projects are in there as well."

Who gives a shit about grades? Trish thought to herself as she took the box from the principal. Peering into it, she saw Kyle's favorite Yankees sweatshirt at the top. The smell of him wafted up … laundry detergent mixed with lollipops. Her eyes welled as the familiar scent engulfed her. She willed the emotions away. The Vicodins helped with that too.

"Also, I have this for you. On behalf of Kyle's classmates." And Principal Gavin held out a large stack of papers in a bundle bound in ribbon. "Many of Kyle's friends have elected to write him letters. Such a kind sentiment, don't you think?"

Trish didn't know how to respond as she accepted the cards, but she managed to say, "Yes, very kind. Thank you, Principal Gavin."

"Please," he said. "Call me Rich."

"Ok. Well, thank you, Rich," Trish said.

"Truly. Anytime. We look forward to hearing good news soon," he said as he came around the counter to embrace Trish in a stiff hug.

With the box balanced in one hand, and the bundle of cards in the other, Trish made her way out of Robert Moses Elementary School and back into her sparkling new black Escalade. She closed herself within the cocoon of leather. Suddenly, she felt warm, too warm. She wrestled out of her cardigan and threw it into the back seat. With a deep inhale and exhale, Trish rested for a minute, eyes closed, against the cushioned headrest behind her.

Reaching over, she grabbed the stack of cards that Kyle's classmates had hand-drawn for him. The first one, written in the large awkward letters of 1st grade, said 'Come back soon Kyle. We miss you.' And below the message, was a crayon picture of two stick figures, one with yellow hair (Kyle, Trish assumed) and the other with red hair, holding hands. She opened the card and inside it said, 'P.S. I hope you are back in time for my birthday party. Your Friend Shane.'

Trish flipped through a few more cards. All of them were heartfelt. All of them were adorable. Or they would be adorable if they didn't remind her of the grotesque reality that they were written for her own son ... for her son who remained gone. Missing. Erased. Blotted out of existence. Suddenly, Trish felt the gorge rise up within her. She threw open the car door, slamming it into the Honda Pilot that was parked next to her. The impact would undoubtedly leave a mark on the shiny surface. But she didn't care. She barely made it to the grassy patch near the fence, before vomiting up the burning bile that was churning inside her stomach. Maybe she should have eaten breakfast this morning; maybe if she had, she wouldn't have felt like pieces of her soul were being dislodged from her very core, but she didn't have much of an appetite anymore.

After she finished heaving, she wiped her dripping mouth on her bare arm and stood up, gulping air, heart hammering in her chest. She went back to her car and grabbed the stack of cards that she had just flipped through. She absolutely could not bear to have them in her possession for a moment longer. They were too real, too honest, too ... threatening. If she took them home, she would undoubtedly bury herself in them. And she couldn't allow herself to sink her teeth into the meaty, terrible truth they contained. That would certainly ruin her. And even though it broke her to do it, Trish was in self-preservation mode. She took those sweet, crayon-flecked cards–they felt waxy in her damp hands–and tossed them into the wire trash can that stood in front of her car. If she was home, she would have burned them and watched with satisfaction as they went up in flames, the twirling gray smoke sent up into the atmosphere, a sacrifice to whatever gods that lived there.

After the deed was done and that bundle of cards lay at the bottom of the receptacle amongst other people's discarded trash, Trish Yardsleigh got back into her car. Before pulling out of the parking lot, she started a new text message thread:

> Hey Janine. Any chance I can get some more of those little uppers? I ran out.

Her breathing became a bit easier; just thinking about those little white pills slowed her pulse. *This is my last batch*, Trish assured herself as she maneuvered her car out onto the main road leading away from the school. *I just need to get through the rest of this week. Then, I'll be done with them. I'll flush any extras down the toilet.* Trish drove home and all thoughts about Kyle's classmates and their sweet sentiments faded by the time she pulled into her driveway. Her mind was on other things.

Chapter Forty-Seven

MIA

Mia couldn't perceive her body's descent as she sank deeper and deeper underneath the surface. The bag of sand attached by a rope to her ankles served to make her path straight and sure. Her bound wrists drifted above her head and her chin jutted skyward as the salt water filled her throat and lungs. Tiny bubbles escaped her nose and mouth marking a trail that no one would ever see—except perhaps the beach gulls that cawed overhead in the 5 o'clock tilted sunlight. While her body fought for air, her mind remained blank, clear, serene. Mia didn't fight her death; she couldn't. The drugs took all the fight out of her. Her consciousness was elsewhere, floating in the abyss of medicated slumber. She remained blissfully unaware.

Not only was she unable to perceive her impending demise, she was also unable to distinguish the force that put a slight tear in the bag of sand, causing the grains to gradually leak out and mix with the sea—slowing her downward climb. Nor could she recognize the unexpected swell of the tide that moved her up-current as she leisurely ascended to the surface—her gaping mouth drinking in the air as she bobbed up and down. And she didn't know how she ended up tangled in the tall marsh grass surrounding the bay house in which Jimmy and Kyle remained hidden away. Through it all, the drugs kept their stronghold on Mia. She had become a puppet, a marionette, directed by a power far greater than, even in the deepest recesses of her mind, Mia would admit existed. And despite the urgency that ticked away with each passing minute, and despite the faraway knowledge that Jimmy and Kyle were in imminent danger of being permanently relocated somewhere else with some other family, Mia remained unconscious, partially submerged and cold as the last rays of daytime faded from the sky.

It wasn't until much later that Mia would have time and energy to speculate about the forces that saved her life that day. And it was a thought that continued to spring to her mind over the years, especially late at night when she found herself unable to sleep or in the clutches of a nightmare. Feeling a connection with the ocean was one thing, but the sort of absurd magic that directed her course that fateful day was quite another. But all of it was too convenient to be coincidence. Too preposterous to be simply providence. Mia came to accept it all with a sort of child-like wonder, a wonder which has remained etched into Mia's soul until this very day.

But at the moment, all of this was far beyond Mia's logical thought as she remained in blissful ignorance sprawled out, half submerged, like a sleeping infant in the marsh grass. For many hours, consciousness lay hovering on the horizon, and although it was drawing closer with each grateful breath of air that Mia unknowingly inhaled deep into her aching lungs, true thought remained a distant echo. As the waves persisted in their gentle, rhythmic rocking, the fading twilight made way for darkness.

Chapter Forty-Eight

JIMMY

Jimmy sat with his arms around Kyle. He felt so helpless watching his friend breathe in and out so slowly. There was a rattling noise coming from inside him. It didn't sound good at all.

He still didn't even really understand how they got here. He thought back to the day at his house. His mom had picked them both up at school. He had been so excited to be dismissed with all the other kids instead of having to go to the Y after the bell. Miss Cindy was so mean there and they only had gross snacks at the Y. Jimmy begged his mom not to send him there anymore, but she told him that he had to go there because she worked and couldn't pick him up at 2:45 like all the other moms.

He remembered seeing his mom, standing a little bit apart from all the other moms, smiling. He and Kyle ran over to her so fast. They couldn't wait to get home and play basketball in the driveway and pirates in the clubhouse next door. He had the treasure, his mom's necklace, already in his pocket. He felt a little guilty when he saw his mom standing there without the locket around her neck, but he was going to give it back later. She wouldn't even know it was gone.

Kyle made three swishes in a row. And then they got sweaty

playing basketball and asked for Capri Suns. It was weird because Jimmy didn't see his mom bring them out, but there they were ... sitting in the bottom part of the driveway. That was also weird, but Jimmy figured that his mom left them there when they ran next door to do a quick run down the twisty slide.

He and Kyle sat in the driveway and poked the tiny yellow straws in the little holes of the Capri Suns. Kyle's straw went through to the other side so he had to slurp his fruit punch up before it all poured out onto the ground. They didn't taste like they came from the fridge; they were warm and stale tasting. But Jimmy and Kyle were thirsty, so it didn't matter.

Then things started to go slow. He had asked Kyle if he wanted to go back next door, but he said that he was feeling kinda tired and wanted to sit for another minute. Jimmy started to feel tired too. His legs felt really tired. He couldn't even really lift them. And there was a car that stopped. He remembered seeing someone's feet, in flip flops, really close up.

When he opened his eyes again, he was in a boat. The dark blue sky was flying by overhead. He sat up and had a big-time headache. Worse than when he had the flu that time. He felt like he was going to puke, but he didn't. He saw the man driving the boat, and the woman was sitting between him and Kyle, holding their wrists, which had thick ropes tied around them. He wondered if she was a pirate and he was going to have to walk the plank.

And then they came here. To this house in the middle of the water. And they had been here forever. And now they were going somewhere else. It was all so confusing.

Maybe Kyle remembered more. Maybe he should ask him. He glanced down again at his friend who was still sleeping. That's all Kyle did anymore. Sleep. Which was weird, because Jimmy barely slept. He got really scared at night, even though he tried not to. It was better to stay awake than see the monsters that haunted his dreams.

Jimmy remembered learning about how bears hibernate in

the winter. Maybe that was what Kyle was doing. Jimmy hoped so, because otherwise it meant that Kyle was really, really sick. Was he so sick that he would die? Jimmy didn't know, but that thought made him more afraid than he had ever been. Jimmy closed his eyes and whispered into the still night air, *Please, Please someone come help us. Mom ... Dad—if you can hear me, please come help us. We want to go home.*

Chapter Forty-Nine

MIA

Despite the cool water she had been submerged in for hours, Mia managed to wake up. Somehow. It was dark ... pitch black in fact, and Mia had absolutely no idea what time it was. Logically, hypothermia should have taken over her extremities, but the fact that she had become lodged unevenly in the marsh grass meant that only the lower portion of her body was completely water-logged. While still damp, her torso, arms, shoulders and face were spared the brunt of the sea. Even though it was June, and the ocean was definitely milder than it had been, this portion of the Atlantic didn't truly warm up until August–and even then the highest temperature it reaches is only about 75 degrees. Not high enough for a body to remain immersed indefinitely without danger.

She regained consciousness slowly as the drugs gradually faded from her system. Mia's eyes darted back and forth as she tried to make out any object whatsoever in her inky surroundings. Slowly, her vision adjusted to the dimness and she could perceive hazy shapes in her periphery. The events that occurred on the boat came back to her, crashing like lightning against the skies of her consciousness. Bob and Dee ... her landlords. It had been them ... all along. Maybe she should have asked them how they managed it—she was curious. She supposed she would have, had they not drugged her, bound her wrists and ankles together, and tossed her overboard. Their reasoning behind their actions boggled Mia's mind; she didn't remember Bob's exact words, but the idea of kidnapping kids, trading them in for an infant, and then taking off to Florida ... it was the stuff of movies! And that was just the theoretical part. What about the logistical side? How could two elderly—albeit healthy—people possibly abduct two young boys from outside Claire's suburban house without leaving a trace? Mia guessed that the how didn't really matter anymore, did it? Somehow, they had managed. And impossibly, as a result, Mia was here. It must have been a perfectly executed and well-planned endeavor. It had to be. And they had gotten away with it.

But then again, would it have been that hard to get away with? Who would suspect an elderly couple, completely unrelated to the families in question, living not 10 minutes from the kidnapping site, of anything at all? The police had looked far and wide, when all they really needed to do was look directly under their noses. Everyone, including Claire, assumed the abductors had fled with their bounty. Who in their right mind would keep these boys, whose faces had become as recognizable as any movie star, essentially in their hometown? Well, now Mia knew exactly who would do that. Two people. She knew them well ... or at least she thought she did. It was brilliant in its recklessness ... in its randomness. Nobody would suspect such a thing. Not even their tenant. Mia wondered if you ever truly know another human being, what he or she might be capable of. How many monsters lay hiding in plain sight? That thought made her shudder even harder.

Mia remembered the last thing that Bob had said. About it being an inconvenient coincidence for them that Mia had ended up living in their upstairs apartment—that she had discovered them somehow. She had wanted to tell him that it wasn't coincidence at all ... that it was something else, something much larger and more purposeful, but she couldn't utter the words as a result of the drugs that had coursed through her bloodstream. At the time, she had thought that it was too late. Yes, she had pieced the puzzle together, but as her eyes closed, she hadn't known what good she could possibly do ... what help she could possibly be if she was dead. But, looking down at her bound wrists, teeth chattering like mad in her skull, she realized that it wasn't too late. She was wet, yes ... in fact, she was soaked. And her body temperature was probably impossibly low; she could feel it in her slowed breathing and numb fingers. But she hadn't died; despite Dee's and Bob's efforts, she was very much still alive. And she was starting to think–now that her thought faculties were working again ... yes, she was muddled, but she was becoming more and more able to puzzle this all out as the minutes progressed–that the ocean ... the waves had somehow intervened on her behalf. Did that make her sound crazy? It was certainly a fantastical thought. But regardless of what had actually happened, the truth surrounding how she ended up miraculously alive–accidental or destined–she couldn't just lie down and give up. She just couldn't. She didn't know how often nature negotiated on behalf of humans, but it couldn't be very often ... and this obligation lit a renewed flame in Mia's heart. And even though she was cold, this flame was enough to thaw her mind and heart. It was enough to force her to keep trying.

A rush of gratitude consumed Mia and through lips that were blue she spoke softly. *Thank you*, she said. She wasn't fully sure what or who she was thanking, but she thought that it was the ocean beneath her, the rippling waves that buoyed her up and saved her life.

Glancing down–amazing how one's eyesight adjusts–she could distinguish the plastic tie that bound her ankles together. She could also discern a long yellow string attached to an empty sack of some sort, tangled in the reeds by her feet. Trying to break the tie she pressed her feet apart as far as possible, straining her legs against the tension; there was no give at all. Despite her numbness she could feel the plastic bite into her exposed ankles.

Once it became clear that her legs were restrained, she focused her gaze on her wrists. Bringing her hands close to her face, she examined the place where both ends of the plastic tie met one another. Was that a slight tear? She thought it was. Or maybe her eyes were playing tricks on her. She brought her mouth down on the tie, ripping and tearing with her teeth. The unforgiving tether ripped into the tender flesh on her inner wrist; Mia's mouth filled up with the metallic taste of blood, but she didn't stop. Finally, Mia felt the tie give, releasing her hands. Relief flooded her, and a renewed sense of hope.

She opened and closed her hands a few times to promote the flow of oxygen and blood into her fingers, and sat up, stretching her arms above her head. The floor of the water beneath her was mushy, but solid. She could feel the mucky sand and dirt seeping deeper into her jeans, into her sodden shoes. She thought about her cellphone, and then remembered that it was in her tote bag, secured under the bench of Bob and Dee's boat. Damn. Not that it would have worked anyway even if it had been secured in her pocket.

She lifted her legs out of the water and yanked on the tie binding her ankles together with all of her strength. Using her fingers, her thumb nail ripped so low it brought a wave of tears to her eyes. No luck. The tie could have been made of iron the way it remained fixed in position, like a manacle. Mia's breath came in ragged gasps through her chest, and she tried to suppress the panic that threatened to overtake her. *Think*, she urged herself. *I'm still alive. I'm not going to die here in this fucking grass.* She looked around. The bay house. Swathed in moonlight, it couldn't be more than a football field away ... what was that? 100 yards? Something like that. Could she make it there?

On numb, sore fingers, she maneuvered herself out of the greenery and found that the water gradually deepened as she moved farther and farther away from the marsh grass. There was no way she could swim that distance with immobile legs. She would have to move edgewise, traversing the reeds, sticks, and tall grass. And that was what she did. Switching between a crab-walk and a restricted crawl, she progressed at what felt like a snail's pace. It was a slow process, made harder by the slimy ground that engulfed her hands and feet with each painstaking movement and even slower by the plants and mud that got caught on her bound ankles. Without a phone, Mia couldn't be sure of exactly how long it took, but it felt like hours ... days even. Mia's sweat beaded on her damp scalp, mixing with the sea water, and she had to rest at least four times, plopping herself down in the sludge. Each time she stopped, she had to will herself to commence the journey again and not just lie down and let the current take her away.

Despite the overwhelming difficulty, Mia managed to reach the foot of the bay house. She held onto the exposed section of one of the wooden stilts that supported the structure. The base of the house was about 4 feet above her head. How in the world was she supposed to get up there? She had to get her legs free. After the arduous job of propelling her body across the marshland, she was almost out of strength. The numbness in her legs and hands worried Mia, but she pushed all concern for herself into some locked box in the back of her mind. She didn't have the luxury to stress about that now.

With the last bit of exertion she could muster, on her back, she propped herself up on her elbows and spread her feet as far apart as the ties allowed. Maybe there were 3 inches of space ... more than before. Mia guessed that the binding loosened slightly as she crossed the distance. Yet, it still wasn't loose enough to free her feet. Maybe she could scrape the binding against the wooden structure. She pushed the tie, now suspended alone between her feet against the solid wood of the stilt, using her knees and hips to give her leverage and strength. At first, the effort seemed fruitless; a dull headache formed between her eyebrows as a result of the strain. *Come on*, she uttered out loud. *Break, you stupid thing.* And then, as she pushed once more, harder than last time, she heard an audible *snap* as the confine gave way. She was free.

Mia stood up on wobbly legs ... made even more wobbly by

the uneven and soggy terrain tugging at her. The water came up to her lower thighs–how insanely lucky that it was low tide–and her limbs ached with weariness, but she would rest later. Now, she had a mission to complete.

Arms shaking and weak, Mia pulled herself onto the wooden dock–if you could even call it that; it was so badly rotted and damaged. With tentative steps, Mia skirted around the loose and missing floorboards and approached the chipped front door of Bob and Dee's bay house. She almost couldn't believe that Jimmy and Kyle were in there; the structure was so quiet, so dark–like something out of a horror movie. Before she turned the rusty doorknob she took two deep breaths to calm her trembling heart, which could undoubtedly be heard over the waves lapping softly against the wooden legs propping the house up in the water. She was nervous, incredibly so; she wasn't sure why exactly, and for a moment there, she thought she might collapse ... from fatigue, from the cold that had worked its way up her spine again, from the pure, unadulterated fear that lurked in the dark recesses of her consciousness. But she didn't collapse. No, there was a great deal more steel in Mia than she had given herself credit for and her hands remained steady as she turned the creaking door knob clockwise; the first crack of dawn pierced the darkness that had pressed down around her shoulders.

Chapter Fifty

CLAIRE

It was seven in the morning and Claire paced back and forth in her living room. She had barely slept last night, which wasn't abnormal for her these days. But thoughts of Mia Rossi raced through her mind as she lay in her bed staring up into space; she had watched the hours tick slowly away until there was enough daylight in the sky to justify actually getting up. Not only had Mia never responded to Claire's first text, but she hadn't responded to the subsequent messages afterwards, nor had she answered the phone the three times Claire had called. It was odd. Mia usually responded quickly. And Claire's texts and voicemails had gotten increasingly harrowing. Especially the last one, which said:

> Mia. Please call me back. I need to tell you about a car that I've been noticing around lately. I have a bad feeling.

Mia definitely would have called her back after hearing that. And on a Sunday night, Mia should have been home, like she always was, getting ready for work the next morning.

If Joe was around, he would have some sarcastic quip to tease Claire about her worry. Something like, *Watch out. Helicopter mom is in the house.* Or, *Clear the landing pad, helicopter mom is hovering.* But Joe wasn't around. And Claire couldn't ignore the creeping feeling that something was wrong. Within the next hour or so, Mia would be getting ready for work; she was scheduled to be in the realtor's office at 9. Claire made a deal with herself that if she didn't hear from Mia before then, she would put a call through to the office ... just to make sure she was there.

Claire worked from home on Mondays, so she showered and made the top half of herself look presentable ... so the attendees of the Zoom meeting she had to lead at 10am would think she was put-together and professional. Sitting down at her desk with a cup of steaming coffee, she logged on for the day at 8:45. She planned to call Long Beach Realty at 9:15 ... the 15-minute grace period would ensure that Mia was indeed sitting at her desk. She had already rehearsed what she would say: *Hi, Mia. I'm so sorry to bother you, but I was paranoid about something.* She would laugh it off and the queasiness in the pit of her stomach would ease as she would undoubtedly hear Mia's cheerful voice float through the receiver.

Claire busied herself with editing the Google Slides she was going to present to a panel of advertising executives in an hour. This was an important meeting and a big deal for her company; it could mean a potential promotion for her later this year, and she could certainly use the pay raise. But the nerves swimming around in her intestines were not due to this career opportunity, but for Mia Rossi–whose earnest face kept appearing in the front of her mind.

Claire glanced down at her phone. No new texts, no missed calls–of course she wouldn't have "missed" any contact from Mia because the phone was resting directly next to her keyboard and the volume was on full blast–she had checked four times. Claire watched as the time display flipped from 9:14 to 9:15. Finally! Claire already had the number to Long Beach Realty up on her phone screen. She pressed the 'call' icon and, balancing her phone between her ear and shoulder, waited as the ringing reverberated through her head. After a few seconds, someone answered.

"Hello. Point Lookout Realty. Can I help you find your dream home today?" said a high-pitched female voice.

"Yes! Hello. Actually, I must have called the wrong number. I'm looking for Long Beach Realty. My mistake," Claire responded, confused.

"Nope. No mistake. The Long Beach branch has routed their calls to us for today. How can I help you?"

"Well," Claire began. "I'm actually looking to speak with the receptionist at the *Long Beach* office. Her name is Mia Rossi. I'm a close friend."

"I happen to also be a friend of Mia Rossi," the friendly voice on the other end of the phone said lightly. "We just met recently. My name is Hailey."

"Hi, Hailey. Mia's mentioned you," Claire responded, unsure of how to proceed.

"From what I hear, Mia was a no-show at work today. That's why the Long Beach calls have been directed my way. I hope everything's ok. It's not like her to just not show up to work."

Hailey's words struck Claire in the gut. It was definitely not like Mia to blow off work. Not like her at all. The fear that had subsided a bit in Claire's soul returned in full force. Where was she?

"Are you sure?" Claire asked.

"Positive," Hailey answered. "My boss specifically spoke to me about how to handle the calls. My boss also said, 'Don't you even think about pulling that no-show bullshit.' He can be a real asshole."

"Yeah, he sounds like it. Have you tried calling her?" Claire asked.

"Yeah, I have," Hailey responded. "I texted her at like 6 o'clock last night thinking she might be up for a quick pre-work-week drink at The Inn. Never responded. I called her this morning when I found out she was out. I was thinking that maybe she had Covid or something … my brother is just getting over it and it was a really nasty few days for him. But again … nothing."

"Ok, Hailey. Thanks," Claire responded, swallowing over the nerves.

"You think she's ok, right?" Hailey asked, her light-hearted demeanor revealing a bit of genuine concern.

"I hope so," Claire answered. "Thank you. Bye," and then she hung up the phone.

Claire immediately and on instinct called Mia again … she had the digits memorized by this point. This time, the phone went straight to voicemail. What did that mean? Was her phone off? Silenced? Had it lost its charge? So many possibilities.

Images of that silver car flashed behind Claire's eyelids. Was she being paranoid? Maybe? Maybe Mia had simply come down with Covid, and was sleeping it off. But maybe not. Claire willed herself to suppress her panic. She had a presentation to deliver in ten minutes, and there was no way she could avoid it.

Ok, she said to herself. *Let me get through this meeting … it will probably be over at around noon. Then, on my lunch break, I'll drive over to her apartment and see what's up.*

The fact that she had a plan allowed Claire to give her notes one last, critical glance before beginning the Zoom meeting. Plastering a fake smile on her face, she pressed the 'Start Meeting' icon.

Chapter Fifty-One

MIA

As the knob rotated in Mia's damp hands, she could feel the lock mechanism engage, preventing her from entering the bay house. But despite the resistance, Mia could tell it was flimsy. Without further hesitation, Mia used her hip to force the door open; it didn't require much effort at all ... just two or three thumps. Squeaking, the old door swung in.

With tentative steps, Mia entered the dimly lit room.

She called softly, "Hello? Jimmy, are you here? I want to help you."

The soft orangey glow from the rising sun shone through the front windows, allowing the objects in the room–if you would call it a room–to materialize before her eyes. The place was pretty stark. A row of ramshackle cabinetry lined the side wall. The high planked ceiling was peaked, and it allowed muted light to shine through the cracks.

Before she could really take it all in, from a far corner, she heard a small voice, "Who are you?"

The sound startled her; maybe she thought the house would be empty. Maybe she hoped it would be. She whirled around.

With her heart pounding in her ears, she said, "My name is Mia. I'm a good friend of your mom. Are you Jimmy?"

"My mom doesn't know anyone named Mia," the boy replied.

Mia approached slowly, not wanting to frighten him any more than she probably already had. As she got closer, she got a good look at him. He was standing up in a protective stance–arms crossed over his chest trying to hide the figure wrapped up in a blanket on the bench behind him. He looked skinny, pale. Mia could perceive his cheekbones protruding slightly from beneath his hollow eyes. In her mind, she compared his face to the smiling image on the television screen. The freckles were still starkly visible across his nose, despite the grime caked to his ears and in the corners of his eyes. His hair was longer and there were no dimples, but it was undoubtedly the same person. It was Jimmy Benicek. Her friend's son–the missing boy. Mia's heart fluttered in her ribcage.

Mia responded to his statement, "Your mom didn't know me until recently. I found her necklace in the ocean by my house and gave it back to her. We have been friends ever since."

A spark of life entered Jimmy's eyes as he said, "You found her necklace? It was in my pocket. I thought I lost it."

Another odd fact that Mia could puzzle over later.

"I did," she responded. "It has your initials on it."

Tears spilled from the boy's eyes and rolled down his cheeks, leaving a clean track in the accumulated dirt.

"Is she mad at me for taking it?" Jimmy asked, barely able to keep his lips from trembling with emotion.

"No. She's not mad at you. She misses you. She loves you and wants you to come home."

Mia watched as the boy cried softly, shoulders shaking up and down, trembling fingers wiping at his streaming eyes. Mia moved towards him to offer some comfort, but he flinched a bit so she stopped and instead, kneeled before him so her eyes were level with his.

A bit of movement behind Jimmy caught Mia's eye, followed by a soft whimper.

Mia's eyes flicked back to Jimmy and she asked, "Is that Kyle, laying on the bench behind you?"

"Yes," he replied. "He doesn't feel good. He's sick."

"Can I look at him?" Mia asked.

Jimmy hesitantly moved a bit to the side and Mia approached the bundle. She pulled the blanket down a bit from Kyle's face to inspect. Her breath caught in her throat. Kyle was staring back at her from glassy eyes narrowed to slits as a result of the crust and pus mixing with the grime that had accumulated. His lips were terribly raw and chapped–there was a cut that had not scabbed over yet in the corner of his mouth, and dried green mucus was caked over his nostrils. She could feel the feverish warmth radiating off of him.

Having no idea what else to do, she leaned close and whispered in his ear, "You're going to be ok. I'm gonna get you guys out of here." She desperately hoped that she could make good on her promise.

Kyle answered in a raspy whisper, "I want to go home."

Mia tried to suppress the tears that threatened to drown her and turned her attention back to Jimmy.

"How long has he been sick for?"

"It started a while ago. Yesterday he got real bad. Is he going to be ok?"

Mia ignored that last bit. She had no idea if he would be ok, or how to get these boys the hell out of here. They were surrounded by water–completely isolated. Her cell phone was gone; who knows if it actually would have worked out here anyway? What is cell service like in the middle of nowhere? No time to dwell on the 'what-ifs.'

"Are you hurt?" she asked Jimmy.

"No ... well, not really. My finger kinda hurts."

Jimmy held out his infected finger to Mia. It seemed like he was warming up to her. Mia carefully took the boy's hand in her own. The wound didn't look great ... actually, it was downright gross. A gray tint had traveled up towards his wrist and the cut itself was festering. *Shit*, she thought.

"Kinda hurts?" she repeated. "It looks like it really hurts."

"I got used to it. It's not so bad," Jimmy replied.

"You're really brave. You know that?"

"I'm not that brave. Not like Superman or anything."

"Don't sell yourself short," she replied. "Most kids couldn't survive what you survived."

"I miss my mom and dad," he said simply. "I want them. I want to go home."

"I'm going to try my hardest to make that happen," Mia responded.

Escape scenarios unspooled through her mind. But, when it came down to it, without a boat, there was no way out. She walked over to the canoe that had been propped up on a few cinder blocks in the center of the room.

"That's broken," Jimmy said as if he could sense her thought process. "There's a big hole in the middle."

There goes that idea, Mia said to herself.

The sunlight streamed, warm and bright, through the windows and open door. For the first time, Mia felt a bit of warmth return to her fingertips. She had almost forgotten about the fact that she was cold and wet–and damn lucky to even be alive.

"That's not good," Jimmy said, alarm rising in his voice.

"What's not good?" Mia asked, puzzled.

"Whenever the sun looks like that, that's when Sir and Ma'am come here."

"What do you mean?" Mia asked, even though she thought she already knew.

"Sir and Ma'am come every morning to bring us breakfast. They're gonna be mad if they find you here," he tried to explain.

And before Mia really had time to process the information she had just been told, or the implications such knowledge could have for her, she heard the unmistakable whirring of an approaching boat.

Chapter Fifty-Two

JOE

What the hell am I doing? Joe thought to himself as he sat in his car outside his house ... not his apartment, but his home. The one he used to share with Claire and Jimmy. But that was before this nightmare happened. Before their son had disappeared.

He hadn't gone into the office today because he had two client meetings: one this morning at 9am in Queens and another at 2pm in Merrick. It was 11:30 now, and he had some time to kill.

Claire's car was there. Maybe she was also working from home today. He hadn't dared park in the driveway. It didn't feel like it was even his anymore. Maybe it wasn't. Nothing was official yet, but no matter what happened with the divorce, he wasn't going to kick Claire out of the house. She didn't deserve that.

Whenever he thought about the word "divorce" it was in all capital letters. D-I-V-O-R-C-E. Such an ominous word. So final. So permanent. To Joe Benicek, it was a word that reeked of failure. And despite all their efforts, they *had* failed. Hadn't they? They hadn't been able to take care of the one thing that meant more to both of them than anything else in the world. Their son, Jimmy. Joe was aware that in his thoughts, he had just used the word "they." "They" had failed. Not "she." In the beginning, it had been so easy to blame Claire. But now, he wasn't so sure he blamed her anymore. Had she really done anything all *that* wrong? Joe didn't know anymore. He didn't know anything anymore.

He turned the car off and listened to the tick of the engine cooling. Did he have the balls to go in? He still had the house keys. Had Claire changed the locks? He didn't think that she would do that. Especially because he hadn't made any effort to even step foot in that house since he walked out all those weeks ... all those months ago.

What would he even say to Claire if he did have the guts to go in? *Hey, Claire. How've you been? Sorry I was such a dick to you.* Would that work? A bitter laugh escaped him. Was he even sorry? He didn't know that either.

With a final sigh, Joe started the car back up again. He wasn't going to just barge in on her. That was a privilege he had lost when he walked out. Instead, he decided to head over to his next meeting. Maybe they would be ready before 2. And if they weren't, he could always just zone out to the classic rock station on *Sirius XM* and let nostalgia take him away.

Chapter Fifty-Three

MIA

Oh, shit, Mia thought to herself as the whirring sound of the boat got louder. Bob and Dee must be pretty close. Her heart was beating so hard and quick that for a minute there, she thought she might be having a heart attack. *Wouldn't that be a happy ending*? she said aloud. She put her fingers to her mouth to indicate to Jimmy that he should keep quiet–hopefully he understood the message–and ran towards the side of the structure ... the opposite side from which the noise was coming from. She pushed open the side window; it slammed upwards with surprising force, breaking the pane of glass encased within. *Oh, God. Good thing for the noise of the boat motor ... otherwise they definitely would have heard that.* Carefully, she climbed out of the open square, mindful to keep her palms away from the remaining shards. Once outside, she pushed the window down and pushed her back against the side of the house next to it, just as she heard the front door of the bay house squeak open. *They're here*, she thought, exhaling a deep breath and trying to calm her fluttering nerves.

She thought about descending back into the water to conceal herself more fully, but she worried that the noise of her footsteps on the crumbling dock would give her away. And there were so

235

many loose boards, what if she fell? Splashing sounds would definitely alert Bob and Dee to her presence. And then what help would she be? She remained, frozen in place–exposed and terrified.

The broken window allowed her to hear a bit of what was going on inside.

Bob's unmistakable voice came to her ears, "Brought you two McDonald's today. Hope you like Egg McMuffins."

The rustling of a paper bag, muted, but unmistakable. Mia's stomach grumbled loudly. She hadn't eaten since she had been on the boat with Dee and Bob, and that measly sandwich had definitely coursed through her system by now, leaving her not only cold and wet, but starving.

"Tonight's the night, boys," Dee spoke. "The night when you finally get to where you're supposed to be." She sounded chipper, energetic.

"We want to go home," Mia heard Jimmy boldly say. *God, that kid is impressive*, she thought.

"You are going home. To a new one. A better one. With parents that will appreciate you, hopefully," Dee said with an edge to her tone.

"My mom and dad do appreciate me," Jimmy responded. "And Kyle is very, very sick. He needs medicine."

Bob retorted, "I'm sure he'll get all the medical care he needs soon enough–"

"Hey," Dee interrupted. "What happened to that window over there?"

Oh, no, Mia held her breath.

"I thought I told you two to stay away from the windows," Dee continued.

Her voice was getting louder, telling Mia that she was approaching. Mia held her breath and pushed her body into the wall, hoping that she would actually melt into the soggy, damp shingles behind her back and disappear. If Dee looked out the window and to her right, Mia was done for. She would undoubtedly be seen. Looking around, there was nothing she could use to defend herself. But if it came down to it, she would fight. She was younger than they were. And she had the element of surprise on her side. Could she take them both? Maybe one at a time? She was exhausted, but she would try. If she had to, she would try. Mia closed her eyes tightly, her only defense against what was to come.

Then, from inside, she heard Jimmy say, "Oh, I'm sorry, Ma'am. I was playing with my plastic SpongeBob and I launched him too hard. He broke the window."

"I told you to be easy with those stupid toys," Dee said. She was retreating; the sound of her voice was getting more muted.

Thank God. Mia exhaled softly.

"Guess it doesn't matter anyways. We'll be out of here soon enough," Dee said lightly.

Bob spoke up, "Well, eat up, boys. Next time we come back, it's gonna be with a man who's gonna take you to your new home. It's gonna be late, so I suggest taking a nap. And don't even think about causing a fuss. No one wants to take care of a bad boy." He continued, "You don't want to end up dumped in the ocean."

Mia shifted her weight from foot to foot too afraid to even breathe. She couldn't believe that Bob could say that last bit to little boys ... but then again, she only *thought* she knew him, didn't she? After what she estimated to be about a half an hour ... although it could have been longer, or shorter, the conversation picked back up.

"We better get out of here, Bob. We gotta go wait for that phone call, and there's no service here." And then Dee spoke again, "Alright, boys. Gimme all your trash."

"I'm not done eating," Jimmy said.

"Let him keep his sandwich, Dee," Bob replied. "It doesn't matter."

Mia could hear Bob's and Dee's footsteps as they walked to the front of the house. A closing door. A few minutes later, she heard the click of the engine starting and then the fading sound of the boat as it went back the way it had come.

For good measure, Mia forced herself to count to 100 before she climbed back into the bay house, and each of those seconds felt like an eternity.

Once she was back inside, she turned around and facing Jimmy, she said, "Superman's got nothing on you."

"What does that mean?" he asked, gazing earnestly up at her.

"It means that you're the bravest, strongest kid I know," Mia explained

"Thanks," he said sheepishly. For the first time, Mia saw his crooked smile light up his face.

"What should we do now?" Jimmy asked plaintively.

"I don't know," Mia responded honestly. "We have to get out of here before they come back."

But how? she said to herself. They were in the middle of the marshland, with no means of communication. She certainly couldn't lead Jimmy and Kyle over the reeds, as she had done to reach the bay house. Kyle for sure, didn't have the strength for that type of journey. And she had no idea how far away they were from any type of civilization ... nor how deep the water spanned. *Think. Think.* What about the other bay houses? She gazed out the window. She could just make out one white structure on the horizon. Definitely too far away ... and who knew if anyone was even in there? From the brief look she had glimpsed of it on Bob's and Dee's boat, it looked pretty deserted. She couldn't chance it.

I have to do something, she thought. The room was pretty stark. Not much here that could help. Too bad that damn canoe was broken; it would have come in handy. She scanned every inch of that room, and even looked in the back room and makeshift bathroom: nothing. *Shit.* Then, her eyes settled on the Egg McMuffin in Jimmy's hand. She had an idea. It wasn't much. A long-shot at best ... and cliché as hell. But it was better than nothing.

The ocean had saved her life yesterday. And it had taken her this far in her journey to return Jimmy and Kyle to their parents. There was a purpose in it all ... *she* had a purpose. Whatever powers were at work here, they wouldn't get her so close and then allow her to fail. She knew that now and could accept the crazed truth of the matter. Maybe the water would help her one more time. Just one more time. She could make things right. She could help these boys, help her friend. So with a desperate plea to whatever forces were listening, Mia Rossi took her chance.

Chapter Fifty-Four

CLAIRE

It was about 1pm–that damn Zoom meeting went longer than Claire had expected. She had even cut the Q&A section short in an attempt to encourage the attendees to leave the chat sooner. She already had her flip flops on and her keys in hand as she clicked the "End Meeting" icon at the bottom of the screen. Mia hadn't returned her calls or responded to her texts, and that combined with Hailey's information about Mia having been a no-show at work today, made Claire's pulse throb rapidly in her neck. *Enough of this waiting*, Claire said to herself. *I'm going to take a drive to her apartment.*

Claire paid no mind to her ridiculous attire–top half in work clothes, bottom half in sweatpants–and grabbing her purse off the living room sofa, raced out the front door of her house. Something felt wrong ... off, in a way that Claire couldn't explain.

Starting her car, Claire opened up the windows to get some air on her flushed face and pulled out of her driveway, into the quiet backroads of her development, and onto Long Beach Road headed south. She didn't need to put the address into her navigation ... she had eaten–and gotten drunk–at Minnesota's many times, especially before she had Jimmy and knew that Mia's apartment was just down the road, a house or two from the beach entrance. It was crazy to think that she had never even been to Mia's apartment; Mia had been to her home so many times. The thought made Claire feel a bit guilty. Should she have made more of an effort to go see Mia, instead of the other way around? Maybe. *Well ... I'm going there now. I'm sure she will show me around when she answers the door*, Claire thought hopefully. She tried to swallow the doubt that she felt creeping up her throat.

It wasn't hard to find a spot on the street on a Monday afternoon, and by 1:20 Claire was already parked directly across from Mia's house. The first thing she noticed was the "For Sale" sign with the rectangular panel over it reading "Sold" stuck into the front lawn. Suppressing the urge to run, she quickly ascended the side staircase leading up to the second floor. Impatiently, Claire rapped on the door. Nothing. She knocked again, louder and more insistent this time. No answer. Using her hands as a shield against the glare, Claire bent down and peered into the small window pane on the door. It was dark inside. Tentatively, with her panic rising, she turned the doorknob. Locked. *Shit*, Claire thought to herself. *Where the hell is she?*

Claire flew back down the staircase and stopped in front of the house. Not knowing what to do, she looked around—as if she would find the answer in the windows of the other houses lining Minnesota Avenue. Her vision caught sight of something that stopped her heart. There, on the other side of the street and down a few houses, was a Honda CRV in the same smoky gray color as Mia's. *It's not her car*, Claire reassured herself aloud. *Mia isn't here, and she's not at work; she probably went back to Sparta to see her family and didn't tell anyone. She's probably driving there right now and that's why she isn't answering her phone.* Slowly, Claire walked over to the car, wanting but not wanting to know. She peered into the window and saw the unmistakably familiar sight of the daisy air freshener that Mia had hanging from the rearview mirror. Then, as if that didn't give away the identity of the vehicle's owner, she noticed the New Jersey license plates. Claire's stomach sank. Despite the fact that she was trying to convince herself that this was all coincidence–there must be other people from Jersey that drive a gray Honda CRV with a daisy air freshener that live on Minnesota Avenue, right?–logic told her that this was absolutely Mia's car. Where the hell was she?

With a sag in her shoulders, Claire walked back to the house. What more could she do? It seemed as though Mia had up and vanished into thin air ... just like Jimmy did. Then, something else caught her eye. How had she not noticed it before? It was right there ... in the driveway. A silver sedan. Claire's pulse fluttered. She moved closer to get a better view. *Hey,* Claire thought. *This car looks a lot like—.* Her eyes focused on the license plate. It read: BLK-D30X. BL. Her mind made the connection before she could really process it. BL ... BL ... BL ... The first two letters of the license plate on the silver car. THE silver car that had been showing up lately–showing up mostly when Mia was around. Could it be the same car? The idea punched her in the gut as thoughts swirled around her jumbled mind. What did it all mean?

With a newfound strength, Claire walked up the front path and knocked on the front door. Mia had told her that Bob and Dee (were those their names?), the landlords, lived directly below her. It had to be their car ... why else would it be parked in the driveway? She rapped three times. No answer. She tried again for good measure. Only silence greeted her. What was she supposed to do? Bust down the door? That seemed a bit excessive, didn't it? She stepped to the side and peered through the window. The room within was swathed in darkness, although ... was that a light on back there? Claire walked slowly around the side of the house on legs that felt like they belonged to someone else. What was she doing? Trespassing in someone else's yard? But she didn't care. Her instincts were screaming at her and she intended to listen. She stood in the dirt of the back garden to try to get a view into the house, and then on the walkway leading to the fenced-in yard, peering inside with a scrutiny that surprised her. Despite a small opening in the blinds of what looked like a bedroom, every other window greeted her with drawn curtains.

She made her way back to the front of the house; it felt like a caged bird was flapping its wings in the recesses of her mind. She just couldn't put it all together. She needed to think. Looking to her right, she saw the wooden stairs leading up to a planked walkway. What better place to unwind your spinning thoughts than on the sand?

She ascended the steps and once the sand engulfed the footboards, she shed her flip flops that she had hastily thrown on before she left the house and proceeded barefoot down towards the ocean. The sun warmed her face, and there was a slight breeze in the air that filled her nostrils. It had gone on and become summer without Claire even knowing it ... well, technically, the first day of summer was still a few weeks away, but she could sense its rapid approach. Aside from a couple of picnickers in the distance, Claire was alone on this stretch of the beach. She stood in front of the swirling waters and thought about what it must have been like for Mia to stand in this same spot and receive those cryptic messages from some otherworldly source. It must have been terrifying ... and exhilarating. Rolling her sweatpants up to her knees, Claire waded in the ocean, relishing the cool feel of the water colliding with her ankles and shins, brushing up against the back of her calves.

She felt her trembling soul begin to calm, and she was able to think more rationally. Mia hadn't responded to any of her texts or calls ... and she wasn't at work; she hadn't shown up. She wasn't at home either, despite the fact that her car was parked a couple of houses away. And then there was that disconcerting silver car resting in the driveway. Claire supposed that there must be a million silver cars with license plate numbers beginning with BL. But still, what an eerie coincidence. Joe's voice played in her head, *Stop being a helicopter mom. You're being paranoid.* Was that what this was? Paranoia? Or perhaps grief? Maybe. But if it wasn't that ... if this was real, was Mia in some sort of danger? And shouldn't she try to find out? Her instincts answered yes to both.

Claire's gaze, which had been fixed skyward, traveled down

when she felt something thud softly against the side of her right calf. A plastic coke bottle. Anger bloomed inside her, *How dare people just throw their trash in the ocean.* But then she looked more closely. The label had been peeled off, so aside from a few tacky remnants, she could see inside. Was there something in there? She picked up the bottle and held it in front of her face. Yes. There definitely was. The cap was secured tightly and for a minute there, Claire didn't think she would be able to open it. Using her shirt to dry off her damp hands, she twisted counter-clockwise and felt it give. She had to dig inside with her fingers to reach the piece of brown curled up paper below the narrow neck of the bottle, but she secured it between her pointer and middle fingers and managed to pull it out. From the look of it, it was a piece of a McDonald's bag or wrapper. She could see the logo along with darker grease splotches along one end. She turned it over in her hands. Just as Claire was about to dismiss this as mere garbage, she was able to make out some writing in between two grease patches. The letters were very light and written in a pencil that must have been exceedingly dull. She had to read the words twice before her mind could process them, before she could believe them. It was impossible ... and ridiculous ... and miraculous. Her hands shook violently as she read the words out loud:

Help! Brown bay house. Reynolds Channel. Jimmy Benicek.

Could it be true? A message in a bottle? But Claire didn't have time to ponder the cliched beauty of the thing. Nor did she pause to consider how it had come to wash up exactly where she had stood. Or if it was intended for her? Or if it had anything to do with Mia Rossi, even though Claire very much thought it did ... it had to. She would think about those things for years and decades to come. But now, she needed to act. And that's exactly what she did.

Chapter Fifty-Five

DEE

"Why the hell was that woman knocking on our door?" Dee asked.

"What woman?" Bob responded.

Bob had been napping on the living room sofa. Ever since they had … disposed … of Mia, he had been extraordinarily sleepy.

"Claire Benicek. She was just here. Snooping around in the yard too. I hid in the bathroom."

That made Bob sit up straight.

"Well, what'd she want?" Bob asked.

"I don't know, Bob. I didn't answer the door when she knocked. Good thing most of the lights were out," Dee spat back.

Yes, Bob had done his job … had helped with the "Mia situation," as Dee had called it and he had contacted McGivern like he was supposed to late last night, but he was starting to annoy her in a way that he never had before. The extreme stress of this business made her edgy and tense.

"Well, tonight's the night," Bob tried to reassure Dee. "By 2am those boys and us will be long gone."

Despite her near-frenetic excitement regarding the thought of getting her hands on their baby, a bit of anxiety nagged at Dee.

Murder was never in her plans, and quite frankly, the fact that she was even capable of it surprised her. She had thought that once they dealt with Mia, the rest of it would be a cake-walk. But now, there was that nosy, snooping Claire Benicek to think about.

"I don't know, Bob. I'm worried. Imagine that after we waited so long and worked so hard it were to all fall apart? I couldn't survive a disappointment like that."

"That won't happen, Dee," Bob responded, getting up on creaking knees. "It's all set. McGivern and his crew are gonna meet us at the bay house at midnight to make the swap. The car's all packed. As soon as we dock back in Point Lookout, we're gonna hightail it south ... baby in tow."

"Are you sure you gave him the right information, Bob?" Dee asked.

"Why do you always doubt me?" Bob responded.

"Because you're a scatterbrain," Dee replied.

Bob's anger boiled, "I helped you kill a woman last night ... an innocent one! We threw her off a boat, Dee. Goddam, I never thought I'd be able to do anything like that. And you're going to call me a scatterbrain?"

"Well, what do you want? A trophy. It's for us, Bob. We put ourselves first. Always."

"I know that," huffed Bob. "Just remember, without this scatterbrain right here, none of this would be happening. Give me some goddamn credit."

When Dee didn't respond, Bob said, "Just make sure you're all packed. I'll worry about the rest."

"Yeah, yeah," Dee responded. "Don't worry about me. I'm prepared."And then in a lighter tone, "Think it'll be a girl or a boy? We better have two names picked out."

"I don't know, Dee," Bob replied. "What are you hoping for?"

Dee thought for a minute before responding.

"I don't care what it is ... so long as it's ours," Dee said with finality.

Chapter Fifty-Six

CLAIRE

Claire blew at least three traffic lights as she raced to the Long Beach Police Department. She didn't care about tickets, red-light cameras. Fuck it. None of that mattered to her as she impatiently jockeyed for position behind lackadaisical drivers. She honked the horn, yelled out the window, and got flipped off a few times on her way down Long Beach Road. Claire didn't even recognize herself. *Come on. Come on. Move it,* she said aloud through pursed lips.

After what felt like an hour, she careened into the parking lot and pulled her car into one of the handicapped spots directly in front of the station. Heart racing, with one hand, she grabbed the bottle with the message inside and with the other hand, she grabbed her purse. Slamming the car door closed, Claire flew up the front steps and burst through the glass double doors like she was on fire. She *was* on fire. Every single fiber in her body was tingling, electric. She was surprised that sparks weren't flying out of her fingers. She didn't bother with the check-in desk; that would take too long and she knew exactly where Sergeant Lackey's office was. He better be there.

"Excuse me, ma'am," she heard behind her as she walked directly to the end of the lobby, towards the door leading to the

247

back offices. "Ma'am, you cannot go back there without being explicitly called."

Claire knew the rules, but she didn't give a shit. Her erratic behavior had alerted the security guard and both he and the lady behind the desk walked towards her as she turned the handle to the back door.

Sensing their approaching presence, Claire said, "I have to talk to Sergeant Lackey ... right now. I can't wait. Please–"

"But ma'am—"

Sergeant Lackey saved her at that moment as he peeked his face out of the office and called, "What's going on out there?" And then his presence filled the hallway. "Mrs. Benicek?"

"I need to talk to you. Urgently," Claire said to him as an explanation.

"Ed, Janet," he said, addressing the two flustered figures behind her. He held a sandwich in his hand and, wiping a bit of mayonnaise off his chin, said, "It's ok. Let her come on back."

Claire turned around gratefully, tears threatening to stream from her eyes, "Thank you. Thank you so much."

Claire walked into Sergeant Lackey's office.

"Have a seat. Let me just clear off–"

Before he could even finish, Claire spoke hastily, "I have a lead that you have to check out."

Sergeant Lackey put his sandwich down on the paper plate before him and looked up at her from behind his desk. "What kind of lead?"

Claire almost threw the bottle at him.

"What is this?" he said, holding the item like it was garbage, which technically it was.

"Open it," Claire instructed.

He did.

"Now take out that piece of paper," Claire continued.

"What exactly is–"

"Just take it out. You'll see."

She watched as the sergeant tried to squeeze his fingers

through the narrow neck of the bottle, his thick knuckles preventing him from reaching in.

"Gimme it," Claire said impatiently. "I'll do it."

She snatched the bottle out of his hands, slid the paper out and thrust it into Sergeant Lackey's open hands.

"Mrs. Benicek," he began. "I don't underst–"

"Look at it," Claire said. "Read what it says ... no. Other side."

Sergeant Lackey turned the paper over. "I don't see anythi–"

"Just look. Between those grease stains. It's very light."

Putting on a pair of glasses, the detective held the paper out away from his face. His lips moved silently over the words printed in dull block letters.

"Where did this come from?" he asked when he was done reading. His tone had changed from skeptical to serious ... as did his gaze.

"It washed up at the beach ... about 15, no, 20 or so minutes ago. You have to check it out."

"Mrs. Benicek ... this is ... a very strange message and–"

"I know. I'm aware that it's strange. It's crazy. A message in a bottle. I know how it sounds. I do. But I'm not crazy. We've been looking for Jimmy for weeks now ... months. And this is the first scrap of real evidence that we've gotten. Do not tell me it is not worth it to at least check it out–" Claire's impassioned speech flowed out of her in a rush of emotion. An accusation.

Sergeant Lackey looked at her; she could actually see the cogs in his brain turning behind his eyes.

"I agree, Mrs. Benicek. It is definitely worth investigating," he responded.

With that little bit of reassurance, Claire allowed herself to collapse into the leather chair opposite the sergeant's desk. Placing her head in her hands, she cried stormily as Sergeant Lackey made a phone call.

"Hello. Can you please connect me with the Point Lookout extension of the Coast Guard? No. I don't want to call back. I'll hold," he spoke into the receiver.

A long pause.

"Hello? Yes. It's Sergeant Lackey over in Long Beach. I need an escort out." Pause.

"Uh-huh. Yes. Today."

He gazed over at Claire, "Actually, right now. I need an escort as absolutely soon as humanly possible. Got a lead in a missing person's case."

Relief flooded Claire; he believed her.

Another pause. He glanced up at the clock hanging on the wall behind him.

"30 minutes. Yep. That works. We'll be there. Thank you."

Claire looked up at him, "What's happening? Are they going to help us? Are they going to take us to the bay house?"

Her fingers found the locket that rested at the base of her throat and she pushed her thumb into that worn-down comfortable spot. She held her breath.

"Yes. Let's go," he ordered.

Claire and Sergeant Lackey piled into the patrol car; she had never ridden in one before, and the knobs and electronic mechanisms were jarring.

He spoke tentatively. "I'd advise you not to get your hopes too high up," he said. "... if I thought you'd listen."

"You're right. I wouldn't listen to that advice, Sergeant," Claire replied, but not in a scornful tone. "A mother never loses hope."

He gave a brief chuckle at that and said, "Well, let's just cross our fingers, toes, and anything else we have to cross, that you're right."

Claire sent a quick text to Joe to give him a short update; he deserved to know, right? Their crumbling marriage didn't negate the fact that he was still Jimmy's father. And then, before she secured her phone back in her bag, she texted Trish Yardsleigh too. It didn't matter that the woman hated her. This mattered more. A whole lot more.

"Might as well switch that phone off," the sergeant advised.

"No service out on those waters. And private cell devices could potentially impact coast guard radar. Not my rules."

Claire didn't need to be told twice. She powered her phone off as they pulled up to a dock surrounded by a barbed wire fence and gate labeled U.S. Coast Guard. She was ready.

Chapter Fifty-Seven

MIA

Kneeling in front of Kyle, Mia tried to clean the goo out of his nose and eyes with her sleeve, which was now dirty and had dried stiff after being wet for so long. She wished she had some antibiotics ... hell, she would have even welcomed some Tylenol to ease the heat pulsing off him in throbbing waves that she could almost feel. A simple tissue would have also been nice. But beggars can't be choosers. She rolled her eyes as her mom's cheesy saying came to mind. She succeeded in freeing up Kyle's nasal passages, but his eyes ... she didn't want to hurt him by rubbing too hard.

Sitting down in between the two, she felt Jimmy slip his small hand into hers. Such a tiny thing. But it brought a surge of warmth straight into her heart. She could not fail. It was almost unreal to Mia to think that she was sitting here with Claire's son—this elusive boy that she had heard so much about and had spent so much time thinking about over the course of the past months.

Mia wished that she had a better concept of the time. How long had she been here? Minutes? Hours? It felt like it could have been days; time was certainly crawling along. The tilt of the sun had changed and if she had to guess, she would say that it was late afternoon. But she couldn't really be sure. She was no expert at interpreting solar positioning.

She had felt so hopeful when she tossed that bottle into the water–optimistic that the ocean had some stake in the outcome of this whole thing. That it would assist her somehow, protect her. But now, the longer she sat there with these two little boys, that hope about her message reaching someone, anyone began to wane. God, what a fool she was. Maybe she had been stupid; maybe it had been a waste of time.

In her mind, she tried to think of some other way. *Any* other way out of here. Some other way to save not only these two little boys, but herself as well. She felt so useless, just sitting here and not doing anything–so completely stuck. She had to do some-thing. Getting up, she gazed out the side window. She could see one other bay house way off in the distance. She had no idea how far away it was exactly; she had never been good at estimating distance, but it certainly wasn't close. Maybe a mile, two miles? Farther? She had no idea. It was hard to tell when the only other judges of proximity were the marsh grass, the gulls flying overhead and the endless blue water standing in between. However, she knew that she couldn't just wait here indefinitely. That was suicide.

A tiny plan hatched within her desperate mind and Mia made a deal with herself. If help didn't arrive within the next hour–or at least what she could estimate as an hour without a watch or clock–she would leave the boys and venture out for help. She could not chance leaving and letting the boys be taken while she was gone. Before night fell, she would crawl over the reeds to that bay house in the distance. Maybe someone would be there ... if not, maybe there would be a boat attached to the dock, or a phone connected to some wall. Something to help, ANYTHING. It would be easier to move over the swampy terrain now without her wrists and ankles bound, at least she hoped it would be. And she would pray, PRAY that she could get help before Bob and Dee returned. When she had overheard Bob and Dee talking to the boys, they had said that it would be "late" by the time they came back. What did "late" mean? Mia didn't know. There was still daylight in the sky, but the sun seemed to be moving rapidly across the vast expanse of blue overhead. She couldn't wait too long.

Chapter Fifty-Eight

TRISH

> I'm going to find our boys. Point Lookout
> Coast Guard Extension Pier 2

Read an incoming text from Claire Benicek. Claire Benicek. God. Trish hadn't expected to see that name flash up on her phone screen. She texted back:

> What the fuck does that mean?

No response.
She tried again:

> Claire. If you know where Kyle is, if you have
> any updates whatsoever, tell me right now!

Again nothing. What the hell? Who just texts someone something like THAT and then doesn't respond? It had been a half an hour since Trish first received that bizarre text from Claire. Half an hour since she ran out of her house headed towards Pier Two as Claire mentioned in her cryptic message.

Trish tried to think of the last time she had even laid eyes on that woman. It must have been about two weeks ago in ShopRite

... on the deli line. Claire had tried to meet Trish's gaze with those earnest eyes of hers; Trish had just looked away. She tried to swallow both the memory and the encroaching guilt as she slammed on her brakes and rolled down her window in front of the barbed wire fence.

"I need to speak with someone immediately," Trish said to the officer dressed in blue at the little checkpoint kiosk positioned outside the gate of what was apparently a branch of the U.S. Coast Guard—at least that was what the sign said.

Straining her eyes to peer beyond, all she could see was a structure, or more accurately a compound. It looked like a school made of stucco—rectangular, flat, unremarkable.

"Hello, ma'am. Name?" the guard asked, completely nonplussed.

"My name is Patricia Yardsleigh," she replied, the panic rising in her voice. "I was told to come here regarding my son, Kyle Yardsleigh. I'm told that there has been some new development—"

"Give me a minute, ma'am," he said, picking up an intercom.

"I have a Mrs. Yardsleigh here, looking for information on her son ... yes, sir. Ok. Yes, sir. I'll relay the message," the guard spoke into the speaker.

Then the guard addressed Trish again, "You can pull your car just over there and wait for Sergeant Lackey and the Coast Guard to return." He motioned with his hand to a small lot next to the dock.

"But—," Trish sputtered. "...what's going on? Has someone found my son? Has someone found Kyle?"

"We are not authorized to provide any information on any cases not manned by our outpost here. And quite frankly, ma'am, we don't know too much."

"But I'm his mother. He's been missing for months. I have a right to know!" Trish was almost incoherent with emotion. "Can't you get in touch with them? You have to be able to tell me something ... ANYTHING."

"I understand your frustration. But it's the best we can do. Please go and wait in the allotted area, ma'am."

If he calls me ma'am one more time I'm going to lose my fucking mind, Trish thought to herself. *And did he say he understands my ... frustration? He has absolutely no fucking idea what I'm feeling right now.*

But because she had nothing else to do, she put her car in reverse and eased her huge, shiny Escalade into one of the narrow parking spaces in the small lot. Throwing her car into Park, she closed her eyes, resting her head on the plush leather headrest behind her. Her heart hammered in her heaving chest. She needed to breathe. In ... and Out. In and Out. In. Out. She felt her respiration slow as she gulped air into her lungs. In her rush to leave the house after she received Claire's text, she hadn't even thought to grab her purse ... which unfortunately meant that her pills were too far out of reach to offer their quiet comfort. Damn. The need coursing through her bones made her feel shaky, and a headache was already starting to form at the base of her skull. What the hell was this all about? Impatience assaulted her, and it took every ounce of her strength to will herself to wait. There was nothing else she *could* do.

A soft tapping on her window startled her. She sat up straight in her seat and looked out. Joe Benicek's grim face filled her vision. *I guess he got Claire's text too*, she thought as she rolled down the glass pane. She hadn't seen him since that awful Ceremony of Life.

"Hey, Trish," he said.

"What the fuck is your wife doing?" she asked. "Where is she? Has she found Kyle?" The questions gushed forth untethered.

"I have no idea. I just got this text." Joe turned his phone around to show Trish his phone screen.

"Yeah," she said. "I got the same one."

Joe ran his fingers through his hair and looked around. Trish wondered when it had turned so gray.

When Joe didn't speak, Trish continued, "What the hell is

going on? Claire better have a damn good reason to send such a cryptic text. I mean ... what the hell is wrong with her? Couldn't she have given us some more information instead of just–"

"Whoa. How about you just cool it, Trish? You have no idea why she did what she did. Maybe she really has found them somehow ... God knows how. Or at least maybe she got some information. Claire wouldn't just send us that text for no reason. And God ... she definitely didn't have to do that ... text US, I mean. Not after how terrible we have been to her–"

"Jesus, Joe. SHE is the one responsible for what happened. Don't give me that bullshit about how WE treated her. SHE deserves it ALL. She just fucking left Kyle ... and Jimmy ALONE–"

"Yeah. That's true, Trish. But what about the time we were at your house and WE ALL left them alone to ride bikes or scooters or whatever in front of YOUR house, while we were ALL drinking margaritas in your backyard? Couldn't this have happened then too? Then whose fault would it have been?"

Trish didn't know what to say or how to answer, but her anger was running out of steam.

"I don't know, Joe," Trish managed to spit out. "I just don't know."

Trish was absolutely not going to dwell on the what ifs. It DIDN'T happen at her house. It happened at Claire's house. It was HER fault.

But she wasn't going to argue about it with Joe, so instead she said, "Whatever. Wanna get in and we can at least wait together? Whatever the hell THIS is."

After a moment of thought, Joe spoke again, "Nah. I think I'm gonna go wait in my car over there."

"Ok," Trish responded. "Let me know if you hear anything."

But Joe didn't respond. Maybe he hadn't heard her.

As Joe walked away with his shoulders slouched, Trish glanced down again at her phone. She hadn't even texted Mason ... not that they texted too much anymore. It seemed as though they had run out of things to discuss, outside of Kyle. They might have still shared a home, but that was about it.

Trish knew that he was at the office; what else was new? She sent him a quick update, then rolled up her window and turned up the air conditioner. She had no idea what it was she was waiting for ... what it was that Claire meant by that frustratingly uninformative text. But she would remain here until she found out. It was nearly 5 o'clock and she had a full view of the sparkling bay out of her front windshield. If she hadn't been so unbearably miserable, she might have admired the unabated beauty before her. But she couldn't see beauty at all ... all she could see, all she could feel, was fear.

Chapter Fifty-Nine

BOB

"It's time," Bob told Dee as he looked up from his phone.

He still hadn't fully gotten the hang of that thing. This rectangular piece of machinery with all its buttons and flashing lights. It was just another trendy gadget to Bob. But in this case, that trendy gadget held his future because he had just received the text that they had been waiting for.

> We make the exchange in 3 hours.

Such simple words. Such life-changing words. Bob had already given McGivern the coordinates of the bay house. It was all set. Finally, their hopes, their dreams that seemed too far away to grasp were hovering right on the horizon.

"It's too early," Dee said. "They were supposed to come at midnight. It's only 7. That puts them here at 10pm."

"Yeah, well. It's now or never. It'll be dark by the time we get there. These aren't the type of people that will wait."

"So I suppose we're the ones who have to wait, huh? He was supposed to be here weeks ago! God. It was stupid of us to take the boys so long ago ... reckless actually. We should have waited longer ... instead of keeping them at the bay house for all these weeks. We could have been caught," Dee said in response.

"Yeah, well, how were we to know that, quote unquote, 'unforeseen circumstances' would have delayed them. We just did what we were told. What was expected. And we *didn't* get caught. No use dwelling on the shoulda coulda woulda," Bob said.

"Hell of a risk," Dee answered. "Mia got close. Too close. And she's a nobody. Imagine if the police were as observant as she was!"

Bob repeated himself, "Well, Dee ... we got away with it. We're ok. All that stress ... all that waiting'll be over after tonight. We'll start the rest of our lives."

"I'm excited, Bob. Nervous as hell, but excited. I can barely contain myself. Look at my hands."

Dee held out her arms to show Bob her trembling fingers. Ever since they came back home after–after the "Mia situation," they had been just sort of plodding about. They slept a little ... intermittently. But mostly they spent the time adding small items and knick-knacks to their already packed bags: nail clippers, a roll of aluminum foil, a few extra towels. Biding their time. Waiting on pins and needles for this one message to set their plan in motion. And now it was here. This was the last piece; soon enough, they would be whole. A real, true family.

"I'm excited too, Dee," Bob replied, pulling her in for a quick kiss on the temple, their earlier bickering momentarily forgotten. Bob continued, "I want to make sure we are there before McGivern and his crew show up. We have to put out the flag to tell them we're there, otherwise, they won't stop."

McGivern had specified to Bob that his boat would not stop at the bay house without glimpsing the white flag hanging out front. That was the signal that everything was ready and in order. Such a little thing that had the potential to change their fate. Bob was not gonna screw it up. He knew how much this whole thing meant to Dee ... to them. He had a brief vision of Dee all those years ago, in the bathtub–the hopelessness, the emptiness in those eyes ... the empty bottle of pills. Nope. That was not gonna happen again. Not on his watch. This baby would fix her. It would fix everything.

"Do you think we have everything we need?" Dee asked.

"We got that flag. And we got each other. We got stuff for the kid. The rest of this junk ... we don't need it," Bob answered.

"Ok. Let's go get our baby," Dee responded with finality.

Their baby. Bob liked the sound of that. All of this fuss would be worth it pretty soon.

Bob looked around one last time, as if to solidify this place in his memory, this home that contained so many of their memories over the years. He held the front door open for his wife. Together, in the gathering dusk, they walked down the pathway and got into the silver sedan parked in their driveway. It was a quick drive to the dock where their boat was waiting for them, and then about forty minutes to the bay house–possibly a bit more; that should give them plenty of time.

As they drove up Minnesota Avenue for the last time, Bob swallowed any remaining nerves along with the creeping guilt–he refused to examine that too deeply–and set his sight on the horizon as they drove towards their destiny.

Chapter Sixty

MIA

Ok ... *Looks like I'm going to have to go with Plan B,* Mia thought to herself as she sat on the bench with Jimmy and Kyle's clammy little hands enclosed in her own. She just couldn't wait any longer. *Shit.* Had it been an hour? Mia thought so ... maybe less. She couldn't really estimate the time ... especially with panic threatening to overtake her with every breath. The moon was already full and visible in the twilight; it was getting dark much too quickly. It was now or never. Despite her earlier optimism, her first plan clearly hadn't worked. Apparently, the ocean had its own agenda, and Mia couldn't help but feel a bit bitter and a bit betrayed. Did that sound foolish? Maybe. Had she been stupid? Naive? Possibly. A message in a bottle? That was her big plan? What did she think this was ... a fairy tale? If it was, where was Prince Charming? Even thinking about it brought a wave of hot shame to her face. She truly thought it would have worked. She had put all her eggs in one basket, as her mother would have said. But she had been wrong. So wrong. She had made a mistake. And now, time was running out.

She released her hands from the boys' grip and crouched down in front of them. Their eager stares almost broke her heart.

"Ok, guys," she said. "I am going to find help. You wait here."

She stood up, knees creaking, and turning away from Jimmy and Kyle, headed towards the door. She felt a tug on the back of her shirt. It was Jimmy.

"Where are you going?" he said, panic rising in his voice. He clutched at her. "You can't go anywhere without a boat. And you don't have a boat."

Mia led Jimmy to the side window and pointed. "See that bay house out there in the distance? I'm going to get there and find help."

"How are you going to get there? That's so far away. Take us with you. Don't leave us here." His desperation was palpable.

"I'm going to crawl over the marsh grass," Mia said, trying to feign more confidence than she felt. "That's how I got here. I'll get wet, but it shouldn't be too deep. And if it gets deep in places, I'll swim."

"But how do you know someone will be there? It's getting dark out. What if you can't make it? What if you get lost?"

"I won't. I am going to get you two out of here. And I can't take you with me. You need to stay here with Kyle. He's too sick to get wet. You need to be brave for just a little bit longer, Jimmy. And I know it's so unfair to ask you to be brave. You have been so brave for so long. But if I don't go now, the people might come back and take you away. I can't let that happen. This might be our last chance."

Jimmy opened his mouth as if to speak, and then closed it again, considering. Finally, he said, "Do you pinky promise you'll come back?"

Mia extended her little finger and linked it with his. "I promise."

He released his grip on her shirt.

She sent up a silent plea that this would be one she could keep. The thought of submerging herself back into the ocean was distasteful to Mia. No. Distasteful was much too kind of a word ... so was unpleasant. Appalling was more like it. She had finally dried off, had finally stopped shivering. But she had to do it. She didn't see any other way.

Jimmy had retreated back to his seat on the bench next to Kyle. Mia watched as the little boy adjusted the blanket over his friend's shoulders and placed his arm protectively around his neck. The gesture brought an iota of warmth to Mia's heart and gave her the courage she needed to step back out the front door. He looked back at her with a gaze that bespoke immense courage ... courage that she thought couldn't exist within someone so young.

She stepped over the threshold of the front door and onto the dock. Before she even secured the door behind her, she heard the distant rumble of a boat engine approaching. *Oh, God*, she thought to herself as she turned around. *Maybe it's the cops. Or the Coast Guard. Or anyone. Please do not let me be too late!* She gazed out towards the sound with a growing sense of horror, dread creeping up her spine like frigid fingers massaging each stiffening vertebrae. *Please, God, let it be someone who can help us ... because if it's Dee and Bob, I can't let them take those boys. I'll have to fight.* The boat came closer and closer still with each breath, with each pulse of her heartbeat that she could feel reverberating in her teeth.

As the vehicle came more fully into view that pit in the bottom of her stomach opened into an abyss, because even in the dimness, she knew that boat.

Shit, Shit, Shit, Mia muttered to herself trying to drown the absolute terror washing over her in relentless crashing waves. *Think. What should I do?* Mia didn't think they had seen her. At least she hoped that they hadn't. How could they have? It was dusk and she was wearing dark colors. And they wouldn't suspect that she would be here ... not after they essentially drowned her hours ago. The element of surprise was on her side. At least she had that.

Turning quickly on her heels she raced back into the bay house and closed the door behind her. Jimmy looked up.

"Ok, guys. Change of plans. They're here."

"Oh, no," Jimmy uttered, tears gathering in the corners of his widened eyes, breaths quick in his chest. "What are we going to do now? You can't let them take us. You can't, Mia!"

"Try to stay calm. I won't let them take you. I promise. I pinky promise," Mia said. She tried to sound reassuring.

She frantically looked around for a piece of wood, something–anything to use against them. There was nothing in this godforsaken place. She had been lucky to even find a pencil when she wrote her message earlier. Her eyes were drawn to the bottom of the bench the boys were sitting upon. It would have to do.

"Get up guys ... quickly," Mia instructed.

"What? Why? What are you–?"

Mia pulled Jimmy up by his arms and then lifted Kyle gently and placed him on the floor. Picking up the bench, she lifted it as high as she could above her head, and hurled it against the floor with all her strength. It wasn't that heavy. It shattered with a satisfying crash. She bent down and picked up one of the legs, now splintered with broken wood.

"What are you going to do with that?" Jimmy asked, panic rising to the surface.

"I'm not going to let them take you. Go sit down against that wall," she pointed towards the left side of the house.

Something in her tone made Jimmy stop asking questions. He helped Kyle to his feet and with an arm around his waist, guided him to where Mia had pointed. She watched them sit down and then took her own place behind the front door, gripping the bench leg in her white-knuckled fist. A surprise attack–it was the best she could do. It was true that she was younger and in better shape than Dee and Bob, but they outnumbered her. And Bob was strong; she remembered his muscled grasp on the boat. Her heart pounded in her throat, and her palm, circled around her make-shift weapon, felt slick with sweat.

Who did she think she was? Was she literally going to fight them? Hit them with this jagged piece of wood? Beat them up?

She had never been in a fight in her life. And she was still feeling weak as an after-effect of being drugged and nearly drowned. But, she would have to. She was absolutely not going to allow them to just sail out of here with these boys. Mia tried to clear her mind, tried to will herself to be able to attack. The tread of footsteps on the dock outside made her breath catch and a small gasp escaped her open mouth. Then, there was the creak of the front door. It swung open hiding her from view.

"Boys?" Dee's unmistakable voice called upon entering.

Mia watched through the crack between the door and the wall as Dee walked into the room.

"What in the world happened in here?" Dee said as she took in the wreckage of the splintered bench before her.

Now was the time. First Dee, then Bob—had to be in that order. Before she could think herself out of it, Mia charged out and struck Dee on the shoulder with the paltry wooden bench leg. It broke in half on impact, and the woman went down, hitting the floor with her knees. She looked up, the shock and surprise in her gaze was unmasked.

Dee finally managed to sputter out, "You?"

"Yes. Me," Mia replied with a calm she didn't feel, getting ready to strike again.

Dee spoke again, "How did you—?"

Before she could say any more, Bob raced through the front door with surprising speed. He rushed right to Mia, ripping the weapon from her hands, tossing it away. It left splinters as it scraped roughly against her palms. He held her firmly by the arms, restraining her. Mia fought with everything she had; she kicked at his legs and tried to bite his shoulder, but it was no use. He was much stronger than she had given him credit for, much stronger than he looked.

"Dee," he instructed. He was calm, "Get me the rope."

"The bitch really hurt my shoulder, Bob—"

"I know, my love. But you have to be strong now. We can take care of your shoulder later. Go get the rope. Now."

Dee stood up slowly, and once she was steady on her feet, she walked right over to Mia and glared into her eyes.

"Dee–the rope," Bob said again.

Dee wound her arm back and slapped Mia hard across the cheek. Mia's head rocked to the left as she accepted the blow. The sensation shocked Mia, but she was brought again to her senses when she heard Jimmy scream from across the room.

"Leave her alone!" he screamed. "Don't hurt her!"

Bob turned to face the boy. "Don't even think about making a scene now. If you do, I'll kill her right in front of you." He yanked Mia down to her knees for emphasis.

Jimmy did as he was told, but his whimpering was still audible.

Mia resorted to begging, "It's not too late. Don't do this."

"You have no idea what you're doing, Mia. We're owed this. And you're not going to stand in the way," Dee spoke in a near scream, as she rummaged through a bag near the door.

Mia watched as Dee handed the thick white rope to Bob, who had her positioned in a way that any movement brought with it a piercing pain that traveled up through her arms into her neck. Dee moved with deliberateness to protect her own injured shoulder, but Mia took no pleasure, no consolation in this. It hadn't been enough. Maybe she should have waited to strike. Maybe she should have known that Bob would soon follow his wife into the house. She thought that she could take them one by one, but she had been wrong. So wrong. Too many *maybes* swallowed up any rational thought in Mia's mind. But one thing she did know for sure was that she had failed. Again, Mia had failed. And now, for the second time, Bob tied Mia's wrists and then her ankles together, pushing her roughly against the wall next to Jimmy and Kyle. How could she possibly help them now? How could she possibly help herself? Could she be fortunate enough to avoid her own demise for a second time?

Mia began to beg, "Please don't take these boys. Don't you see that what you're doing is wrong! They have a home. A family. They don't belong to you."

Dee spoke, "And what about us, Mia? Don't we deserve a family too? Some happiness? This has been in the works for a long time, girl. And it is not your battle to fight. We told you to stay out of this. You managed to escape with your life last time. And you're lucky for that. This time, you won't be as lucky. I promise you that!"

"You're going to kill me ... again?" Mia responded.

Now Bob spoke, "If we have to. You're not gonna get in the way of this–"

"Well, I AM in the way. You are NOT taking these boys with you. I won't let you."

"Oh, yeah?" Bob spat out. "And how exactly are you going to stop us?" Bob gazed intently at Mia with a savagery in his eyes, a hardness that she had never seen before.

Mia didn't answer. She couldn't. Bob was right. She couldn't save them ... couldn't protect them. Not now. She averted her eyes as the tears welled up.

At that moment, a familiar sound reached them. Another approaching boat.

A small smile played at the corners of Bob's mouth, and he cocked his head to one side as he said, "Hear that boat, Mia? A little bit early, but just in time all the same. That's my friend. He's gonna take these boys. Whether you like it or not. And I'm sure he'll help us deal with you too."

Mia didn't say anything. The fear silenced all her words. She had no idea who this "friend" was; maybe it was the elusive "Mr. M." Bob had mentioned yesterday? Or was it a million years ago? Time had gone slippery on her since she had been dumped off the side of that boat. But as the whirring sound of the engine grew closer, Mia closed her eyes and sent up one more invocation ... to the ocean, to a higher power, to anyone who might be listening, that whatever was coming would allow her to keep the promise she made to the little boys sitting next to her.

Chapter Sixty-One

MCGIVERN

This whole situation has been fucked from the start, McGivern thought to himself as he expertly navigated through the water. He lit himself a cigarette, the cherry the only bright spot in the darkness. *I'm too nice; that's my problem,* an ironic notion coming from a smuggler. He had to chuckle to himself despite it all.

He never should have agreed to help Bob in the first place; he knew that now. There was too much emotion involved. It had been reckless of him to put himself in this situation. The guy knew his identity for Christ-sakes. Bob just looked so pathetic that night in the bar, blubbering about his depressed wife and yadda, yadda, yadda. McGivern had been a few shades to the wind himself when he proposed the idea; Bob had always given him healthy pours of Johnny Walker, and most nights he visited Fenley's, he basically had to stumble back home. He almost took the offer back, but Bob's big old hopeful eyes, the tears ... *Ahh, fuck it,* he had thought then. He'd always been a sucker for a good old sob story–those crappy Hallmark movies around Christmastime sometimes made him tear up. *Plus,* McGivern thought to himself, *this guy won't rat me out.* He genuinely liked the guy and wanted to help him.

McGivern still didn't think Bob would rat him out. That wasn't it. Bob would be ratting on himself too, if he did. It was this Benicek/Yardsleigh case. It just got so much damn publicity. And if McGivern hated one thing, it was publicity. Why would Bob and his wife have chosen kids from middle-class, white suburbia? Stupid. It was part of the reason for the delay ... he had to wait a bit for the media coverage to die down. Maybe he should have given Bob more direction, but it wasn't his responsibility to run a course on Kidnapping 101. The whole scenario gave McGivern a bad feeling. He didn't want to be anywhere near this thing–didn't want to touch it with a ten-foot pole.

Yet here he was. And once the ball started rolling, it was hard to stop. There had been delays, even aside from the need to wait for the news outlets to stop plastering pictures of the boys on the television. The damn motor of the boat blew and needed to be repaired. And his contact in Russia had been under heat from the Feds. It felt like everything was working against him for this job. But delays were expected in this line of business. Very rarely did all the stars align perfectly. He tried to explain that to Bob a month or so ago when he had called worried about the fact that it was all taking too long. People are always so damn impatient.

He glanced over at the baby. It hadn't been easy to come by this one. He always thought of the barter material as an "it." Allowed him to put a human on the same level as a product, which was, to him, what they were. Products. All humans ratio-nalize their actions somehow–no matter how sordid–and this was just how McGivern rationalized his.

At the moment, "It" was asleep in the carrier on the floor, in between the feet of Lucia ... or whatever her name was. She had been quick to accept his offer when he approached her in the Gateway Motel, where she worked as a maid. Three grand: a lot of money for an illegal immigrant. But the price didn't really matter ... not when it came down to it. McGivern had no intention of actually paying her. He just needed to get her to agree to help him. He couldn't steer the boat and take care of a baby–hell, he didn't even know how to change a diaper. That's how it always worked. He would find some non-English-speaking hotel maid or nanny; a few times he even went with an escort, which was really just a glorified hooker. Those girls always ended up getting too paranoid and shrieky, so he tried to stick mostly with the quiet girls with no family. Girls no one would actually miss–or even notice if they just happened to go missing. Their fate was always the same anyway–a burlap sack, weighted down with rocks at the bottom of some body of water. Just like the infants or children he traded in, they were products too … commodities needed for barter. How many women–commodities–had he disposed of in his career? He lost count years ago.

Almost there, he said aloud to himself. McGivern couldn't wait to wash his hands of this job. Once he got all these products where they needed to go–and disposed of the ones that needed to be disposed of–he was going to treat himself to a vacation. Mexico sounded nice. Some cigars, some tequila, some Spanish-speaking women on the beach–just what he needed. This whole affair would certainly put a nice chunk of change in his pocketbook. Hey, maybe he could retire soon. He was getting sick of all this bullshit anyway.

Flicking the stub of his cigarette into the ocean, his eyes scanned the horizon. He could just make out the bay house in the distance with the white flag tied to the post. He was almost there. Almost home free.

Chapter Sixty-Two

CLAIRE

Claire stood right next to the Coast Guard pilot as he expertly maneuvered the boat through the waters. The choppy waves looked like polished onyx in the growing darkness.

Who would have thought there would be not one, but two brown bay houses in a 20-mile radius? Claire thought that Mia–she now knew for certain, knew in her heart, that Mia was the one responsible for that note–hadn't known this either … she might have specified if she had. When they knocked on the door of the first one, Claire's stomach had been in her teeth, and when no one answered, and Sergeant Lackey had burst into the structure with gusto, Claire couldn't even draw a single breath. But after they had done a thorough search and found no one there, nor any evidence that anyone had been there, that flame of hope began to flicker a bit.

Much to Claire's frustration, she learned that traveling 20 miles by boat was very different from traveling 20 miles by car. The guard had warned her that it would take nearly an hour, even at a higher speed, to reach the next bay house, especially in the dim light. She could tell that he was getting annoyed at the errand by the comment he made to the sergeant after they had been unlucky at the first stop. He had said something like, "What are we ... just gonna go to each of these houses and see if anyone's home?" But Claire didn't care what he thought. She saw the grim determination in Sergeant Lackey's eyes and tried to remain undeterred. Mia's letter remained gripped in her fist–proof that there was hope. Tangible proof.

"Can you give me a bit of space," the guard, a new hire named Bill, said to Claire as they skirted over a small swell in the tide that caused her to wobble on her feet.

She had accidentally grabbed onto his shoulder to stop herself from bumping into the dashboard–or whatever that panel in front of the steering wheel was called.

"Sorry." She had to raise her voice to be heard over the sound of the engine. "I'm just so anxious to get there."

"I get it," Bill said. "But it's a little hard to steer with you standing so close."

Claire took the hint and moved away from him towards the front of the boat, to where Sergeant Lackey was holding onto the rail.

"What do you think?" Claire managed to sputter out.

"I don't know, Mrs. Benicek. We'll be at the only other brown bay house in about 40 minutes. Remember what I advised you about earlier? About hope?"

"I remember," Claire responded. "You told me to not get my hopes up too high."

"Yup. And now, I'm going to tell you the same thing."

Claire didn't say anything in response. She couldn't. Because her hopes were high. Impossibly high. In her mind, she had concocted a vision that seemed so real–a scenario in which she was reunited with her son. And with each passing minute, she had been adding more detail to it ... the way one might add flowers to a growing bouquet, making it more vivid with each new bloom. She could almost feel the curve of his head nestled into the crook of her neck. Her arms ached to hold him to her chest. Jimmy. Her sweet boy. God. Once she had him in her grasp, she might never let him go.

A cool wind nipped at her eyes as the boat careened through the water, and she wiped at them with her forearm. Her loose hair whipped around her face, tangling itself into knots, but she didn't care. Claire and the sergeant remained like that, standing side by side at the front of the boat, as the night pressed down upon them.

Chapter Sixty-Three

MIA

Crouched on the floor in between Jimmy and Kyle, Mia watched as Bob opened the front door of the bay house, with Dee standing close behind him, hovering. Mia didn't know who this "man" was on the other side of the door–or what he was capable of–but she definitely did not want to meet him. Anyone who could do what he was doing ... the reality was unfathomable.

She turned to the boys. "Boys–it's going to be ok."

What else could she say? What else could she do, now that she was restrained, but offer them some comfort for what was about to happen? She had failed ... epically. She had failed them, and she had failed Claire. And what was to come of her? Mia felt sure that her life was over, but these boys. She thought that they would be ok ... maybe not right away. But eventually. A vision of her little sister popped into her mind. Gabby would be devastated. Would she and her parents think that Mia had simply disappeared? Taken off without saying goodbye? Or would her body eventually surface from the depth of the ocean to provide her family with a sense of closure. It was weird, thinking about herself like this ... like some commodity. Logic allowed her to compartmentalize her terror and raw panic. At least for the moment.

Before Bob opened the door, he turned to Mia and said almost with a tinge of sadness, "You should have stayed away. These are not the kind of people you want to cross."

"I would never stand by and just let you do this," she responded, tightening her grip on the boys' small hands.

If Mia was being honest with herself, a part of her wished that she had listened to her mom all those weeks ago. This was a side of humanity to which she wished she had not been privy. It was too dark, too sad, too hopelessly awful. She might have been better off remaining blissfully ignorant to such sordid deeds. To people who could swap kids like one would trade Pokemon cards. The terror swirling around in her roiling stomach was all too real, and she wished briefly that she was back home, tucked away in her child-hood bedroom in Sparta.

But yet ... she did not regret moving to Long Beach, or meeting Claire Benicek. Once she had met Claire, all those weeks and months ago, after having heard her story, and seeing the pride swell in her eyes when she showed her Jimmy's bedroom ... there was just no way she could have defied that kinship. That sense of responsibility. Especially when the ocean had been egging her on.

Giving Mia one more backwards glance, Bob began to swing the door open as he said to the person on the other side, "You're early. I'm glad I got to put that flag–"

Mia watched in horror, Jimmy grasping tightly to her bound hands, as the door swung open allowing in whatever fate awaited.

Chapter Sixty-Four

CLAIRE

"Excuse me, sir," Sergeant Lackey began, holding up his badge. "I have a warrant to search this property."

"Huh," the man said as he leaned up against the doorframe; he seemed genuinely confused.

There was a woman behind him with a similar expression of perplexity painted on her face. They were an older couple, but not that old. In their late 60s, maybe ... or early 70s.

The sergeant patiently repeated himself, "I have a warrant to search this property."

Claire waited behind Sergeant Lackey with a growing impatience; she noticed a white flag whipping against the house at the edge of her periphery.

Then, as if a switch flipped in his mind, the man in the doorway screamed out, "No!" and he attempted to slam the door closed.

The sergeant was quick and put his hand out to stop it and barreled into the room with his firearm drawn. Despite Sergeant Lackey's warning to remain behind, Claire was on his heels, unmindful of whatever danger awaited them inside. This was the place. It had to be.

As the sergeant had his pistol trained on the couple hovering in the corner of the room, he brought out his intercom and spoke into it, "It's Lackey. I need backup at—"

But Claire Benicek didn't hear the rest because her swooping eyes focused on a small area of the room in the opposite corner. With the help of the moonlight streaming through the front windows, she could discern three people huddled together on the floor–their reflective eyes turned her way. The next word she heard that came to her through the darkness pierced her heart, and she fell to her knees in the middle of the space as a small shape ran at her.

"Mom?" a faint voice uttered.

Was she really hearing that? Or was it the vision from her mind? A fantasy concocted from the wall of grief she had built up. Maybe she had snapped; maybe she was hallucinating.

Then again, louder this time, "Mom!" Followed by approaching footsteps.

But before she could truly question her sanity, or her logic, or the complete absurdity and ridiculousness of ending up here after receiving–of all things–a message in a bottle, as if by muscle memory, she knelt down, and her arms wrapped themselves around the thin frame of her son as he cried stormily into her neck. After all the months, all the waiting, all the hoping, he was here, with her. At that moment, the floodgates within her opened and the tears coursed freely down her cheeks. She kissed his head, his eyelids, his ears, his fingertips. Grasping him by the shoulders, Claire held him away from her for a moment, just a moment, so she could look at him, so she could be sure that it was all real. That *he* was real.

"Let me look at you. I missed you so much. My sweet boy."

Her eyes roved over him, taking in the dirt on his face, the way his clothes seemed to hang on him.

"I missed you too, Mom," Jimmy answered.

"Are you ok? Are you hurt?"

"I have a cut on my finger. But I'm ok. Mia saved me ... and she saved Kyle too."

Claire embraced her son once again as her vision blurred with tears. And as she gazed over his shoulder, her eyes sought out Mia. She saw her there, sitting next to Kyle Yardsleigh with a smile tugging at the corners of her lips. Relief flooded Claire with a forceful intensity and her soul knew peace for the first time in a long time.

Chapter Sixty-Five

MIA

From the far corner of the room, Mia watched Claire's reunion with Jimmy outlined in the moonlight. She didn't even know she was crying until her tongue tasted saltwater in the crevices of her mouth. There was so much to take in. Dee and Bob handcuffed together. A cop's gun pointing at her landlords–crazy that she still thought of them as such. Kyle's tiny shivering body pressed up next to her. But the only thing that filled Mia's soul at that moment was the scene in front of her. Her beautiful friend–Claire ... a woman who had taken Mia's life by storm–rocking her son against her heaving chest. Everything was going to be alright.

Mia held herself back for a few minutes to respect the gravity of the situation before her. Claire deserved that ... Jimmy deserved that. But when the crying seemed to ebb a bit, Mia spoke.

"You got my letter," she said simply–a statement, not a question–as Claire, still holding her son's hand, approached Mia.

"I got your letter," Claire repeated, bending down to her.

Mia would never forget Claire's shining, grateful eyes.

"Thank you," Claire whispered, almost overcome with emotion. "Thank you for my son."

Claire hugged Mia tightly around her neck and called over to the sergeant, "I need something to cut these ties."

With his firearm trained on Dee and Bob, the sergeant took his free hand and reached into his pocket, removing a Swiss Army knife. He tossed it over to Claire, who with one deft motion, flicked it open and cut through the binding restraints at Mia's wrists and ankles.

Mia rubbed at the soft skin above her hands; the area felt raw. The amazement about what had happened had not been fully realized yet. That would take some time to sink in, and it would be many, many years before Mia could truly come to grips with the power, the baffling, awesome, graceful forces that saved her ... that saved them all that fateful night. And she truly believed that it was fate that had intervened on her behalf. It had to be. What other explanation was there? The ocean hadn't let her down after all.

The spell was broken by Dee's harsh sob echoing through the room, "This isn't the way it's supposed to happen." Then she glared directly at Mia and continued, "You ruined this. YOU! I'll never forgive you. Why couldn't you just die when you were supposed to?"

Mia spoke back calmly, "Because I *wasn't* supposed to die. That was never the plan. Remember the first night I moved in? You invited me over for dinner?" She didn't wait for an answer. "I told you that I had moved here for a reason. Some calling in my soul." Mia pressed her hand flat against her chest. "Well, THIS is my reason. I finally figured it out. I guess I really have found my ground. "

Mia looked at Bob as she said that last sentence. She almost felt sorry for him ... almost; the hurt, the shame, the bitter disappointment was so visible on his face.

Sergeant Lackey spoke up, "Can someone tell me what the hell is going on?"

Claire responded, "This is Mia's tale to tell." And then she turned her eyes towards Mia again. "Will you tell it?"

Mia responded back, "Of course." A small smile played at the corners of her lips.

"Well," Sergeant Lackey's voice brought them all back to attention. "It seems like all of you have some stories to tell. And we can do that later on tonight, back at the station. But for now, you all go with Bill back to the pier. It looks like Kyle Yardsleigh over there needs some immediate medical attention."

"So does Jimmy," Mia added. "He has a nasty infection on his finger."

"Alright. I'm going to wait here for backup to arrive. They should be here within 20 minutes. You four, you should get going."

Pulling Kyle up to a standing position, Mia helped walk him out the front door. Claire and Jimmy followed closely behind.

Before they crossed the threshold of the bay house, Mia heard Claire address the sergeant, "Hey, Sergeant, remember our conversation about hope?"

"I absolutely do, Mrs. Benicek. And you proved me wrong. Thank you for that. Now go on. I'll meet you back at the station."

Mia filed this exchange away in her mind; she hoped that she would remember to ask Claire about it at a later date.

Then Jimmy said, "I want to go home."

"Me too," Claire responded. "Me too."

"Me three," Mia added with a tiny, stifled laugh.

Mia tore her stare away from the two and gazed out towards the horizon, which was now barely perceptible as night settled over Reynold's Channel. Was that another boat ... just over there? She could make out a dark shape in the distance. Some rippling in the surface of the water. Maybe a rumbling in the distance? Was that the sound that filled her ears? Could that be the man, Mr. M., who was supposed to come take Jimmy and Kyle off to some other family, some uncertain future? Could there be an infant in tow ... ready to be handed over to an elderly couple looking for absolution? She didn't know, and the harder she strained her eyes to see in the shadows, the less sure she became that there was anything there at all.

Mia lifted Kyle over the gap between the edge of the dock and the boat–he seemed to weigh almost nothing. She sat quietly with him on her lap while Claire and Jimmy settled in on the bench next to her. He still felt feverish–she could feel the warmth radiating off him–but there was a tiny smile playing on his face. The sight of the small gesture eased some of the tension in Mia's neck. *He's going to be ok*, she thought to herself gratefully. *Good thing kids are resilient.*

"I can't wait to see my mom," he said in a raspy voice.

"She is going to be so incredibly happy to see you," Claire responded. "In fact, I bet she'll be waiting at the pier when we get back."

"Will dad be there too?" Jimmy asked.

"I think so," Claire answered, planting a kiss on his temple.

"It's over," Mia said. "It's really over."

"It is," Claire answered back. "It really is."

Circumstance had brought these two women together, and love and kinship had solidified their bond ... and oh, yeah–the ocean. The ocean helped too.

"Thank you," Mia whispered softly to the cool comfort of the night air around them.

"Did you say something?" Claire asked.

"Nope," Mia said. "Just a yawn."

"Well, we have a long night of explaining ahead of us," Claire responded.

"Yes, we do," Mia agreed. "Think Beach Beans is still open?"

"Not a chance," laughed Claire. "But I'll buy you a cup of coffee ... and a chocolate croissant in the morning."

"Can I get one too?" Jimmy chimed in.

"This time, it's my treat," said Mia as she snuggled Kyle closer to her.

Her heart felt very full as the boat cascaded through the waves headed towards Point Lookout. Somehow, they had all come out on the other side. Miraculously. Safe at last. Despite it all.

Mia wondered what would become of Dee and Bob, but that was a thought for another day. There would be plenty of time ... years upon years ... to dwell upon the ugly. But right now, right now, Mia only allowed the happiness to flow through her body as they bobbed up and down on the small boat. The waves were happy too. Mia could feel it, that sense of peace vibrating through her bones. She had come home. Come home at last. And that sense of belonging flickered throughout her entire being as the four friends headed towards home. She had finally found her ground.

Afterword

MIA

Three weeks later

Mia had to move some of the boxes out of the way to get a comfortable spot on her couch; this endless unpacking and sorting and reorganizing seemed to go on forever. Her new place wasn't as cozy, nor as close to the ocean as her place on Minnesota Avenue, nor did she have an ocean view, but Mia thought it would do just fine. Claire had offered to pop over tomorrow to help her make a dent in this mess, and she was grateful for the gesture. Hopefully, Jimmy would tag along with her. She couldn't seem to get enough of that little boy. Mia couldn't wait to finally feel settled in her new space and enjoy the rest of the summer.

Tucking her legs beneath her, Mia pressed the "on" button on the remote, lighting up the television that had not yet been mounted to the plaster wall. She had been eagerly waiting all day for this segment on *News12*—a special interest story, they called it. And she certainly had a "special interest" in what they had to say.

On the screen, a blonde anchorwoman dressed in a navy blue blazer and matching pants was standing outside Bob's and Dee's house; it was weird seeing her old residence on the television …

weirder still, was being so personally invested in the story. Mia could even make out a bit of the side staircase leading up to what was until recently, her apartment. The anchorwoman began her report:

Behind me is the former residence of Robert and Dee Forman, the individuals responsible for the abduction of Jimmy Benicek and Kyle Yardsleigh in March of this year. Their involvement has come as quite a shock to this quiet, Long Beach community. Most residents who knew the alleged abductors describe them as a quiet and kind couple, who spent most of their time either at home, on the beach in the summers, or out on their boat. Tomorrow morning at 9 we will hear from some of their neighbors in an exclusive broadcast called Untraceable. *Make sure to tune in to get the full scoop that only* News12 *can give.*

But on a happier note, while Robert and Dee await prosecution, the Yardsleighs and Beniceks are enjoying some much needed family time with their sons who, after receiving two days of medical care at Southside University Hospital in Rockville Centre, have returned to their homes. The whole Oceanside community, along with the neighboring towns, welcomed the boys back with open arms. While much of their miraculous story remains a mystery, residents are waiting with baited breath for the trial, which will be aired on News12, *estimated to begin in early September. We will have more updates on that over the course of the next week. The Beniceks have asked that we respect their privacy during this emotional time and have declined any interviews, but Patricia Yardsleigh, mother of Kyle Yardsleigh, has committed to a full exposé, which will air this coming Sunday evening at 7pm ...*

Mia couldn't help but let out a sarcastic chuckle hearing the news that Trish Yardsleigh had agreed to a media appearance regarding what had happened. Of course the woman had. While Claire expressed no interest in sharing the murky details of Jimmy's kidnapping with the world, Trish couldn't seem to get enough of the attention. It seemed as though her heavily made-up face was plastered across every television channel in existence. Mia had only interacted with Mrs. Yardsleigh for a few brief moments over the past few weeks, but that woman was insufferable. At least Trish's crusade against Claire seemed to have abated. She hadn't openly acknowledged Claire for the role she played in rescuing the boys, but at least she had stopped publicly shaming her. That was probably the closest Trish would ever get to offering Claire that well-deserved apology. Mia cleared her thoughts and turned her attention back to the screen:

As the police continue their investigation, I am sure there will be much more evidence to provide clues into what really happened, but for now, let's go over to Lauren Harding to review what we already know about—

Mia flipped off the television. She didn't need to hear about the evidence, what they "already knew" ... she was there. She had lived it. She had even told the cops about the mysterious Mr. M. who was supposed to come to take Jimmy and Kyle and give Bob and Dee a baby in return. Even thinking about her landlords' rationale behind what they had done sounded twisted and beyond belief–like a movie. But they never did locate this man ... or the infant.

The thought of testifying in a trial against Dee and Bob–coming face-to-face with them in the courtroom–was not appealing to her, but she tried to view it as just one more unpleasantry to get through in order to move on with her life. And she desperately wanted to move on.

With a sigh, she slipped her feet into her Old Navy flip flops, grabbed her keys, and walked out the front door. At least she managed to secure a first-floor apartment this time ... even though she did have to walk nearly two full blocks to get to the beach entrance. Oh, well, beggars can't be choosers–there was her mom's saying again. Even thinking about her mom brought a wave of contentment to Mia–contentment and relief. After the harrowing experience at the bay house, she had told her mom everything. No more lying. No more pretending. That feeling of being torn between a rock and a hard place had gradually subsided, and in the aftermath, her mother had become her biggest support system—as, deep-down, Mia knew she had always been. Her whole family was planning on visiting next weekend, and Mia couldn't wait to see them.

It was warm—summer—when Mia walked outside, and she could feel the prickle of sweat behind her knees, even though she was wearing only shorts and a tank over her bathing suit. Bob had been right … two blocks felt a lot longer when you were carrying a beach chair and a cooler, as Mia was now. She was scheduled to meet her friend Hailey at 5 for dinner and drinks on the sand—apparently pizzerias around here actually deliver to the ocean. It was only 4 o'clock, but Mia wanted to get there earlier.

After a ten-minute walk—*not too bad*, Mia thought to herself—she plodded up the wooden plank stairway … there was a similar one at every entrance to the beach on the West End. Shedding her flip flops as the boards gave way to powdery, tan sand dotted with seashells, Mia held her breath as she contemplated the view before her. Vast and deep and sparkling in the late afternoon sunshine. So much blue—possibly every single shade. There was not a cloud overhead as Mia dropped her belongings at her feet. She shimmied her shorts down over her hips revealing that deep mocha birthmark about which she used to feel embarrassed. She thought to herself, *Who cares about such a small blemish now? Life's too short to worry about such nonsense.* Her gray tank joined her shorts on the sand, and Mia walked towards the place where the waves rolled softly against the shore. The foamy ripple cascaded over her toes as the sand engulfed her feet.

But this time, she didn't stop there, at the brink of the ocean. No, not this time. The water undulated against her ankles, then her shins as she waded deeper; it mixed with the perspiration behind her knees. Then she felt the welcome shock of cool water rush against her thighs, her belly, her breasts, her shoulders. Mia Rossi held her breath and submerged her head under the rippling waves that moved her gently onto her back, supporting her weight, embracing her in their cool comfort. Mia inhaled, pulling the salty air deep into her lungs as a feeling of utter peace radiated through her very being. Thrumming deep within her core was the whisper of the ocean, but this time, there was no accompanying fear ... no dread ... no confusion. Only love ... only light ... only peace ...

The End

When I graduated from college and landed my first teaching job, my then boyfriend, now husband, and I rented a tiny apartment in Long Beach, New York. I would come home from work, grab my beach chair and a book, and spend the afternoons spread out on the spot of beach at the end of Minnesota Avenue. He had already been living in Long Beach for a few years at the time and if it wasn't for him, I never would have discovered the magic of the location and the setting for Mia's and Claire's story. So Brian, thank you for not only exposing me to the beauty of Long Beach, but for being my first reader and biggest supporter. I love you and the life we have created together.

It takes a village to publish a book, and I would be remiss without extending my sincerest gratitude to a few special people. One of the reasons I started writing was to show my own children, Jack and Max, that we can all accomplish difficult tasks if we put our minds to it. They push me to be better, strive for greater, and reach farther every single day. I hope that one day–maybe when they are a bit older–they read my stories with pride and the knowledge that everything I do, I do for them.

Without Dave Goldman–my dear friend, colleague, editor, soundboard, and unfailing cheerleader–Mia's and Claire's story would have never seen the light of day. His advice, interest, unyielding encouragement and positivity helped shape this story into what is contained between the covers of this book. I am forever grateful.

I also have to thank my friend Michelle, who helped me find Mia's story. The manuscript had been sitting unfinished on my computer for months because I couldn't put the puzzle pieces together. She graciously and generously helped me see the full picture.

Also, Monica and Jenn—my lifelong friends—read my story when it was still a Word Document. Their enthusiasm for my story and my writing has given me the confidence to put myself out there and share Mia's and Claire's story with the world. Thank you for being there ... through it all.

I want to acknowledge my parents—my mom, who made me a reader in the first place and who is the proudest, fiercest, most loving advocate for my story and every other facet of my life ... and my dad—who would stand by my side regardless of what I did. When it comes to family, I truly hit the jackpot with you two ... and of course this includes my brother, Evan, too.

My endless gratitude and appreciation goes to Stephanie Larkin at Red Penguin for taking a chance on a new author. Her belief in me, passion for her work, extraordinary patience, and dedication to helping me make my story the best it could be became the wind behind my sails. I am so proud to be part of the Red Penguin family and look forward to what the future has in store for us.

And to all of you readers who have spent time with my story ... thank you. It means everything to me to have your support. I truly hope you enjoyed unearthing a bit of magic hidden within the crevices of reality. If you feel so inclined, an Amazon or Goodreads review goes a long way for us newbie authors.

Melanie Murphy is a writer and high school English teacher from Long Island. She loves to include the diverse settings of New York in her fiction, as she explores nature's capacity for magic and the inherent strength hidden within us all. She lives in Massapequa Park with her husband, two sons, and her Labradoodle, Winnie.